THE TIDE OF TIME

The Tide of Time

An Experienced Goods Detective Squad Mystery, Volume 3

Barbara Schlichting

Published by Barbara Schlichting, 2026.

THE TIDE OF TIME

First edition. February 2, 2026.

ISBN: 979-8993014029

Written by Barbara Schlichting.

Also by Barbara Schlichting

An Experienced Goods Detective Squad Mystery
The Forger
Ila Looking Out
The Gin Game
The Tide of Time

White House Dollhouse Middle School mystery series
Spangled to Pieces
Word to Pieces

White House Dollhouse Mystery series
Spangled to Death
Word to Death
Clued to Death
Suffragette to Death

Standalone
Body on the Tracks

The Broken Circle

Watch for more at www.barbaraschlichting.com.

Written by

Barbara Schlichting

Books by Barbara

An Experienced Goods Detective Mystery
The Forger
Ila Looking Out
The Gin Game
The Tide of Time
Single Titles
The Broken Circle
White House Dollhouse Mystery Series
Spangled to Death
Word to Death
Clued to Death
Suffragette to Death
Historical Fiction
Body on the Tracks
Middle School
Spangled to Pieces
Word to Pieces
Clued to Pieces
Suffragette to Pieces
Poetry
Blood Red
Bike With Me
Picture Books
Red Shoes by Barbie Marie

The Tide of Time

Chapter one

John knew he must face the day, he couldn't let his Inga down. He pushed himself up to sitting and heaved his legs off to the side of the bed, letting gravity take over for his feet to finally plunk onto the wood flooring. His slippers were right there and without moving too much, he flexed his toes and worked his foot until the first one slipped onto his right foot. He did the same with the other foot. All set, now he could stand. First he must wrestle with the knowledge that his Inga waited for him, just as she always did in the morning. He could almost smell the bacon frying and hear her call out that the pancakes were ready. Yesterday it was eggs, sunny side up, his favorite. The toast must be warm with peanut butter, and she always had apple jelly or orange marmalade. How many more years until he could kiss her again, he wondered, before pushing himself up to standing with a "heave-ho!"

Out in the kitchen, he stood before the cabinet with his favorite picture of his late wife and greeted her with a smile and a, "Good morning, honeybunch!" Next on his agenda, he rearranged the rose printed sealed vase that held her ashes, and he said, "Honey, I miss you." At night he'd remember to say the Lord's Prayer with her just like they'd always done together before closing their eyes.

As he stood in front of the stove, contemplating whether or not to fry the morning bacon or just have a bowl of oatmeal, the phone rang.

"Doggonit! I thought I could make it through one day without that woman pestering me!" John tried to ignore the ring as he began to dig out a cooking pot, but it wouldn't stop. Reluctantly, he answered.

"Hello."

"I thought you'd never answer. I almost came round to make sure you're not dead!" Frances said. "Good grief. You almost gave me a heart attack." He could picture her clutching her chest. "I've got breakfast and a favor to ask of you."

"What are you having?" John reached for the coffee pot and frowned. He'd forgotten to dump out yesterday's brew. "Got fresh coffee? Enough for a thermos full?"

"Get over here, you old buzzard." Frances slammed down the phone in disgust. She called to Leif, "John's coming by. Get yourself dressed and put that phone and all your stuff away. He'll make something out of you, if it's the last thing I do."

"Grandma, I don't care much for John, he's so ornery and has an attitude." Leif appeared in the kitchen. "I don't care that he's my grandpa."

"You should! Now go look in the mirror for once in your life and comb that mop on the top of your head and wash your face. Better yet, take a quick shower. You stink. Hurry it up!"

"Grandma, you're mean sometimes." Leif walked from the room.

"Just wait. I'm only getting started. Now git!"

Frances turned back to the stove to begin breakfast. The bacon started sizzling as the doorbell dinged and the door opened.

"I'm here," John said, entering. "I've got something for you." He walked in and set his thermos on the countertop before handing over a small butter dish. "I thought you might like this dish seeing as you two were such good friends." John looked around the room. "Where's he hiding?"

"He's in the shower. Can't you hear the water running?" She rearranged the bacon strips. "You're gonna take him with you this morning."

"I am? Why?"

"Punishment." Frances began to whip up the pancake batter. "Get the syrup out, don't just stand there."

"Good Lord. What did I ever do to deserve this?" He went to the refrigerator and removed the butter and syrup for the table. "Anything else?"

"Yes. Pour yourself a cup of coffee. Fill up the thermos."

"Yes, ma'am." John filled it and placed the thermos near where he planned to sit. After, he poured two cups full and set them on the table. He took a sip from his full coffee cup. "Good and hot. Very good."

"Bacon's done." She set the plate of hot bacon on the table in front of John. "Don't eat it all up, there's three of us, remember?" She flipped the pancakes and dashed toward the bathroom door. "Hurry up in there! We're ready to eat."

"Okay, Grandma. I get the message." Leif got dressed and walked out to the kitchen and sat beside his grandma. "Sure smells good."

"You got it made, kid," John said, cutting up his pile of three pancakes. He took a bite. "Mighty good."

"What's up?" Leif said, dishing up his plate of four pancakes and most of the bacon. He glanced from John to his grandma. "I was planning to get in touch with my mom today." He thought the statement might wake up the two old people he was forced to be around for the summer.

"You see, Leif, you're going to spend time with your grandpa this summer," Frances said. "You'll be with him every day, helping to remove graffiti and learn something about the forest and the trees plus help to keep the pathways clean from garbage since there's so many people who visit the park on any one day."

"Grandma? You've got to be kidding? All day long with this old man?" Leif glared at one and then the other. "He hates me! My grandpa hates me." He pushed his chair back as if to leave. "I won't."

"Sit down, young man," John growled. "Your dad was a brilliant man. A soldier who fought bravely in Iraq, and you're going to listen to me." John leaned over the table and stared at him. "Down! Now!"

"Yes, sir."

"You call me Grandpa, not Old Man." John bit into his forkful of pancakes. "Beginning now."

"When you, Old Man, respect me by calling me your grandson," Leif said. "It doesn't count if you blurt it out right now because it's not meaningful."

"Okay, you two." Frances stared at each of them. "That's enough. The both of you are going to spend time together and that's final. And, you're going to love it."

"Yes, ma'am," John said, lowering his eyes. "I'll be a good boy."

"Finally, you've got it right," Frances said, sipping her coffee. She turned to Leif. "You, pay attention to John. Your mother is having a terrible time and you know it. She can't handle anything right now."

"You know that she remarried and lost a baby, and that man left her," John said. "She hasn't gotten over her mother's death, either, and neither have I, which is why she isn't around. Then there's your father who was killed in Iraq. She'll never get over Gary's death and neither will I. Do you know that his picture is hidden in her wallet? She told me that the last time I saw her. It pains her to be here."

"I must remind her of my dad," Leif softly said. "When can I see her?"

"Someday, we'll go together to visit her or we'll get her here," John said. "In the meantime, you're listening to what we have to say."

"Well, okay, as long as I don't have to call you Grandpa."

"That's fine, kid. We'll get there eventually." John sliced more of his pancake and ate. "Be ready every morning at nine, we'll walk together down to the park."

"No car?" Leif dived into his meal as if he hadn't eaten anything for seventy-two hours. "I want a glass of juice or milk, Grandma."

"Get it yourself," John growled.

They watched as Leif stood up and poured a glass full of orange juice. To each other, they raised a brow.

"I've got sandwiches made. They're right inside the refrigerator in a brown paper bag. It'll get you through until midafternoon when you return home."

"Okay, Grandma," Leif said, still eating.

"Well, I must eat up and get going," John said, taking his last bite. "It's time to get down to the park before the gang bastards come and ruin the engine."

"You mean for me to wipe all the graffiti from the engine," Leif said, then finished drinking. "And you expect me to do the climbing to the top and wipe it all down, right?"

"Ja, most likely. You're younger than me and I don't have good legs," John said. "You can do it really good without any difficulty."

"How much you payin' me?" Leif dished up the last of the pancakes, then poured syrup over them so it looked like a lake. "Huh?"

"Shame on you," Frances said. "Talk that way? My goodness, you know better than that."

"I do? Who taught me?"

"Here now, young man," John said. "You can get up off you duff and come and help me out and learn something or stay back and become an idiot or bum for the rest of your life."

"Who am I to you?" Leif said with a mouthful of food. "Who am I?" He shoved his plate back. "I'd like to know."

"Tell you what, you tell me who I am." John stood and looked at him. "I'm leaving. Thank you, Frances." He took the sandwich bag, thermos, and walked out the door. When he opened the front door, he called, "Bring you fishing pole, if you come, but only if you want to." He grumbled to himself as he walked away about the youth nowadays being lazy and good for nothing.

The six block long stretch to the Minnehaha Falls Park located in South Minneapolis never seemed to bother him. Walking amongst the old great-grandfather maple and oak trees was a blessing. The walk along the Minnehaha creek bed and hearing the water ripple and bounce across the rocks was music to his ears. He remembered fishing with his daughter when she was a little girl. Her first catch was a small perch that had to be let loose because it was the length of his index finger. She cried and cried, so he let her keep the next one and they ate it. So very many years ago. He flipped his cap up and down after brushing back the few hairs he had left on his head.

As he turned the corner and walked straight ahead to the stop lights, he thought of the years he'd ridden with his dad on the train to Chicago, Florida, and California. His dad had been an engineer for the Milwaukee Road. While on the train rides when he was a kid, he'd hear stories about the gangster Al Capone when they'd have the layover in Chicago. His dad taught him how to ride the "L" train around the city. When his daughter became old enough to travel with him, together they rode the "L" train.

At the park, John walked straight to the old Minnehaha Depot.

"I wonder if Diane will make it today?" he wondered out loud.

The old steam engine, one of the first in Minnesota, sat out front. He stood with his hands on his hips and grinned. His heart went pitter-patter from the beauty and magnificence of the spectacle in front of him. The engine commanded adoration and reverence. It brought America together as a nation. The Gold Spike in Utah was the last nail pounded. It sewed the United States together, and the magnificent engine carried the world across the United States by bringing passengers from all different nations. The thirty-six states were at last united after the Civil War.

As John was about to sneak inside the building, he heard from behind, "Hey, Old Man! I'm here!" He looked around and saw Leif hurrying toward him.

"Hurry-up, boy! The day's beginning!"

Leif rushed to him, stopping by the depot's door. "You can't go in here, can you?"

"Shh! It's a secret," John said, setting his thermos down. "A nice old ranger came by and handed me a key and told me to keep it under my hat. I've never told anyone that I have it. You're the first to know." John motioned to the two lawn chairs hidden inside. "How about setting these two chairs out there somewhere so passersby can see us and ask questions?"

"That's what you do all day?" Leif picked them up. "Well?"

"Huh?" John took the bucket, poured soap into it, and made sure the large sponge was where it should be. He stood with the bucket. "What did you say?" When he looked toward the doorway, no one was there. "Oh well." He walked out and found the chairs set in an odd location.

"How does that look?" Leif asked. "Hey, Old Man?"

"What?" John set the bucket down near the back of the engine. "I didn't hear you." He saw what Leif was referring to. "Over here is better, boy, it leaves room for Diane. She'll pass out homemade cookies until they're gone."

"What? Someone passing out cookies! For free!"

"Yes. Let her tell you all about it, boy."

"Boy? Again?" Leif moved the chairs to the designated place. "From where they were, we'd be able to watch the road."

"Back here, it'll give the guests a chance to ask questions about the engine, and they'll see Diane. She'll wear a uniform cap," John said. "That's important."

"Whatever," Leif said, shrugging. "Anything else?"

"Yeah. Get me some water in the bucket. Right over there is the stream. You can do that for me, can't you?"

"Sure." Leif took the bucket and left.

John settled in the chair to wait for Leif's return. While waiting, he poured himself a cup of coffee and took a drink. Still hot, he thought and took another drink. As he did, people began to walk toward him. They waved and a man stopped while the women continued.

"This one of the first steam engines?"

"Yep, cowcatcher and all. Carried visitors across the country."

"Amazing," the man said. "Just amazing." He walked away.

John yanked his dad's old railroad watch from his pocket and read the time. "The boy should've been back by now," he grumbled.

As the cars drove past on avenue where the roads split and became Hiawatha and Minnehaha Avenues, he watched two policemen walking with their eyes focused downward as if searching for something. At the same time, Leif returned.

"You'll never guess, Old Man, what's going on around here. Never guess in a million years!" Leif set the bucket down with a jolt, splashing out water all over John's feet.

"Can't you be more careful?" John brushed his shoes off.

"It's not as if—never mind." Leif stared down at John. "It's like this—Grandma said I must get along with you or I'll be sent to some foster home. So at least try to be friendly, will you? You are my grandpa."

"I am, aren't I?" John said. "What's got you jumping around like a bouncing ball?"

"The cops are searching for a missing person," Leif said.

"A missing person?"

"Right! Someone who went missing in 1970," Leif said. "You were like a hundred already then, right?"

"Watch it," John said. "I used to play football with George Washington."

"Wow! You are old, Old Man." Leif grinned.

"Was it a man or woman? Do you remember?"

"A young girl. High school. She went—"

"Vicky Storbakken, Diane's daughter. Missing during prom pictures right here over by the falls. The falls were the backdrop of the pictures. Her boyfriend never did know what happened. She disappeared. Went to the bathroom and never returned." John snapped his fingers. "It was just like that. Her brother never married, spent half his lifetime wondering what happened to his sister and the other half, keeping his mother, our Diane, company."

"Unbelievable. She's probably dead by now. That's ancient history," Leif said, looking over at John. "I mean—well?" Leif shrugged, knowing his grandpa was much older or at least the same age as the missing person.

"I feel for the family." John glanced toward where Leif was looking. "Diane is with them. That's her with the cap." He pointed. "See the cap and she's carrying the basket."

"Cookies in a basket? Wow!"

"They're no closer to locating Vicky. It's a shame." John gave Leif a sideways glance, realizing this may have been their first decent conversation. "Well, let's get busy washing the engine."

"We need a right good name for it." Leif removed bottled water for himself and took a drink. "What do you say? How about Big Mama?"

"You don't think Carl, after my dad, would be a good name for the steam engine?" John said.

"Nope. Big Mama," Leif said.

"We'll go with Papa."

"Okay, your choice." Leif shook his head because this guy just didn't give him an inch. He couldn't figure out why mama was any different than papa. "I suppose you still expect me to climb up on the top, eh?"

"Yep. I'll get the ladder and long handled brush for ya," John said, heading for the building. Inside the depot near where the chairs had once been, against the corner, were the needed items. He went out and set the ladder up right in the front so the windshield of the engine would be first cleaned. "There. You can start climbing up and I'll be right back."

"Hey, Old Man! What are you going to do while I do all the work?"

"Watch." John glanced over toward where the investigators were searching. "Looks like Diane's heading this way." Walking toward her, he waved.

"John! The basket is getting heavy." Diane stopped to wait for his approach. "Will you finish carrying this for me? You know, it's hard for an old granny like me to carry all these cookies. So foolish of me."

"Foolish? People love it, especially the older people who remember the women and Red Cross helping to feed the soldiers as they left for the war. You stood out here when your husband left for World War II, and how many years ago was that? You're doing wonderful, young lady."

"Ahh, you're a dear to say so. I'm ninety-two."

"I thought you were thirty-nine." He took her basket and they went to the engine.

Chapter two

"Would you mind if I sit in the comfiest chair today? My back hurts." Diane tried to sit in the designated one for her but stood almost immediately.

"This one?" John asked. When she nodded, he moved it to the correct spot for her to sit upon it. "There now, this will be perfect for you."

"Hey! Can I have one of those cookies!" Leif strode right to her. "Heard about you. I'm so sorry. I hope they find your daughter."

"So do I, young man. You must be John's grandson? We've met before." She smiled at him. "You look just like him too. Mostly like your mother."

"I look like my dad?" He ate the cookie in two bites.

"Oh, yes. Somewhat. Didn't know him very well."

"These are really good."

"Thank you." No sooner had Diane gotten herself situated by opening the basket and removing her small thermos and poured a cup of coffee than a young woman approached her.

"What do we have here? You remind me of my grandma."

"Would you like a free cookie?"

"Sure, but why?" She reached for a chocolate chip cookie. "It smells fresh." She bit into it and her eyes opened wider. "Wow! Tastes like hers too. Thank you."

"In World War II, I served food to the soldiers when they were going to war. They'd hop on the train and off they went."

"You're sweet. Thank you." The woman walked away.

John and Leif scrubbed the engine down, Leif close to the front windshield and John with a large sponge across the sides, each glancing from time to time toward where the search party walked the grounds.

"You okay up there?" John hollered up to Leif.

"I can't hear you very well up here, Old Man," Leif hollered down to him. "Whatya say?"

John glanced upward and noticed Leif stood on top of the engine and was almost directly over him. "You can fall from where you're at. Don't stand! It's wet and slippery!"

"Hey, Old Man. I'm done. Faster than you!" Leif dropped the handled brush, and it almost hit John on the head. "I'm sorry!" Leif climbed down and pushed the ladder together, then carried it inside the depot doors. "You okay?" he asked upon his return.

"Sort of. Don't be a fool and do something like that again. You've watched too many movies, boy. It's the real world now. Help me take care of the rest of the engine. I'm almost done." John continued to wash off fingerprints and gang markings. "Bastards, I wish they'd leave Papa alone."

"You can't even say 'thanks,'" Leif said. He kicked the bucket over and left with his fishing pole, shouting over his shoulder, "I'll be back."

"What am I going to do with him," John muttered to himself. He finished with what little water was still in the bucket before calling it a day. He brought the bucket and cleaning supplies back inside of the building and placed them in their designated location.

After rearranging the chair on the other end from Diane to showcase the engine, John sat down and reached for his thermos. The leftover remnants in his cup, he threw out into the grass before pouring himself a fresh cup. Steam from the coffee wafted upward, and John breathed in deeply. "At last some peace and quiet." He shut his eyes for a moment and pictured his Inga. He opened his eyes and saw two men standing right in front of him. John took a moment to size them up from the top of their heads to the bottom of their feet where they stood. The tallest had a crown of hair while the other, a full head, both were gray and wore glasses. Nice jeans and shirts, fitting for a leisurely day walking in the park. Both had a nice new pair of tennis shoes. He could tell the clothes were new because of little or no rips or stains and the shoes weren't very dirty. The boy must've been right, he thought, the police were up to something. He wondered if it went back to his dating days, and if they'd found anything new?

"I must've fallen asleep," John said, massaging his chin. He began to stand, but the men motioned for him to stay seated. "What can I help you with?"

"Is that your son we saw or grandson?" the taller one said. "I'm Detective Mark Anderson. This is Detective Ronnie Johnson."

"Your son—" Detective Mark Anderson said.

"Grandson, so they tell me," John said. "Why? What did he do now?"

"He hasn't done anything," Detective Ronnie said. "Actually, he told us about you."

"See? He did do something," John said, frowning. "How can I help?"

"Don't worry about anything," Detective Mark said.

"I think I remember you two from Roosevelt. So many years ago. Anyway, I know what this is all about." John removed his engineer hat, scratched his forehead, then placed it back on top of his head. "You're obviously looking for Vicky, right?"

"Yes. I believe we did grow up together, so you were living around here in 1970? May?" Detective Mark asked.

"Yes, of course! I grew up here and went to Roosevelt, is that what you're asking?" John said. "The boy—"

"What's his name?" Detective Ronnie said.

"Leif."

"Just Leif? What's his last name?" Detective Ronnie asked. He crossed his arms and looked down at John. "Everyone has one."

"Dahl." John stared at him. "Is that all?"

"Nope. We'd like to know if you graduated in 1970? Our classes at the time were so huge, we can't remember everyone. Do you remember the missing person, Vicky Storbakken? Does that name sound familiar?"

"Different year. Yes, I do. Vicky and I dated. When I met my wife I broke it off with Vicky," John answered. He took a minute and said, "My God. You don't think I had anything to do with her disappearance, do you?" His heart seemed to beat faster and he clutched his chest.

"You all right, sir?" Detective Mark asked, placing a hand on John's left shoulder. "Sir?"

John nodded, took in a few deep breaths. "Yes. Yes. I'm doing fine." He lowered his arms after the next deep breath. "Well? Do ya?"

"Not really, no," Detective Mark said, stepping back. "But you see? We're trying to gain further knowledge about the incident. No sighting of her over the years. No communication with the family. No body. No murder weapon." Detective Mark stepped back to observe him. "Can you think of any one thing that may come to mind about Vicky?"

"I see you and Diane get on, maybe between the two of you, you can talk about the dates and something will pop that will spark a memory?" Detective Ronnie suggested. "Since you dated Vicky, do you possibly have pictures? Any memento? Anything? No matter how simple or stupid it sounds, whatever it is, it just might help the investigation progress." He stopped a moment before proceeding. "We graduated with her, and I wonder if we both don't remember you? I bet you were in '69?"

"Yes. '69. We broke up right after I graduated. Let me take a good look at you two," John said. "It's impossible to remember everyone from my class, let alone another."

"I know. We had at least seven-hundred and fifty classmates, and your class had about a hundred more than we did. I basically remember only a few, and they are mostly from grade school." The detectives moved to stand in front of John. "Now take a good look."

John studied them once again from top to bottom. "Yes, I do remember you two, but not for anything in particular. It must've been from dances or language classes. I took Norwegian, that's what charmed my Inga into dating me."

"Any men around her?" Detective Mark asked. "We're curious. It might give us a spark or idea."

"Her dad worked at the Old Soldiers Home." John remembered. He massaged his chin. "You see, she'd bring friends there to see her dad and sometimes, we'd hear stories about the Civil War veterans. That was all fine, but there was someone there, an old WWII vet, who gave me the willies. I told her I never wanted to return to that place."

"A patient?"

"Yes."

With the fishing pole across his left shoulder, and a big smile, Leif marched toward them, stopping beside John. "What's up?"

"Can we take down your name?" Detective Mark asked. He opened his notebook to write.

"Evans. John Evans."

"We'll call if we have any more questions." He slapped his notebook together to slip it into his pocket.

"I'll be happy to help," John said, giving out his phone number. "Anything else?"

"Yes. Go through your old pictures and if there's anything that comes to mind or a picture that might be helpful, please contact me." Detective Mark gave him his contact card after placing the notebook back where it once was. "Please do this."

"I'll make sure Grandpa here will do it," Leif said, smiling.

"Didn't catch anything?" Detective Ronnie said. "By the way, what's your dad's first name?"

"Gary. That all?"

"Should be," Detective Ronnie said. "You folks can call us by our first names when you see us. We're retired and doing this to find our classmate and to give the family some kind of closure, which will hopefully ease the pain after all of these past years."

"I get it. If you need me, I'm here hanging out with the old man."
Leif removed his earbuds and phone from his pocket and started his
music.

"See what I have to put up with?"

"How old is he?" Mark asked.

"Fourteen."

"He'll grow out of it," Ronnie said.

"I can only hope," John said. He turned to Leif and pulled out an
earbud. "There's spectators coming so don't be a smart mouth brat."

Leif paid little or no attention as he placed the bud back into his
ear. John watched the two men go over to speak to Diane for a short
time, then leave.

John stood as a passerby approached after speaking to Diane. He
stopped to talk, already chewing a bite of cookie.

"Good morning for a stroll, sir," John said, nodding to him. "Good
cookie, eh?"

"I teach these engines in school. They were remarkable in their
day. Without this engine, our country never would've been settled or
populated as early as it was," the spectator said.

"True. This engine ran on steam. Oils from coal, oil, or wood," John
said.

"Absolutely clean. Boy, a person really had to know how to run it
too, or you'd end up over the edge or crashed or—"

"Blown up!"

"Nice talkin' to ya. Thanks for keepin' this old beauty sparkling."
He began to walk away, then called, "The cookie's wonderful!"

"Come by anytime," John said, barely able to contain himself with
delight from the compliment bestowed upon him. As he glanced
toward Diane, he said, "Good cookie, the guy said."

She returned a smile.

John returned to his chair. Few sightseers passed by, which allowed
him time to think about the missing woman, Vicky. Vicky Storbakken.

The poor girl. She'd disappeared during her senior prom, but he'd already graduated. His mother told him Vicky had accepted an engagement ring from her prom escort. She was engaged.

John scratched his chin. The man's name alluded him, but John felt better about his memory lapse because Vicky's date wasn't a Roosevelt grad. When he returned home for the evening, John planned to ask Inga where the photo albums were and dig them out. He also must remember to clue Frances in on the investigation since she'd grown up in the neighborhood too.

John noticed another group of spectators headed his way. He nudged Leif and said, "Take time and listen to what these people say."

"I'd rather not," Leif said. "I'm getting bored."

"So am I, but I won't tell you what from," John said. "Talk to Diane, she might give you another cookie if you're nice and take those buds from your ears."

"Okay, I will." Leif carried his chair away from John to sit near Diane.

The approaching group, presumably a family with three children about middle school or high school age plus the parents, stopped first with Diane, then made their way to John.

"Hello to you all," John said. "This type of engine was first in use in Scotland, the year was 1817. George Stephenson was the inventor."

"How interesting," the man said.

"Why is the front so big?" the youngest of the three children asked. She wore her red hair back in a ponytail and had freckles. She reminded John of his daughter at that age.

"It's called a cowcatcher. Funny, isn't it?" John said.

"Cowcatcher? Makes no sense," a child said.

"I agree," the oldest of the children said.

"Catch cows? That's ridiculous," the boy said.

"It really was, though," John said, chuckling. "There were cattle drives out west, most especially. I'm sure that you've read or heard about them, right?" When they nodded their heads, he continued. "There were avalanches, also, which needed plowing through. Think of them as some kind of a snow plow for these parts with all the snow we get in Minnesota."

"Very interesting," the dad said. "Well kids, we've wasted too much of this man's time."

"Let's keep moving," the mom said, ushering her kids onward.

"Thanks for stopping. It's been a real pleasure," John said.

After the group of spectators were on their way, both John and Leif looked out across to the where two women stood talking to the retired detectives.

"I know they are looking for Vicky, and I dated her, but why look around here?" John walked closer to Diane and Leif. "Your husband worked there, didn't he?"

"He did and would take Vicky with him sometimes. I remember when you went with her."

"Me too, but why aren't they searching the hospital grounds?"

"They must've had weirdos down there," Leif said. When John glared at him, he said, "Sorry, I didn't mean that your husband was a weirdo."

"It's okay, I knew what you meant," Diane said. "I only baked two dozen cookies today, and they're almost half gone. I bet you would like another."

"Don't encourage him," John said, "but I would like one." Diane opened her basket and he took one. "Thank you."

"There were some really creepy inmates there. Vicky called one, 'Crazy Eddie.'"

"Still, why are they searching in this area?" John said.

"There must be a reason," Diane said. "Fifty years? I can't imagine ever finding her. I've hung on and hung on to see this happen. I can't or won't rest in peace until it happens."

"I don't blame you for thinking like that," Leif said. "I always wonder about my dad and how nice it would be to have a mother who is well."

"Leif? Don't say anymore. It'll only hurt." John thought for a minute. "I wonder about the old Stevens House? That's been there since 1849. It's where Hennepin County and the school district was organized."

"I thought for sure they'd searched this area thoroughly," Leif said.

"You go and spy on them for me, then come back and report."

"Got it. Then lunch?"

"Yep."

"What do I get for doing it?"

"A soda."

When Leif was out of hearing distance, John brought his chair closer to Diane. "I know you're leaving soon but while we're alone, do you remember anything from when I dated your daughter? Anything in particular? I only remember picking her up and going to dances. She was a flirt and danced with other boys besides me. I'm not saying that to hurt you or your memory of her, it's just the way it was. We went to a few movies too and then the drive-in for a root beer and French fries or onion rings. That's all I remember. What about you?"

"This is what I told the police recently," Diane said. "She continued to wear the half- heart shaped necklace you'd given her for her birthday that year and it's not in her jewelry box, at least I've never found it. She loved playing with Barbie dolls when she was little. I've turned what was in her room over to the police for further DNA testing since there wasn't such a thing when she went missing. Maybe they can tie it in with Vicky and the person who took her?"

"That's something about the necklace. It makes me feel really good because now I know that giving it to her wasn't in vain. I wondered if she'd thrown it away or sold it."

"Nope. My guess is that, you find her and you'll find her half of the necklace."

"Oh my word," John said. "What about Tom in all of this? He ever date? I know he never married."

"He's dated but is afraid of abandonment, which is what the therapist has told him. He can't seem to get over it."

"That's really a shame. Well, I suppose I should walk around a little."

"I'm done for the day. I'll pass out what cookies I have left on the way. I'll stand by the falls, and they'll be gone in a jiffy."

"When will you be by again?"

"I'm not sure when the next time will be." Diane closed up her thermos and basket. "Nice talking to you and meeting you, Leif."

"Bye, Grandma."

"Take care."

Before John inspected the engine, he carried Diane's chair back inside of the depot. Afterward, he wiped out spots as he slowly traveled around the large engine. Just as he sat, a bird flew over and splotched the wheels. He got up to clean it with the damp sponge.

Leif returned with a can of soda and plopped onto the chair. "Ain't you done yet, Old Man?" He drank from the soda. "I'll get the sandwiches. Then you're done, right?"

"You betcha." John finished rubbing the fingerprints from the engine and went to plunk the sponge into the bucket.

Leif stood, opening the brown bag.

"What kind are they?"

"I think one is roast beef. It must be for you because the other one is peanut butter and jelly." Leif looked at John. "Second thought, Grandma told me to eat the roast beef to get more meat on my bones." He kept the beef one and handed the other to John. "There you go."

"Well boy, let's get out there and eat before more people come by. It's impolite to eat in front of other people, especially strangers." John took the sandwich and smiled to himself. Frances always made a pbj for him simply because she knew it was easy to chew and swallow when in front of strangers. He sat and began to eat. "Tell me what the heck is happening over there? Why are they stomping around near trees and brush?"

"Because of the grounds. The mounds and piles of dirt near those old trees. They're bringing in some person who knows how to run an imager or whatever it's called, to look for bones or bodies underground." Leif began to eat. "We should have chips."

"Be thankful with what you have," John said and chewed for a few minutes. "There probably is a load of bones underground around here, seriously. If you think about it, the Native Americans were here, and I bet the Falls area was sacred."

"Yeah, you're right. Then, there's animals or old people just dropping dead right where they stand and no one finds out for sure what happened to them. They've gone missing forever, just like that girl that went missing." He finished his sandwich and drank his soda. "Don't ya think?"

"By golly, this time, you may have gotten something right no matter how serious it is or historic." John finished his meal. "I dare say, that hit the spot."

"Now what, Old Man? We hang out around here for a while?"

"Guess so. Why not go fishing again?" John looked over toward the woods. "I hope they find Vicky."

"What is it that you've been asked to do?" Leif asked, folding his chair. "I'm ready to leave."

"Tell you what, go fish for an hour and we'll call it a day." John stood and took in a deep breath. "I've got a few things to do."

"Okay, back in an hour." Leif took off with his fishing pole.

"Good luck."

No sooner had Leif walked away than another set of spectators walked over to John.

"Hi, sir!" the man said. "I bet you know a thing or two about this here beast?"

"You bet! My pa used to drive one of these. Took me all across the United States, east and west. He was an engineer. "I learned how to get around those large cities. We went everywhere. School got in the way."

"I can see that, but did you work for the railroad?"

"No, I went in another direction, teaching. However, I met my lovely wife through the railroad. She lived in Glenwood and I drove the train there and back. I kept going back with Pa, and now I'm a happy man."

"What can you tell me about this beauty?"

"The first steam engines in Europe were invented in 1784. The steam engine brought the nation together. Abraham Lincoln pushed for it while the Civil War was raging," John said."

"The man was remarkable."

"Oh, yes. He started the process of a Transcontinental Railroad before his presidency. He saw the future."

"Most of our forefathers did." The man began to walk away, then stopped to say, "Thanks!"

"Anytime."

When the man was out of view, John looked over to the flowers and thought how pretty they were and could understand why Vicky had wanted prom pictures taken in the park.

The river of memories invaded his thoughts. Leif's parents, Janet and Gary, had their wedding picture taken with the falls as the backdrop. They married and Gary was sent to Iraq.

Gary never returned and Janet was pregnant.

Chapter three

John sought out the old picture albums from days gone by and set them on the living room table. At first, he'd thought of perusing them in the kitchen but liked putting his feet up after the walk to and from the park. Without wanting to admit it, old age was creeping in. It was hard to breathe comfortably hiking across those rough grounds and then waiting for the pedestrian lights was tough. The sound of the traffic blasted his ears and the diesel fuel from the buses made it worse. All this wrapped together added to his distain of growing old.

As the microwave heated a chicken potpie, his favorite, John wondered how long before Frances would appear at his doorstep? Certainly, she had many pictures from when the children began to play with each other, her son and his daughter. Frances always lived next door. She and Inga were fast friends and stayed that way, no bickering or fighting, and he got along with her husband who died suddenly from a heart attack. The doctors were now telling him to slow down and quit drinking so much coffee. When the dinger went off to signal his meal was ready, he snapped to it and reached for the potholders to lift it out before turning it upside down on a plate. With the plate and utensils in hand, he carried them to the living room.

It felt good to sit in his lazy chair and put his feet and legs up. The time was five o'clock. When the news program was turned on, he watched it as he ate. "Five thirty and she'll be here," he told himself as the program began. While drinking coffee and eating, he wondered what to have for desert and decided upon ice cream. Later, popcorn.

When the plastic fork and other garbage was thrown in the sink beside the rest of the dirty dishes, he grabbed a beer and went out to sit. There were three big picture albums before him and luckily enough, they were dated. He began to look through the albums.

Every so often, a memory popped up as he flipped through the pages. Pictures from when Gary and Janet were little and sitting in the small swimming pool in the backyard. They played croquet and badminton. The net was also set up as they grew older. Pictures of them riding bikes to the nearby lakes, Nokomis and Hiawatha. They stopped for ice cream cones at Baskin Robbins and got caught kissing, he remembered being told. Afterward, he had to send Janet to her room for doing such a thing. Inga made him do it, she was strict. He would slip Janet money when she went out with girlfriends so she could buy something for herself. Inga took care of finances like a bank vault. The final picture in this album showed Vicky at Gary's tenth birthday party eating ice cream. They had celebrated alone because their other friends teased them for being friends.

The next album didn't show anything different, just the two growing older, taller, and Janet beginning to fill out with Gary developing muscles. The final album was much the same. He stood to carry them back to where they came from, returning with the final, older album dated from high school days.

"Should've started with this one." He plopped down into his chair once more and turned the station on the television to the *NCIS* show. Just as he began to study a picture of Vicky, the back door opened and he heard, "Hello! Where are you?" It was Frances.

"Out here!" She knew her way, so he didn't get up. He waited a beat and then it came, "Want another beer?" Frances said.

"You betcha! Get something for yourself."

"I have an album but am not sure if this is her in it, you know? That Vicky girl." Frances pushed a picture in front of him. "It's her, isn't it?"

"Give me a minute," John said, pushing his glasses farther up on his nose. He held the album closer to the light and took his time just to annoy her. He cocked his head and kind of pursed his lips, getting ready to speak, when—

"It's her, isn't it? Hurry up and say something." Frances leaned in to look at it again. "It's the eyes. They match with what you have here." She pointed at a picture from his album. "They're identical. Same hair, size, everything's the same."

"By golly, they are! You hit the nail on the head with this one, Frances. Where was it taken?" John studied it further. "It looks like she's all dressed for a date."

"It wouldn't be with you, would it?" Frances looked down at the date from the black and white photo. "She's in a dress so she has to be going somewhere."

"They wore dresses back then, you know that. What were you doing at the time to have a picture of her?" John noticed that she started to blush. "You were up to no good, weren't you?"

"I was a good girl. Let's get back on task."

They each drank from their beverages.

"Tell you what, I met Inga and that's all there was to it. Did you ever go to the Old Soldiers Home? Take pictures of the falls and catch her in it on prom night?"

"No. This is the only one." She set the album aside and made herself comfortable on the couch. "Let's see what you have."

Car doors slammed outside on the street. John looked out, shaking his head afterward.

"The boy went somewhere with his crazy friends."

"He told me he was going out, but he's supposed to be home by ten o'clock."

"Those guys looked like bums. I don't like it. You should've sent him over here," John said, frowning. "We have to keep a closer eye on him."

"Help me get him to church," Frances said. "He needs direction."

"The boy needs his parents."

"That's true, but he also needs a grandpa who treats him like a grandson."

They sat silently for a short time, then Frances stood to leave. "What should I do about the picture? You might have a few more in that album of yours."

"Give me it, and I'll turn it in with my own tomorrow. I'm sure that someone will come over and ask what I've found."

"Here." Frances handed him the right picture from the album, took the empty cans, and went to the kitchen. She threw the cans away and noticed all the dirty dishes. Before leaving, the dishes were hand washed and set in the drainer to dry. "Good night," Frances called and left the house.

"Thanks!"

For the rest of the evening, John spent time going through the final pictures. There were several of he and Vicky going out the door taken by her parents since he always drove to her house and picked her up in his 1962 Chevy car. She'd slide over and place her hand on his knee, and he'd almost lose control of the car because it was so exciting. Her kisses sent him to the moon and back. If only she hadn't gone out on him, he thought, they may have married. Sighing, he removed the chosen pictures and laid them on top of the one left behind from Frances. The pile was taken to the kitchen table so they wouldn't be forgotten in the morning rush to leave.

John went to look out the front window but didn't see Leif. He hoped that kid returned home at an early hour. Having Leif beside him was comforting.

The evening was long. It was time to say, "Good night" to Inga. He stood in front of the ash vase on top of a China cabinet.

"Inga, what to do with Leif? Poor guy, I do feel sorry for him." He dried his eyes. "I suppose I should look out for him better, eh?" He blew his nose. "Please help me to know what to do with the kid." Lastly, he said, "I miss you something awful, my Inga. Good night." John turned and walked away.

After his evening bath, John went to the office and dragged down his pile of steam engine books. There were three of them. Once belonging to his pa, the two used to sit and comb through them together. He always thought of Pa as being brilliant, and these books made him that way. With the heavy books in his arms, he sat back down on his chair. The covers had fallen off the textbooks, and the spines were broken apart, which made it a little difficult to read the pages in order. The pages were smudged, worn, and ripped. John saved these three books because of the remembrance.

Opening the front page, he began to silently read about the wonderful, amazing steam engine. He read:

The steam engine wasn't invented by a single person but an accumulation of ideas and discoveries over a long period of time. The ancient Greeks knew that steam produced movement by using a model windmill. When the coal mining industry developed steam then it seemed like a viable power. Steam power was patented in 1698 by Thomas Savery. It was a means to raise water to drain mines but had no moving parts. Steam was fed into a downpipe going into the water, cooled, condensed to create a vacuum which drew the water up. Limitations meant that only low pressure steam was used to raise the water but only in a shallow mine. Few were used as there were a number of explosions.

A car door slammed shut and the cars' engine sounded loud. John looked outside and noticed Leif a little unsteadily walking to the house. The clock dinged eleven times. Opening his door, John watched while Leif tried to enter his house. When unable, Leif stumbled toward the back of the house, presumably to enter through the back door. John put on his slippers and went to open his back door. Across the yards, he watched Leif pounding on his back door. It wasn't too long of a wait until Leif glanced over at John.

"Get your sorry ass over here, boy! Right now!" John called out to him. "It's my bedtime."

"Coming, Old Man!"

While John waited by the screen door, he glanced over to Frances's windows but didn't detect any movement. He had a gut feeling Frances did this on purpose—locked the kid out as a form of punishment for him and Leif or else she used some kind of psychology to teach them both a lesson. Evidently, he and Leif needed to find common ground.

"Get in here," he growled at Leif as he entered. "You smell of alcohol. You're too damn young, and I'm too damn old to deal with it. Go shower."

"No clean clothes."

"I'll give you a big towel. Your grandma will bring your clothes over in the morning if she wants or else you'll have to run like a bunny home. Got it?"

"Got it." Leif headed for the bathroom. "Where should I put my dirty clothes?"

"I'll give you a plastic bag."

While Leif showered, John realized it wouldn't be long before the kid asked for the offered towel. He took out one from the hall's linen closet and set it on the floor outside of the bathroom door.

John set the books aside on the table next to the chair and went to bed. No sooner had he shut his eyes than there was pounding on his bedroom door.

"Where's a towel?" Leif asked. "I only see the dirty one hanging up."

"On the floor in front of the bathroom door." John rolled over and covered his ears with the blanket.

Leif began to throw-up in the toilet. The awful noise kept John awake. He went in to see if the boy needed any help.

"You sound like shit."

"I feel like it," Leif said. He heaved up more. "I suppose you're enjoying this?"

"Yep."

"At least you're honest." Leif stood. With the washrag, he wiped his face. "I think I should shower again."

"Good choice."

"Where will I sleep?"

"I believe know where," John nodded towards Janet's room. "Right in there."

"Got it." Leif went to his mother's bed.

Morning brought John into the bathroom with a sore throat, but he figured he'd be able to manage throughout the day. If only this kid would learn something about the steam engine, then he could do the talking, thought John. In the living room John placed said books back on top of the table in full view, right in front of Leif, for him to see. Hopefully, John wasn't going to hold his breath, but maybe, would he please do a bit of reading from the old pages? Surely, there was something the kid was interested in, right?

After dressing and getting ready for the day, John hit the "on" button for the coffee maker and pulled from the cupboard a box of instant oatmeal cereal. It was his favorite. When finished eating the bowlful, he drank a cup of coffee and poured his thermos full for the days' routine. Next on the agenda was to make a peanut butter and jelly sandwich. Fresh peanut butter and apple jelly from one of Inga's sisters. It was so good, it made him think of her and how happy they'd been together. It really hadn't been too long since she'd left him, only two years, but it seemed as if an eternity. When the sandwich was ready, it was set next to the thermos, but what to do with that kid?

He went to check on Leif and found him sprawled out with his mouth wide open. John wondered if he hadn't seen Gary asleep, watching a movie with Janet and had his mouth open like that? As he scratched his head, John went to stand in front of the ashes.

"Honey, shouldn't I wake him? He needs to come with me. The kid needs to learn how follow rules, be dependable, reliable. What should

I do?" John waited for a few minutes before turning to look over at the kid and shrug his shoulders. "I guess I'll leave him alone."

As soon as John picked up the photos of Vicky, the wall phone rang.

"Hello, Frances."

"How'd you know it was me?"

"No one else calls. He's still sleeping. Wait, I hear movement." John set the phone on the cradle and looked. Returning, he picked up the phone. "He's starting to wake up. It's eight thirty and I'm on my way out of the door. Yes, I have a sore throat, but it'll get better with another cup of coffee."

"Bring some water and cough drops."

"Yes, ma'am." John hung up the phone and headed out the door, shutting it loud enough to wake the boy up. "Stupid. Going out when he's supposed to be working all day. It's time for me to be strict but not mean, like my mother always told me."

As John came to the stop light, he realized the thermos, pictures, and sandwich were still sitting on the kitchen table. Certain the kid was still sleeping and probably wouldn't take them with him to the park, John turned around to march back home.

The kitchen was as he'd left it, but there was an odd sound coming from the living room, and it wasn't the noise of a television set blaring. He peeked around the corner.

"What on earth are you doing?" John said loudly.

"What do ya mean?" Leif slammed the book shut. "I thought you left this here for me to look at or read?"

"I thought you didn't know how to read," John said, quieter. "I'm sorry. You took me by surprise. Go ahead and read it. If you stay here to read from this book, I'll be a happy man."

"You happy?"

"I'll ignore that."

"Look at this picture. Tell me about it."

"It's the first successful steam engine. Read this section here, it explains it all. He pointed to it. I had just read it when you came in last night. I like to review when working at the park to refresh my memory."

"Now?"

"Yes. Go ahead and read it. When you're done with this section then read the next paragraph. Come on down to the park when you're finished."

"What's this paragraph about?"

"Look at the picture and think about it."

"I'll read and then see you at the park."

"Good. Don't forget to pick up a sandwich from Grandma and something to drink." John grabbed the thermos, sandwich, and left. "Read up, then come and surprise me with what you've learned."

"Got it!" Leif said. "Now I can show the old man up with my brilliance when I get to the park." Leif dressed and went over to his grandma Frances'.

Chapter four

At the light, he felt in his breast pocket and realized he still didn't have the photos nor would he head back for them. The boy would only laugh at him and call him "Old Man" or something else just as disrespectful. He took a deep breath and crossed on the green light. It was the same intersection he'd crossed since he was a little boy on his way to grade school. Julia Ward Howe, the author of the Civil War hymn, "The Battle Hymn of the Republic," grew up near Louisa Mae Alcott in Boston, Massachusetts. Every so often he'd hum or sing it to himself, but it'd gotten to be less and less since Inga died. He knew he'd lost his center and had a hard time each day making it through to the night. But then, the night...

As he approached the park, there were two familiar looking women stomping the grounds over by an area that was barely visible. It was an area where he'd go walking with his dates late at night and had walked with Vicky when they still dated. It caught his curiosity, so he went straight toward them. He stopped short before approaching them because the two women were old friends from school. One was Nancy, she'd been in his Norwegian class, and Judy in required art. He waved to them as he approached.

"Hey, Nancy, Judy!" John called. "Remember me?"

They stopped what they were doing and looked over to him.

"Not sure, but you're awfully familiar," Nancy said. "Who are you, anyway?"

"I know exactly who he is," Judy said. "The guy who used to date Vicky, aren't you?"

"As a matter of fact, yes. Yes, I am," John said, reaching out to shake their hands. "It's been so very long."

"Yes, of course. Neither of us can believe it's been fifty years since graduation, and for you fifty-one. Time flies," Nancy said. "So you're here checking up on us?"

"Is that you standing and sittin' over there?" Judy motioned toward the steam engine. "It is, isn't it?"

"It sure is," John said. "Finally, the case is reopened, eh?"

"Yes. We've been sorting through pictures and lookin' through this and that for all hours of the day and night," Nancy said. She straightened up to show her full height of five feet nine inches that shown her slim form.

"Look at this old picture of Roosevelt High, so many years ago. Not much has changed," John said.

"Nope, not really, maybe the sign," Judy said.

"You two are gray like me," John said, "but still beautiful."

"Yeah well," Judy said. She stood shorter and fuller than the last time John had seen her. "We should get busy."

"If I recall correctly from the paper, Margo passed away. When is her funeral?" John asked. He removed his engineer cap, wiped his brow, and placed it back on his head. "It's getting hot out."

"Her daughter told us it'll be at Nokomis Lutheran on Friday at ten o'clock," Nancy said. "You comin'?"

"Plannin' on it."

"Come and sit with us," Judy said. "Us sad sacks will need some company."

"I'll see you there." John raised his arm as he walked away, calling, "Thanks!"

As he walked to the depot, he realized again that he'd forgotten about the godforsaken photos. He frowned. Once he'd passed the lilies and other multi-colored flowers he didn't know the names of, he reached his destination.

A boom box blared music so loud it hurt John's ears. He went right to it to try and shut it off but couldn't figure out which button to push.

"Don't you touch it! I swear—Old Man! Don't!" Leif climbed down a few rungs of the ladder and finished by jumping down just as

John pushed the power button. Silence rang out like a freight train. "Now you did it!"

"I didn't know it was your radio. I never saw you," John said. "Couldn't you have at least asked before turning that on so loud?"

"You weren't here, were you?" He slipped out the photos and handed them over to John. "Here. You forgot them."

"Thank you." The items were slid into his breast pocket.

"Why can't I have the radio loud? Music needs to play like that." Leif stood with his arms crossed. "I mean it, we're going to have a big fight pretty soon if things don't change around here."

From the corner of his eye, John noticed some passersby walking toward them.

"Here's why," John said, nodding toward the people.

"I'll get it," Leif said, showing John up. "Listen to this."

"Beautiful, isn't it?" John said to a spectator.

"I got this," Leif said, stepping in front of John. "Got a question? I'm your man."

John rolled his eyes and stepped to the side of Leif to be able to take over when needed, which he figured would be after the first word uttered.

"Young man, you're keeping the engine nice and clean," the spectator said.

"Yep, wouldn't dream of it getting all dirty," Leif said. "Did you know that the first successful steam engine involving a piston was developed by Thomas Newcomen? Its purpose was to pump water."

"Water? Really? Amazing," the spectator said. "That started manufacturing, didn't it?"

Another spectator said, "My goodness."

"Thanks a lot, kid."

Leif walked back to the boom box. He picked it up and went into the depot where it was set on the floor.

"Thanks," John said, grinning. He followed Leif into the depot. "Man, you really caught me off guard."

"Pretty snazzy, eh?" Leif smiled. "We could be a team, ya know, if you'd give a little." Leif reached for his chair. "Let's sit and talk about it."

"We'll do that later, after we've scrubbed the engine all down," John said, reaching for the bucket. "Go fill it."

"Can you at least say, 'please' and be polite? You're too bossy, just like Grandma." Leif took the bucket. "I swear, school can't come soon enough."

"That's for sure."

John picked up the large sponge, then set it down to wait for the water. Clean fresh water, right from the creek bed, that's what the engine would've run on. The pumps pushed the hot water right up into the coils, which in turn, would turn the engine. The temperature required was phenomenal, amazing, but it worked.

As he waited for Leif to return, John slowly walked the circumference of the engine, making mental notes of places where there were large splatters from birds and gang signs. The ladder, he kept where it was located for Leif to climb up on. He must've been examining it for dirt, John decided and went for the long handled washer sponge and leaned it on the ladder. By the time he'd finished the engine's inspection, Leif arrived with the bucket of fresh water.

"Let's get busy. It's full of bird shit."

"That's what I'd found when you rudely interrupted me earlier," Leif said, speaking his mind. He set the pail down near where the ladder stood. "You're welcome."

"What?"

"You're welcome," Leif said, climbing up with the apparatus.

"Oh, yeah, you're welcome," John muttered.

"No, you say thanks. What? I can't hear you above the noise," Leif said, cupping his ear. "What?"

"Thanks."

"It's a start," Leif muttered out loud. "Where's the grandma with the cookies?"

"Not sure. She comes whenever she wants. That's nice that you sat with her yesterday. Very good for her."

"No grandchildren, I suspect?"

"No, sad to say. You've come a long way, Grandson." John saw Leif smile and it warmed his heart. "There is hope."

With his attention on the engine, John's memories turned once more to the train rides with his pa. "Pa was such a brilliant man." His thoughts went to the books sitting in his living room and wondered how far along Leif read? But, he'd been great with the spectator. Onward, John and the sponge slowly traveled around the engine, cleaning, scrubbing it, and making it shine like a newborn's butt. Afterward, he called up to Leif, "Are ya done?"

"Just about." Leif finished with the final section of the top. He'd made like puzzle pieces in his mind and followed the routine of first wash this piece, then that one until the entire top of the engine sparkled. As he climbed down, he noticed a pair of grizzled looking hands wrapped around two legs of the ladder, holding it steady. When he'd reached the bottom, Leif said, "You're welcome." He grinned more to himself than to John.

"Thanks," John said, stepping back.

"Progress." Leif kept the grin on his face as he folded the ladder to carry into the depot and laid on the floor. Glancing at his chair, he reached for his lunch bag, soda, and went out, setting it all in front of the engine. Then the chair went up to sit upon.

"Too close to the engine. Move over a tad bit," John said, motioning to where he'd arranged his chair. "I've dumped out the dirty water, so you won't need to do that."

"Thanks."

John poured himself a cup of coffee. After his first sip, he cupped his ear. "What?"

"Excuse me," Leif said. "And?"

"You're welcome."

"Now down to business," Leif said, taking a few more swallows of his soda. "It seems to me that even though I'm a volunteer, I should still have some rights."

"Like what?" John took a bite of his sandwich as did Leif. "It's so nice and peaceful around here, isn't it?"

"That's for sure." Leif began to eat his lunch and opened the bag of chips. "I know! No debris. Pick up after yourself."

"I'm glad you have learned something," John said, continuing with his meal, "but you see, that's not the issue. You're well versed in picking up around you as we sit here."

"Then what are you getting at?" Leif crunched his potato chips and finished his sandwich. "I'm waiting."

"You must have patience, for one thing. I am old."

"I get it. For your information, I already know that. Now go on." He continued crunching the chips and soon finished them.

"Do you hear the birds? Their chatter is so beautiful."

"Sure."

"Can you think when it's noisy?"

"Nah. I just groove with it."

"What about when you read this morning?"

"It was quiet."

"You were brilliant. Now do it again with these folks coming along." John leaned his head toward the advancing couple. "Go ahead. Stand up!"

Leif popped up, took a few steps forward, and said, "Glad you came by. Let me tell you about the steam engine, if I may?"

John wondered where he learned to sound so sophisticated, then decided it must've come from the juvenile delinquent center he'd been in for three months two years ago for shoplifting. He focused on Leif.

"In 1698 Thomas Savery patented the machine to raise water so it could be used to drain mines. It had no moving parts. Steam went down the pipe into the water and then cooled. A vacuum drew the water up. Only low-pressure steam could be used, meaning the maximum height that water could be raised was about nine meters. It was only really of use in a shallow mine. Few were used because of explosions."

"You're telling me that the steam engine was first designed for miners? I suppose we're talking about England, Scotland, and so on?" the spectator said.

"I believe so," Leif said, looking over to John who nodded.

"Very good, young man. Thanks for the info," the spectator said, and they continued to walk away.

As the couple left, Leif smiled from ear to ear before going back to sit down to finish his soda. John followed suit but poured himself another cup of coffee.

"You were spectacular," John managed to say. "Very, very good. Where did you learn to be so polite? The delinquent center?"

"That's not very nice. Very rude." Leif pursed his mouth. "We're not speaking of that place ever again. I don't ever want to remember it. It was awful."

"I take it you've learned your lesson, however. They must've drummed in the manners and how to be polite. You were excellent." John finished all of his coffee. "I really must go to the restroom. You can hold down the fort with ease. You're almost better than me."

"Now that's a compliment. Go ahead. I got it."

John took off and headed toward the pavilion where the restrooms were located. It was an old cement building built back in the day of horse and buggies. The grounds used to host a circus near it or was this here first, he wondered as he entered the building. The dampness made his breathing a little tough. He finished his job and left but not before stopping to purchase a bottle of water. Pondering the circus and all the animals, and the old Longfellow library, he was happy to have been born around all this history. Hubert Humphrey had been at the park as well as President Johnson and maybe Kennedy. Either way he'd at least seen Humphrey. The circus and the animals hadn't lasted too long, and he figured its demise was due to the weather, but there had been monkeys, elephants, zebras, lions, and tigers in the cages. Closer to the boy, who in his mind was starting to act like a decent human being, stood one of the ladies. From the distance, it looked like Nancy. She was there for a reason, so he hurried over to them.

"Nancy? What's up?" John said, huffing and puffing as he approached. "Something happen?" John immediately sat down.

"We found some bones," Nancy said, talking with her arms, pointing over by where the authorities were digging. "Right off over in that direction."

"Someone's going to come with one of those newfangled thing-a-ma-jigs that can look down into the ground." Nancy stuffed her hands in her pockets so as not to accidentally knock someone with them or slap anyone. "I'm so excited!"

"When will we learn the outcome?"

"I don't know," Nancy said, glancing over to the crowd gathering around the area where the bones had been found. "I better get going."

"Sounds great. Keep me informed," John said.

Both John and Leif watched as she walked away.

"I'd like to go watch," Leif said, watching the crowd grow larger. "You won't mind, will you?"

"No, but first tell me if anyone else has come by?"

"Not yet." Leif started to move, then stopped. "Don't worry, you'll be able to wow the spectators with your charm."

"Thanks."

As Leif walked away, John wondered if Leif would ever learn to not be so rude. After opening the water, John drank from it. It soothed his throat and made it not feel so scratchy. He kept his eye on the crowd for a little while even though there were too many people to really see what was happening. Finally another person rambled up the path and stopped.

"What's going on over there? Do ya know?"

"Some bones were found. They hope it's from a missing person dating back to the '70s." John shrugged. "It's a cold case."

"Got anything to tell me about the engine besides what most people know, like it ran on steam?"

"Sure do." John took another swallow of water. "The first successful steam engine involving a piston was developed by Thomas Newcomen. It was installed to pump water. Along with collapses and explosions, flooding is one of the great dangers of working underground. When we think of steam engines we tend to think of locomotives. Here we see that the need to drain a mine led to the development of the steam engine about a century before it was first used for transport."

"Excellent!" the man said and walked toward the crowd.

When John sat, a train of bike riders zoomed past. As he finished drinking from his water bottle, another stream of riders zipped past and eventually, they were out of sight. The afternoon progressed and still Leif hadn't returned. Casually, a young woman strolled over to him and stopped right in front of him.

"Can I see inside of that monstrous machine? I think it would be so cool." She wore a pair of short-shorts with a bikini pink top. Her curly hair was the color of a banana cream pie.

"Actually, you can't. I would show it to you, if possible, but I can describe it to you, if I may?" John waited for her to step back before standing so as not to be nose to nose.

"Cool." Finally, she moved backward and to the side.

"Follow me," he said, raising his arm and showing which section he was speaking of. "Right here is where the engineer sat. Inside is a bunch of gears and buttons that keep the engine going, such as more pressure. Of course, the windshield. However, the engineer must climb onto a ladder and reach over to clean it because there was no such thing, back in the day, as wipers nor washer fluid. Onward, the cowcatcher is what it sounds like. You know? Cattle, animals in general, and then add in snowstorms, blizzards, and avalanches. This other side? This is where the boiler was. A man stood beside the engineer and continually fed the hold with coal or wood to keep the water within and the pistons pumping the steam through the pipes and the engine moving."

"Cool!" She grinned. "It must've been really, really hot."

"It was so hot, that it would've made your toes curl." John grinned.

"Really?" Her eyes opened wide, showing him the sky.

"You betcha!"

John watched as she walked away before he finished telling her that in the next car was where the coal was stored. Going around the engine, his mind went to how beautiful the young girl looked and how much she reminded him of his daughter. If only Gary hadn't been killed in Iraq, they'd be a family. Janet and Gary with Leif.

As he sat again, John looked over to where the crowd had been and saw people had begun to disperse. Just when he wondered where the kid was, Leif appeared and was briskly walking toward him.

"You'll never guess! Not in a million years."

"Tell me. I'm dying to know. Is it Vicky?"

"An awful lot of research must be done and another autopsy and stuff," Leif said like an authority.

"What don't I know? Should I guess at something since it might not be Vicky?"

"You'll never guess what else, but let's leave and then we can tell my grandma at the same time. It's time to go home. I bet she's making supper as we speak."

"Ahh, you're probably right." John stood and folded his chair. "It's better this way."

"I think so too."

"We do agree on a few things, boy."

"We do, Old Man."

Chapter five

In the cemetery after the funeral services of the friend, Margo, who had passed away, John stood to the side, not knowing which side to stand with—the family or close friends. He was neither. The fateful night of the last time he'd seen Margo came to mind, and he wished it hadn't. Vicky was involved with this other man so many years ago. He moved over to stand near Diane because he knew she was hurting too, just like him, only for other reasons. Diane was thinking of her missing daughter and he of lost friends.

Sure, they'd all grown up together but now, they weren't really strangers, or were they? John shrugged and began to walk away but stopped.

"Diane. Would you like a ride home?" John motioned for her to come along. "I'll bring you right up to your door. Beats the bus."

"I would appreciate it." Diane looked him over. "I wasn't sure if you'd be here."

"Tell you what, I wasn't sure myself, but Nancy said that I should go so here I am." They locked their arms together, and John led her to his car, which wasn't too far from where they stood. "Another friend passed away, one that I hadn't seen in years."

"It's going to catch up with you. Soon there won't be many school friends left."

He brought her to the passenger side of his car, opened the door, and shut it once she'd sat down then went around to the driver's side and climbed in.

"I don't believe it. You still have the same car!"

"Of course! I never would've traded it. Inga said I should, but I put my foot down to that. I love this car and sometimes think of Vicky." John glanced at Diane then turned the key to start the engine. "I usually walk or take the bus. We have taken the train to Glenwood to visit

Inga's relatives. She didn't mind at all, and Janet loved to walk up and down when it wasn't full of passengers."

"We took the train out West to see the mountains once. It was great fun."

John turned the corner of 42nd Street, continued to 44th Avenue, and parked in front of her house.

"Come in for a few minutes. Leif is probably doing great without you. Either way, come in and see what Vicky wore to prom."

"Okay," John said. He walked around to open the door for her. They locked arms once again as they continued to the front door.

Diane unlocked the door, and they entered.

"Nothing has really changed." John stood inside the doorway and glanced around the room. "Oh, I see her picture, it's right on top of your China cabinet." He walked over to it and held it up for a better view. "She was so beautiful, just like her mother."

"Thank you, but we may never know, will we?" Diane said, shaking her head. "I know you want to get going, but there is something else I'd like to talk to you about."

"What's that?"

"Vicky said that you became mean to her. She went for walks by the Old Soldiers Home, you see? And she said that she'd meet up with you there. It never seemed right. Her dad never said anything to me about it. He never did see you down there unless you were with her. She always said that he knew, but he never did. Nothing ever added up right," Diane said, cocking her head to look at him. Her gray hair shone in the bright sunlight.

"I was never mean to her." John shook his head. "Never. Ever."

"I believe you," Diane said. "Look at the picture. You see? She's wearing your necklace."

"She is, isn't she? I don't believe it!"

"If you'd been mean, she wouldn't have worn it for prom."

"That's true, but I'm really upset over that, Diane. I can't believe it. She'd say that she went to work with her dad. I didn't understand the implications at the time that she may have been meeting up with other men. Was she raped or some such thing? Did this start before we dated? Boy, it makes me sick. Why couldn't I have seen that?"

"Why did you two break up? Can you tell me?"

"She went behind my back and dated other guys. I found her in a frat house down by the UofM one night and the other girls too." He looked at her. "I'm so sorry to tell you."

"I had a feeling she went out on you but didn't know for sure. Thank you for telling me," Diane said. "You do know you'll probably be questioned, don't you?"

"Oh, yes. My grandson keeps me informed of the goings-on."

"Good for him. Have you been able to find pictures for the authorities or remember more information?" She walked him to the front door.

"Oh my word, I have old pictures in my pocket." John removed them. "See here? It's before I met Inga. "

"This was in the fall," Diane said. "Look at the turning leaves. The water had quit running."

"She was lovely. She always took my breath away," John said, wiping his eyes. "It's sad. I hope they find her. I believe that she's alive somewhere, but where?"

"I do too. I force myself to think that way. I'm ninety-two," Diane said. "I can't die until I know what has happened to my baby girl. My beautiful, precious baby girl."

"We're all praying for an answer." John slid the photos back inside of his pocket. "If I see them out there working, I'll take them right over to them. Will I see you tomorrow?"

"I must bake the cookies. The funeral has brought me down a little so I'm not sure. I'm tired." Diane gave him a smile. "Take care of yourself, John."

"Do me a favor."

"What's that?"

"Do you still have your old uniform? Not just the hat?"

"It's stored in the closet downstairs."

"Wear it next time you bring cookies." John leaned over and kissed her cheek. "She'll be found. Keep your chin up." John stepped out and the door closed behind him.

In the car, John wondered if he dared park in the park's lot but decided against it. Quickly, he drove home and parked in the garage, then briskly walked to the engine.

As John tried to follow a path around the trees, he found it difficult to walk to the engine. The tangled roots from old trees and underbrush were hard to maneuver, and the ground wasn't flat because of it. Slowly, he made his way to the detectives, Mark and Ronnie.

"Mark!" he waved his arm to catch his attention. "I have a few pictures!" He kept going in the right direction until at last meeting up with him. "Sorry about this. I keep forgetting to turn them over."

"Thanks," Mark said. "I do hope we find her." He took the photos and flipped through them. "I'm not really sure they'll be of much use."

"Me neither, but take them," John said, "compare them with what you have. Maybe a clue will turn up?"

"I suppose you were at Margo's funeral?" Mark sighed. "I wish I could've gone, but it's more important to keep searching."

"I agree, but have you spoken to Diane? She told me a few things now, that maybe you don't know." John furrowed his brow and studied him.

"Like what?" Mark took out his notepad and pen in case there was something worth writing about. "Tell me."

"I drove Diane home and we got to talking. I did not know that Vicky told her she'd go for walks down by the Old Soldiers Home. Her dad didn't know she had, but she'd tell her mom that he knew. Also, I was shown a photo taken the night of the prom before she went out, and she wore the necklace I'd given her. She might still have it in her possession."

"Which means you'd recognize it," Mark said. "It's very odd she didn't tell her dad when she was near the Old Soldiers Home. Diane must be remembering more as time goes by. I'll have another go with her when the time is right." Mark wrote down what was said.

"By the way, if it should come up—"

"What's that?"

"I was never mean to her. Never. Why she'd tell that to her mom, I haven't a clue."

"Most likely to throw suspicions off from what she was up to," Mark said.

"I'll let you get back to your work. Keep me posted or my grandson."

"Will do," Mark called.

John wondered where the girls were or should he call them the women? He was all confused. He found it harder by the day, the older he became, to know what was right or wrong when talking about the other species. He gained better footing and was soon able to walk on the paved path that brought him to the engine. Initially, he couldn't spot Leif, but then he stood out. Several young boys were setting something up. What in the world?

John hurried toward the table and artwork until within calling range and waved toward Leif, who finally responded with a motion to "hurry." It took only a few moments before he stood in front of five long tables with two young high school boys standing behind them and setting up artwork.

"What in the world?" John stood with his hands on hips. "I don't believe it. You boys are invading the space so no one can walk over and ask questions. What are you doing here?"

"Hold your horses, sir." The ranger came out from inside the depot. "We can almost call you a squatter, so don't get grouchy and turn into an old bugger. These kids know what they're doing."

"Tell me," John said, looking over to where Leif stood. "Get over here."

"It's on the up and up. You'll be surprised." Leif smiled and began to help the kid nearest to him. "I'm staying right here."

"Good grief. So tell me, what's up?" John said to the ranger.

"It's a contest of how well their steam engine works. It's a first of many competitions. As of now, we're facing off with the schools in Minneapolis. Next round is the St. Paul high schools."

"Then what? This sounds exciting. What I've dreamed of." John relaxed, giving the ranger a nod to go ahead.

"You see? Kids need to be busy and the park board set up this competition. Get the young ones out and into the parks, especially since we have this beautiful iron horse right in front of us and the old depot. Good idea?"

"Couldn't be better."

"We're setting up dioramas with explanations. Also," he nodded toward a farther away location, "There will be a small model of the first engine."

"It couldn't get any better than this."

As the spectators meandered toward the tables, John listened to the young men describe the machines and what the parts of them were used for.

"Yes, it directed steam to a windmill."

"Really?"

"Yes. It was fed into a downpipe."

"Why?"

"It forced the water out."

"How interesting, young man."

Spectators continued all day to ask questions, then continue to the next table. John went over to Leif who busied himself constructing a smaller version of the first engine.

"I'm going to order what's needed and build myself one of these things. What do you think? Want to help me out, Old Man?"

"I will." John massaged his chin, took out his railroad watch, and glanced at the time. "We could call it a day?"

"Nah, not yet. I'd like to stay for another hour, at least until these guys are ready to leave. I can watch over it all."

"Thank you. What do you suppose I should do?"

"Go see what they're doing off over there, or set up your chair and enjoy the warm weather."

"Great advice."

John decided to walk over to the falls area and as he did, it came to him they hadn't heard any more news about the pile of bones found a day or two ago. Now would be a good time to ask, he decided, and looked toward where the authorities had been searching but no one was in view. Switching directions, he went over to where the miniature version of the first steam engine was being built.

"Hello there," he said, walking toward the boys. An older gentleman worked with them, so John directed his attention to this person. "What school are you from?"

"Roosevelt. I'm their industrial tech teacher," the man said. "Mr. Tiffany. You're the man who sits and tells whoever asks about the engine, aren't you?"

"You betcha! Lovin' every minute of it." John's eyes sparkled with happiness.

"Bet you were a teacher."

"Yep. Long time ago. Same as you, in case you ask."

"Two of a feather. So, how I'm doin'?" Mr. Tiffany was screwing the pipes onto the overhead windmill.

"I've always thought how strong the men were because they constructed it with ancient tools that stripped out easily. How did they know that the windmill would work?" John said. "It's like having a fan. The steam engine brought us the automobile, in a roundabout way."

"We don't give enough credit to these guys, do we? They had to use their head, now we can look it all up. Knowledge at our fingertips." Mr. Tiffany finished lining up the windmill. "I wish they'd have allowed us to dig a small trench to demonstrate the power of this contraption. How it could bring up the moisture and then spit it out in steam."

"Just like we used to see when a train passed us by. We'd wave to the engineer."

"Oh yeah, I remember doing that too." Mr. Tiffany slowly walked around the engine. "Something just doesn't seem right. Come here and tell me what you think? Maybe I'm not looking right."

"It could only raise the water twenty-nine feet, that's all the strength the vacuum created to lift out the water. It's such an odd looking thing, though," John said. He glanced upward at the windmill. "It's upside down."

"How can you tell?"

"It's spinning in the wrong direction." John removed his engineer cap, ran his fingers through his hair, then replaced his hat.

"How could I be so dang stupid? Thanks!" Mr. Tiffany waited a beat then continued. "I've looked all over for a cap like that, can't find one."

"It was my dad's."

"Really? Your dad was an engineer?"

"Yes. Milwaukee Road."

"Thanks again."

"No problem."

John walked back to the engine and stopped near his chair Leif had provided for him. It had been one heck of a day, he thought, plopping down into it. The seat used to feel soft against his rear end, but now it was hard as a rock. John began to think that he was the antique beside the engine. After a short while, Leif walked over to him with his chair in hand.

"Hey Old Man, how're ya doin?" Leif asked, plunking into the chair. "Soft and cushiony." He looked at John. "You don't look so hot."

"Thanks. I don't feel so hot either. Any news to report today before these guys took over the show?" John asked, sounding grouchy. "I am tired."

"Well, a few people came by. Two old buggers, they may have been your age. Oops! I'm sure they were older because they knew more about the engine than you. One bugger had experienced it suck the water from a mine."

"Really?" John's eyes opened wider. "No one has ever told me that before. You just listened, didn't you?"

"Yes. I've also found out about the bones." Leif grinned from ear to ear.

"What's it about? You look like you're ready to split a gut. What's the find?"

"Animals. A zebra and a monkey."

"Oh, my word. There used to be a circus back a few years ago. Must be where they came from. There's something else too, isn't there?" John took off his engineer cap and swept back his hair before replacing it while Leif held back what was on his mind. "Speak up!"

"Native Americans buried their dead," Leif furrowed his brow.

"it's not right to muck about when there is a cemetery," John said. "That's a good question."

"When should we leave? I'm getting a little anxious. I want to tell Grandma about the bones and the high school students."

"Any friends of yours?" John asked, leaning back to relax. "They were your age."

"Two were. I never did anything with them. Wasn't interested in mechanical stuff, but now it's getting really interesting."

"Go see what Mr. Tiffany is up to. He never taught at your school, did he?"

"No, but I know he teaches at Roosevelt." Leif stood to walk over to him. "Can we leave when I return?"

"You betcha."

John watched Leif swiftly walk to the machine and begin to speak with the teacher. In the distance, cars honked and drove past, down the road. His thoughts went to the funeral, and he realized he hadn't a chance to speak to Nancy or Judy. He wondered if they'd make an appearance to see what was happening or if there was news about the bones. As he closed his eyes, he heard his name called and quickly opened them.

"John! Wake up, it's still daytime!" Nancy called, scolding him.

"John! We didn't get a chance to talk earlier at the cemetery," Judy said.

The two bounded toward him from the walkway instead of across the grass and winding among the trees like he had.

"I didn't see you."

"We saw you drive off with Diane. She stayed kind of by herself, which makes sense. Poor woman, I bet she still prays that Vicky's alive," Nancy said, standing in front of him. "My heart aches for her, always has."

"She's still hopeful, isn't she?" Judy said, lowering herself into Leif's chair. "I don't blame her, if she is."

"It's very possible she believes Vicky is alive somewhere. There's always, 'hope,' she said. I've always liked her."

"We're going to look elsewhere these next few days," Nancy said. "It's hard to say what we'll find, but we've discovered where that boyfriend of hers lives, so we'll search the nearby grounds."

"You can't possibly do anything on his property." John frowned at her. "It makes no sense."

"We've since learned that where he lives, it's a new development. The strangest part of it is that it's old farmland, and his parents purchased the lots for development years ago. There is a tiny area that's never been touched," Nancy said.

"And we're going to walk it. What if there's a sunken mound? Or a mound? We're going to walk it together by holding hands," Judy said.

"I wish you luck and keep me informed."

"Will do," Nancy said.

The two girls turned to walk away as Leif returned.

"Ready?" Leif asked.

"Yes. It's been a very long day."

The two took care of matters and walked home.

Chapter six

The minute John stepped inside of his back door, he let out a very long sigh. Since it was summer and hot in the kitchen, he left the door open. It wasn't that it was stifling hot, it was the loss of his friends. His treasured old friends. Not that he'd really kept up with them like a lot of old classmates did over the years. No, he'd stuck to himself. It was always Inga and Janet. Janet, surely would make him feel better, wouldn't she? He decided to ring her up and was surprised when she answered almost immediately.

"Dad. It's good to hear from you," Janet said. "It's been quite a while since we spoke. How have you been?"

"I'm doing okay, honey. I get out every day." He reached for a nearby chair and pulled it over to sit upon. "I'm sitting now, honey. These legs of mine can't handle much anymore."

"You shouldn't stand all day like you used to. You do have a chair, right? I've heard through Frances that you're now spending time with Leif. How's that going?"

"Pretty good. He calls me, 'Old Man.' I don't like it." John shrugged. "But what am I goin' to do?"

"You could try calling him by his name instead of, 'boy' or 'kid,' Dad. Really, it's only polite."

"I guess I'm a little lost without your mother." John glanced over to the vase. "I speak to her all the time but forgot the last few days."

"I've heard there's some excitement going on around the park?"

"Oh, yes." John told her about the bones.

"Since we're on the subject of death and dying, I'm still in therapy over Gary and my second husband. I really wish Gary was with me. I truly miss him," Janet said, and John heard the tears in her voice. "And Mom."

"Honey, we both miss them deeply. Leif especially. When will you be able to come back home? I know Leif wants to live with you and have a normal life, not with two old buggers like me and Frances."

"I'm thankful for you two." Janet frowned. "I'm being motioned that my time is up. The nurse's aide is making the time out signal. Good night, Dad."

"You too honey. Be good to yourself."

John hung up the phone and wondered if he should try to drive that distance? It was a lengthy drive, and he hadn't driven on a highway for a very long time. There was so much traffic and more horns honking and people driving recklessly. He really didn't want to do the drive. If only Leif had a license, then he could drive. John wondered if he'd let him though.

John got up and pushed his chair back to its original position and walked over to the vase. As he walked, thoughts of Janet and family outings came to mind. Instead of telling her about the search for Vicky, should he speak about Leif?

Standing in front of Inga's ashes, he spoke to her. "Sweetheart, Leif and I are having a great time together. See? I called him by name. I'm getting used to the idea that he really is my grandson even though it doesn't seem like it. We should've been able to have a backyard picnic with the little guy and bounce him on our knee like our friends were allowed to do. Instead she took him to live in Seattle. You know what happened then, the bastard married her and left her right away. Now, she's in Fergus Falls under psychiatric care, and we have the kid bouncing back and forth between us. What a mess. It shouldn't have to be like this, but here we are. Frances is trying to mold me into a good grandpa. I sure wish you were here to guide me, be my guide in the darkness. Well, I am kind of expecting that kid to come over at any time. I'll say, "goodbye" for now, honey, until we meet again. Love you." John collapsed in the chair and blew his nose, wiped his eyes as Leif entered.

"You crying?"

"No. My nose is running." John blew it again for emphasis. "What are you here for?"

"It's that first steam engine. It really wasn't a steam engine, was it? There wasn't an engine. It couldn't have been, right? Tell me I'm right." Leif plopped onto a kitchen chair. "You didn't eat, did you? The kitchen doesn't look a mess."

"No, I haven't. Did you bring me a plate of something?" John sat straighter and slightly smiled. "I am hungry. Tell you what?"

"What? I know, go and get you a plate." He stood with his hand on the door handle. "Then what? We'll try to build one of those simple steamer things?"

"Yes. Right from the bottom up. We'll see if it's possible. Shoot! I'm not sure that I have the needed parts, but we'll give it a try."

"Tell you what, Grandpa, I'll bring over the food and while you eat, I'll scrounge around in Grandma's basement and garage."

"Do you think I should look in mine at the same time?" John figured he should ask since the kid was finally taking charge and not calling him Old Man.

"Whatever." Leif walked out the door, whistling.

"Good kid," John said.

While Leif was gone, John hurried downstairs to the basement to search for copper tubing but only found a short, three-foot tube. Not very long but useful for experimental purposes. When climbing the stairs, the back door opened and the screen door slammed shut almost in unison. Leif entered.

"Here you go. A hamburger hotdish complete with corn, onions, tomato soup, and browned hamburger. Lumped together to make something totally unexplainable to anyone outside of the state of Minnesota. There is also a salad. Another item that will only be allowed in the state of Minnesota."

"I bet I know what it is," John said at the top of the stairs. "Jello."

"What kind?" Leif held the small bowl behind his back. "Guess."

"Since it's not a funeral and yesterday it was green, I'm betting on a strawberry or raspberry." John placed the tubing on the floor near where Leif stood. "Am I right?"

"Nope!" Leif shifted the small bowl to his front and set the blue colored jello in front of John. "Blueberry."

"Good grief. I didn't know there was such a thing. Blue jello. Can you beat that?" John reached for a fork. "Thanks."

"Copper tubing?" Leif said, picking it up. "Not long but useful."

"Right. A boiler must be constructed to build up steam. That other thing we saw today went into the ground, right?" When Leif nodded, John continued. "Now steam is brought up through the use of a boiler."

"I'll see what's available over at Grandma's. She's happy I'm finally enthused about something instead of chasing off with the bums."

"Me too."

Once ketchup was distributed on top of the hotdish, John dug into and quickly ate it down as well as the jello, certain his mouth and tongue would not be the same looking for at least twenty-four hours. It would be the shade of blue. The plates were rinsed and set on the table for later.

Leif stepped inside and held an old iron Dutch oven. "Will this do? It's all there was. The garage has been cleaned out except for the mice, Grandma told me."

"I suppose and anything in the basement was tossed out or I took it. This is all that we have to work with."

"It's a learning experience." Leif placed the pot on the table. "She'll look the other way if we destroy it because, and I quote, 'It's giving me something constructive to do instead of bugging her as she knits. She's tired of recounting stitches because of 'you talking too much.'"

"I can imagine. Go get the book and meet me in my garage."

With the tubing in hand, John walked out to his garage. The side door key hung on a hook on the side of the doorframe. He unlocked it and entered but left the door wide open for Leif to follow. He showed up almost instantly.

"Let's move the car out. Want to back it out?" John dug the keys from his pocket.

"You're asking me?" Leif stood with his mouth wide open, pointing at his chest. "Me?"

"Don't be stupid. Yes or no?" John held out the keys and Leif grabbed them.

Leif climbed inside, admired the dash, steering wheel, tried the pedals, then put the keys into the ignition before turning them to start the engine. "Wow!"

"Crank the window down."

"There." Leif rolled it downward. "Even these little ones?"

"No." John stood right beside him. "Barely step on the gas pedal."

Leif inched the car backward and when out of the garage, he slammed on the brakes.

"Now put it in park." When the car was in park, John ordered, "Shut off the engine by turning the key."

"Got it!"

"Now get out." John took the keys, which were dropped back into his pocket.

"Thanks, Grandpa."

They shook hands.

John looked around at the levers and knives and lathes he'd used for making wood products. He massaged his chin as he considered all the tools in front of him.

"Wow! You used to make furniture, didn't you Gramps?"

"I sure did, before Grandma passed away."

"Any chairs out here or small tables? All I see is dust and wood chips."

"We should go back inside. This place is a mess."

"I'll drive the car back inside."

"Okay." John gave him the keys and watched as he drove it inside the garage. They shut down the overhead door.

They each grabbed what they'd entered with and went outside. John locked the door, and Leif noted where the key hung.

"I called your mother when I got home," John said, climbing the back few steps. "She's doing fine."

"Did she mention coming home?"

"No. The subject was changed."

"Per usual."

"I told her that you need to live with her, not these two old buggers."

"It's okay."

They set everything on the kitchen table after John moved whatever was on top of it, like the small container of condiments. He swiped off any dry crumbs.

"Let's figure this out," John said, placing the iron pot on the top of the table. "This is the boiler, and we'll have to pretend from here on out."

"We are already," Leif said, opening the book to the marked pages. "This will be interesting. Mr. Tiffany's model had that windmill on top."

"Correct, but we won't need it because this one is more advanced. The drilled hole won't be necessary with the pot. Do you know what the function of a boiler is?"

"Tell me." Leif watched as John carefully angled the copper tube so it looked like a "u." "That goes into the boiler. That end."

"Right, but we don't have a piston or another tubing, so we'll pretend that the 'u' is sealed off to allow the pressure to build. Then it expands and the steam will go here," John said with his palm on the pot. "You see? It actually is fairly simple."

"Sure it is, but how does it work?" Leif asked, sitting back. "I don't understand."

"A piston isn't attached because the engineers back a few hundred years ago hadn't experimented enough. Somehow, this brought water up and out, but it was dangerous." John found the picture of the first steam engine with all the tubing and boiler. "It almost looks like the pot that's sitting here, doesn't it?"

"It's what Grandma uses for boiling potatoes for a large bunch, and she'll put a roast in it and bake it. But why is it called, 'Dutch'? Do you know?"

"Nope. Look it up in the encyclopedia." John chuckled. "That's what my mom always told me to do. Do you think this pot is still considered dangerous, if so, why?"

"Explosions, I suppose, if there isn't enough moisture in the bottom when it's in the oven at over four-hundred degrees. Also, if it didn't suck out much water for fires in the mines. The ground was used as the boiler, and now the boiler is invented to do the job instead of the ground. Right?"

"Right. Now we've both had our history lesson for the day. Let's call it quits. I'm really rather tired," John said, stifling a yawn. "Why don't you do some research on the engine. Let's see what we have around here, and I'll give you cash to buy a few necessary parts."

"I like that idea," Leif said. "Mind if I take the book with me?"

"Go ahead."

Leif grabbed the rinsed dishes as well as the book and headed out the door, the door slamming behind him.

"Kids," John muttered to himself. It thrilled him to know Leif took to mechanical devices. He hoped teaching might be on the horizon for him to study. Both Gary and Janet had discussed using the GI Bill to go to college. Get an education. Gary would have certainly been able to do it, he was very intelligent, in John's mind. Leif reminded him of his dad. John wondered if he should tell him? It might please him, John thought. He knew Janet would love for Leif to get a degree in industrial arts, it'd be similar to his own teaching degree.

John went about his night business and when he'd finished the mail hadn't been looked through. When he'd plunked into his easy chair and put his feet up for the evening, the mail was opened. Briskly he read the bills and tossed them aside, muttering about the price of electricity and heating. The television was tuned on to CBS, and he settled in to watch his program. With the noise from the television in the background, he read the newspaper. There was a short article about Vicky's open case. He read it through and wondered what, if anything, was discovered where Nancy and Judy said the man Vicky had dated lived? The paper mentioned new clues were found, but of course, they didn't expound on what they were. Neither of Nancy's nor Judy's phone numbers were readily available in his notepad, so he went after the phone book. The numbers weren't easy to find, and then he wondered if they still had house phones since so many people used a cell phone nowadays. He got up and went to the phone to dial Nancy's number since she was usually the person who spoke to him first.

"Hello."

"Nancy?" John said when she answered.

"Yes. Who is this?"

"John."

"John? You're calling so late. It's nine-thirty. I was just going to bed."

"I'm so sorry. I didn't realize the hour was so late. I can call back tomorrow." John almost hung up the receiver on the hook, but Nancy spoke.

"It's okay, don't worry about it."

"I'll ask a quick question—"

"I bet I know what it is. We didn't find anything, and neighboring individuals questioned what we were doing traipsing around the open field. Also, we were stopped by her former fiancé and asked questions. He, of course, doesn't know anything about the case, no more than what we do, he said. I'm going to have to believe him. We don't have any leads that I'm aware of. Have you heard anything? Anything at all?"

"Yes and no, mostly no. I can't seem to get her out of my mind, and that's unusual since I haven't seen her for fifty years and it's longer since we dated."

"I know what you're saying. I do hope there's a break in the case."

"Me too. You know, I've saved all the paper clippings from when she was taken. I wonder if I shouldn't locate them and read them through," John said.

"I have mine too. That's a thought, though, really John. We should just sit and read everything that's in our possession concerning the crime."

"It would be wise to do, actually. Besides it'll refresh our memory," John said.

"Exactly. We don't know what might jump out and bite us. There must be something that will scare up a certain incident that may possibly lead us to her," Nancy said.

"I really wonder about that guy who was the patient at the Old Soldiers Home and always acted sort of nutty like, don't you?"

"Did he walk the trails around the falls area frequently?"

"Yes, and us guys would run into him in the biffy," John said, shaking his head. "Ish."

"I bet it was, ish."

"Well, I'll say good night and thanks for talking," John said.

"We'll keep in touch. Us Teddies have to keep in touch," Nancy said. "That's right! Go Roosevelt! Go Teddies!"

"You betcha!"

They disconnected and John went into Janet's old room. When she married Gary, it still was her room but when he'd been killed and Janet took the baby, it was converted into a sewing room. Inga used to make a lot of clothes and had purchased a new machine. It had become her room. Scrapbooks were on a shelf inside the closet, so he carried them to the living room.

He turned the reading light on, put his feet up, and began to read the newspaper clippings, getting no further than the first article before he fell asleep. Waking, he read the time, one o'clock. The lights were shut off and John went to bed.

Chapter seven

John and Leif arrived at the normal time. The sky seemed a little hazy, but the promise of another warm summer day was on the horizon. Each time the sun shone its rays, the temperature rose. At the moment it was seventy-five degrees.

"Let's get started on cleaning the engine. Look at all of the graffiti." John motioned to it. "Why do kids have to do that?"

"Not sure, but you can't always blame it on kids." Leif shrugged. "I'll go fetch the water."

"Good idea. I'm setting up an extra chair in case Diane should happen to arrive."

Leif carried out the bucket and soon was out of sight. John noticed that the search crew hadn't arrived for the day and wondered when they would show up. The article about Vicky he read while accidentally falling asleep said that not one piece of clothing was ever found. He hoped it meant she was alive, but if so, where was she? All these thoughts wound through him like a slow moving creek bed. Each day, it seemed, thoughts always brought him back to Vicky. It used to be Inga that he'd dwell on, but now it was Vicky. He circled the engine in pursuit of smudges and gang signs. No sooner had he finished the trek around it than Leif returned.

"I'll get the ladder set up," Leif said, setting the bucket down. "Get started. I'm sure I saw the St. Paul kids coming from the parking lot to set up their model steam engines for the competition."

"We better hurry."

"Diane is almost here," Leif said, climbing up. "Hi, Grandma!" He waved down to her. "Save me a cookie!"

Diane strolled with the stride of a sixteen-year-old as she approached John and Leif. She wore a brown skirt, starched white blouse, brown sash with two badges sewn on it, and brown beret, but the red bowtie topped it off. She reminded John of a very young woman, actually her daughter.

"How does it look?" Diane looked up to Leif and gave him a "thumbs-up" sign.

"Diane! You're beautiful. A young woman with cookies!"

"Still have the coffee and pie badges too. Just as if my mother had sewn them on for me because I was too busy serving the troops." Diane grinned and opened the basket of cookies. "Who are these kids?"

"Have a seat and you'll find out."

John grabbed his large sponge and got busy and so did Leif who fell in step right with him. Instead of climbing the ladder, he helped to make the engine shine. As soon as they'd finished polishing and cleaning the lower half, the St. Paul students arrive. Leif paid little attention and climbed up to scrub the upper half of the engine clean. John hollered out, "Hello!" from around where the ladder was located before walking over to them.

"Another great day in the park, I see," the teacher said. He held out his hand to shake John's, who responded by doing so. "And the lady?"

"That's Diane. She passed out food to the soldiers on their way to the European front during World War II." John stretched his suspenders. "It's a great day. You'll enjoy yourself."

"I'll take time to sit with her during the day and pick her brain about the war."

"She'll love it. Always nice to have school kids come around, but this—most especially. What's in store for today?" John didn't give him a chance to respond. "As you know, I am an old industrial tech teacher too. I used to teach about these engines."

"Really? How interesting."

"My classroom students, well they would dig into constructing their own steam engine. I'd begin with the copper tubing, showing them how to place them, and then we had an old tin pan used for oil changing, you know? And that's where the steam would go, but I'd have to construct the windmill for the top of it with aluminum foil, and of course, that didn't work."

"You sure had fun, didn't ya?"

"You betcha." John removed his engineer cap, swiped the hair from his forehead, and plunked it back on top of his head. "You see? My dad was an engineer for the Milwaukee Road, and he was the first to pilot the Zephyr to Chicago and back again. I used to ride with him as boy to Florida and California and points in between. It was a grand childhood, especially summertime when there wasn't school and I went with him."

"Oh for heaven's sake, you had a wonderful time," the teacher said. "My name's Mr. Olson, what's yours?"

"John. Nice to meet you. Didn't mean to talk your ear off, but it just came a rollin' on out. My missus used to laugh at me when I did such a thing."

"No problem with that. So tell me—"

"What's that?" John pulled on his suspenders.

"Would you be interested in coming into the classroom and talking about this here machine behind us? You know? You can talk about how it was riding along with your pop. I bet he had stories to tell."

"Give me a jingle, anytime," John said. "Here's my number." He waited as Mr. Olson found a pen and paper to write on. "It's Parkway 7044."

"Got it." Mr. Olson finished by writing John beside it and slipped it inside of his pants pocket.

"By the way," John said, "let it ring. I'm here all day. It's an old fashion wall phone. Never upgraded to one of those walk about phones."

"I'll keep that in mind. Now I must see to the kids," Mr. Olson said, then walked over to them.

When John turned to where the trays and tables were being set up, a group of young children were walking on the pathway.

"Good morning, little ones," he said. "How are you today?"

The young woman didn't look to be over twelve to John, but she had on a wedding ring and stood as tall as him and had a sparkle in her eyes.

"They're going into first grade in the fall. We're on an outing. The little imp that holds my hand is my daughter," she said. "What can you tell us about this massive engine?"

"It ran on steam. Coal was shoveled into the furnace, pistons pushed the steam upward, and that's what moved the train."

"I see. Interesting. However, we'd like to know about other things such as how much fun it was to look outside."

"Oh, sure!" John smiled at the kids. "When we'd ride down the tracks, they always made the clackety-clack sound, which was fun to listen to. It's really loud inside too. People, sometimes, would sit in chairs next to the tracks and wave at us while we went by. I'd always wave back, and if it was on the other side of the room, then my dad would wave too if he noticed them." John looked over to the teacher. "How'd I do?"

"Great!" To the students, she said, "Questions?"

"Did you blow bubbles with bubble-gum?" her little girl asked.

"Sometimes." He grinned, looking at the teacher. "Anything else?"

"Did you blow a whistle?" a little boy asked.

"No, but there was a rope or chain. When pulled it sounded like this: 'whoot-whoo.' That's not right, but it sort of sounded like that."

"Tell them why it was pulled."

"At intersections to warn drivers and pedestrians that the train was coming because a train can't just stop like cars can. Stopping could take them almost a mile to complete."

"Really?" a little boy said.

"You betcha!" To the class, he said, "Thank you for stopping by."

"Thank you," the teacher said, then motioned for them to follow.

John was reminded of his years in grade school as he watched the children. They all held hands, walked in a straight line, each behind the other. Turning his attention to the students behind him, he watched them construct their models on the set-up tables. To John, the interest was in the placement of each boiler. Each model was slightly different from the other, and he surmised this was how the engine was improved upon. One experiment led to another differing approach until the engine of today. Automobiles, planes, and cruise ships. He noticed their teacher was sitting beside Diane and having a conversation.

Most of the spectators who passed through stopped to speak to the students to inquire about their models. Among those who stopped, many had learned about the engine in school and gave pointers or further information to the students. It was a good day listening to the enthusiasts. He hadn't seen much of Leif and wondered what kept him away. As he gathered his possessions for home and placed the chairs back inside of the depot, Leif appeared.

"Hey, Grandpa!" Leif rushed over to him. "That time?"

"Yup. Where you been?"

"The search team was down by the home, real close to the water."

"Really?" John stopped what he was doing. "Did they find anything?"

"Put your stuff down, and let's walk over there. It ain't far."

"Okay, Leif."

"Wow! You called me by name."

"Show me the way."

Together they walked the distance to the entrance of the area and stopped. In front of them was a team of investigators instructing uniformed officers to dig in two locations.

"Why aren't they using machines and equipment?" Leif wondered.

"They probably have an injunction against it because it may be Indian burial grounds or something like that."

"Oh sure, or else a Civil War cemetery?"

"Possibly. We'll have to wait and find that out," John said. "Should we get closer, do you think? Where did you stand earlier?"

"Right down, over there." Leif pointed. "Over by those two women you know."

"I wonder if we can't squeeze in next to them?"

"Let's try," Leif said.

"The ground looks good to walk on. Okay, let's go."

They began to inch toward the digging. Mark noticed them and motioned directions to go near Nancy and Judy, which meant they had to walk farther around the perimeter before they arrived beside them.

"What's up?" John asked.

"Not sure," Judy said, "but it sure has me ready to jump to the moon. I'm so nervous. What if we finally found her?"

"I know, me too. That's what I think," Nancy said. "I won't believe it, but I don't want her to be dead."

"Not only that, what if her body is mutilated?" John said, crossing his arms. "I hope not. I'd hate for that to happen."

"You and me both," Judy said. "How could you tell Diane about it? How awful."

"You couldn't tell anyone's mother," Nancy said. "Let's pray that she's all in one piece."

"Agreed," John said.

Leif balanced back and forth, from one leg to the next until, at last, he said, "You three are all wrong. You're already thinking she's dead. What if she's not? It's almost as if you want her to be."

"Oh my God, just when I began to think you really had—" John said, shaking his head. "We're just scared Leif. We're scared of what'll be found."

"We've waited fifty years," Nancy said. "We want to see her again. Sure we do. But we're trying to prepare ourselves for almost anything."

"I suppose." Leif kept his eyes on the digging, first one plot and then the other. "Over there, it looks like they may have found something."

"Where?" Judy said, looking toward the further dig. "That one?" She pointed.

"Let's see if we can sneak in closer," Leif said. He begun to slowly move closer to it and the other three followed close behind him. "Sure. They're putting something into a bag."

"No bones?" John said.

"Don't look like it," Leif said. "What do you think? More to come?"

"Maybe," Nancy said. "They might find a tooth or something that could lead to who the owner is."

"Yes, but we don't know what was found. We're going in circles. I think I'm going to go home. Someone call me later. It's been a very long day." John glanced over to Leif. "You comin' or stayin'?"

"Stayin'. I'll stop by when I go home."

John left the area and retrieved his possessions before walking home. It gave him time to think about the day. When the students were dismissed, he thought about how wonderful it was to see them and their models. The future looked good with young, bright, knowledgeable, inquisitive youngsters like them. The two days of students made him feel young again because he remembered teaching and the thrill of each class.

As he approached his house, Frances called out to him, so he went toward where she stood in the backyard.

"Good day?"

"Terrific. Yesterday and today there were students making models. Loved it." John still held his empty thermos and lunch bag. "I need to go and sit."

"Where's Leif?"

"He stayed for a little while. They're digging and looking for Vicky. In case you're wondering, he's doing great."

"Are you finally calling him by name?"

"Yes."

"Treating him like he's worth something?"

"Of course. Now may I go?"

"You go right ahead. I brought you over a plate of food since you're not eating much."

"Thanks." John started walking away but was stopped.

"I cleaned your house too. Get a cleaning lady."

"Yes, ma'am. Thank you."

John felt like those little kids from the morning who were instructed to hold someone's hand and walk in a straight line. Once inside, he set the thermos and bag down, grabbed a beer, and sat out in his easy chair, then kicked his shoes onto the floor. Before the beer can was empty, he fell asleep. He woke an hour later with a note on his chair arm that read, "found a headband."

"I don't believe it." John sat up to finish drinking his beer. "Warm." Then he took the plate of food to heat and sat by the table. When finished, he rinsed the plate and went to the bathroom. Afterward, with his shoes back on, plate in hand, he walked next door.

"Come in, John. Leif figured you'd be by," Frances said.

John entered. "Where's Leif?"

"Coming." Leif walked from his room. "Caught you snoring, didn't I?"

"Guess so. Tell me about the headband."

"Nothing much to tell. It was blue."

"Wasn't it full of dirt? It should've been black."

"It wasn't though. It looked normal like."

All three slid into a chair around the kitchen table.

"It came from the ground. Positive." Leif's brow furrowed. "You're right. It should've been covered in dirt."

"But, it could've been in a coffin," Frances said. "Or wrapped up inside clothes."

"She was in a prom dress when she went missing," John said. "I wasn't at the prom to see what she wore but presume it was a gown. Blue was her favorite color, if remembered correctly."

"No dress or anything else," Frances said, puzzled.

"If she'd gone missing, then it's possible the assailant wrapped her up like a mummy and stuffed her somewhere," Leif said, scratching his head.

"She went missing before prom. Pictures were always taken by the waterfall," John said. "During the prom, I would guess that rumors began to spread about her and the fiancé missing."

"During the dance?" Frances said, removing her glasses and rubbing her eyes. "It's likely she fell into the falls, isn't it?"

"Yes, but where was he? Her date?" Leif said. "That's what doesn't make sense."

"I haven't a clue," John said. "Remember? I wasn't there."

"Right." Leif said.

"Good grief!" John said. "It's a mystery."

"No motive, either," Leif said. "I'm going to start watching detective shows."

Both adults looked at him then slightly shook their heads.

"I think there's something to this bit about a stranger from the hospital who was 'off' the mark quite a bit," John said. "Well, it's all speculation, isn't it? The authorities have another clue they can pursue."

"That's right," Frances said. "Thanks for returning the plate."

"Thank you for the good meal and cleaning my house. Leif, you're a wonderful grandson."

"I am?"

"Of course!"

"Wow."

"I'm leaving. I'll see you when the sun rises."

John got up and left, heading straight for his back door.

After he'd showered, the scrapbook with all the newspaper clippings was still on the living room table. When the television was turned on and he was comfortable, the book was lifted into his lap.

Chapter eight

Morning came with wind and rain. John pulled blankets over his head and crawled farther down into them. Wind lashed against the windowpanes. What to do today, he wondered, falling back to sleep.

When reawakening and reading the clock, John realized Leif most likely was setting up the ladder, but the wind still blew hard so he wasn't sure. He sat up, then dropped one foot to the floor, then the other. Each foot landed neatly inside the well-placed slippers. The robe lay across a chair and was easily reached. When his arms were shoved into it, he stood to tie the belt. Shuffling out to the phone, John wasn't quite sure how to admit he'd overslept after giving Leif the berries for being late a few days ago. At the phone, he dialed Frances's number.

"Still sleeping?" John said when she answered.

"Guess so. Obviously, you're not down there?"

"Nope. The wind and rain. It'd do me in for a few days, if I went. Can't take the weather so much anymore."

"Neither can I," Frances said. "Heard any more news?"

"Nah, not yet. I'll let you know when I do." John waited a minute before continuing. "Send him over when he wakes up and you want to be rid of him."

"Will do."

They disconnected. John continued shuffling to the coffeepot to pour a cup and make something to eat. He fried an egg, made toast, and sat to eat. Leif would want to make a model like what he'd seen or try for something entirely different, John thought. While dressing for the day, a list started in his mind.

The back doorbell rang, then pounding on the door before he heard the doorbell ring again.

"Hold on!" John shouted as he zipped his pants shut. "Coming!" He walked to the kitchen and opened the door, stepping aside to let Leif enter. "I should've opened it. Knew you'd be by."

"It's soaking out there. Like a flood." Leif shook himself a little, stomped his feet. "I'm glad this storm hit while we were still home."

"Let's sit," John said, pouring himself another cup of coffee. "Grab something if you want."

"I've got water." Leif followed him. He spread out on the couch, and John got comfy in his chair. "I've been thinking about that engine. You know? Something wasn't right with it."

"People experiment all the time. That's how we got the engine of today." John sipped from his coffee cup. "Did you bring over cookies?"

"No, but Grandma's baking cinnamon rolls with caramel frosting."

"Oh my God. That woman. I've never tasted anything so delicious in my life. Sneak me a couple, if you can."

"Will do, now back to the engine."

"I have a list made up. We need to make a steam engine with a cylinder or at least try." John leaned over to look Leif in the eye. "I'm not sure that we'll get it right, though. I hope you won't mind."

"Nope. This is fun. Grandpa teaching me, but I wish it was my dad," Leif took a breath, "and Mom was around."

"I think you will live with your mom someday. I'm pretty sure you will. She has good sense and will eventually snap out of her depression."

"And she'll remember me. Move back home with me. Grandma wouldn't mind her moving in, I'm sure of it."

"Son, I think what will happen is you move in with me because she'll want her old room back. It sounds right, doesn't it?"

"I guess. Maybe she'll get a job and then we'll have our own place," Leif said, eyes sparkling. "I hope so."

"Me too," John said. "Now back to the engine. We should have a bike chain and a small curtain rod. There needs to be a rod."

"For the copper tubing?"

"I believe so. For the rod to work up and down and force the steam out," John said. "It sounds complicated but really isn't."

"We could wrap cardboard around the tubing?"

"Very possible. Great idea. See if you can find some cardboard. We could use a box if it's not cut more than once. We'll unfold the corners," John said. The phone began to ring. "How about gathering the items?"

"Sure." Leif headed for the basement to look for the pieces needed.

"Hello," John said into the mouthpiece.

"John? This is Nancy."

"Oh! Nancy, got more news?" The phone cord was long so he was able to walk out of the kitchen and sit, talk comfortably in his easy chair.

"Mark called. It's really quite odd, but there was a can way off in the woods that they opened. An old coffee can. Inside was a dress sash, like what was worn years ago. It looked like something Vicky would've worn to prom. He said that the shades of blue between the headband and sash were almost identical."

"That sounds really weird," John said. "Why in a can? Why wasn't it found previously?"

"No idea. Mark's having it checked for fingerprints," Nancy said. "Judy is beside herself, trying to make sense of the situation."

"I don't blame her. It makes no sense. Here's what I think—"

"Tell me," Nancy said.

"I think it was recently planted there. I also don't think she's dead, but that's only a gut feeling."

"That sounds like what a deranged person would do," Nancy said. "No one in their right mind would think of it."

"How true." At that moment, the back door opened. "Leif is here so I'll say, 'goodbye' for now. If anything else comes up, call me."

"I will."

Nancy disconnected before John got himself out of the chair to hang the receiver back on the hook.

"Back? Find it all?"

"Yes. All set to figure this one out." Leif displayed the few pieces, cardboard, bicycle chain, and curtain rod. "Perfect. Before we start, I must call Frances to tell her about the new find."

"I'm listening in!"

"Do you even know how to dial one of these old phones?" John said, reaching for receiver. "Do you?"

"Not really, no." Leif shook his head. "Show me."

"I presume that you know the number?"

"Of course."

"Watch." John lifted the receiver and held it to his ear. "Easy?"

"Sure." Leif nodded. "Never mind, I get it now." He held out his hand to take the phone. "Got it." In front of the phone, he reached up and pressed his finger onto the hole where the first number was and said, "To the right?"

"Yes. Pull it around to where it stops, then remove your finger. Then the next, and next until finished. It'll ring. You'll hear her voice."

"And I speak into this end and listen on this." He held the receiver to his ear. "Like this?"

"Exactly correct."

It didn't take long for Frances to answer the telephone.

"Hello?"

"Grandma, Grandpa taught me to use the phone. I'm glad for my cell phone and that you use yours, but here is Grandpa." Leif handed the receiver to John.

"Nancy called."

"What did she say?"

"A coffee can was found with a dress sash shoved inside. It's blue like the headband. The shades seem to match. It's weird, really. Someone had to have recently left it. They may have thrown the headband to keep the search going."

"I don't like the sound of it, but I have rolls in the oven and the buzzer is ringing."

Suddenly, the connection went dead.

"She's taking rolls from the oven," John said, staring at the receiver for a second before hanging it up. "Let's get started on the engine."

"You bet!"

"Let's go into the living room. There might be more room."

"Nope. We're starting this dang thing, and it'll stay where we leave it. We'll go into Mom's old room. Okay?" Leif said. "I've got the book."

"Good! Let's get going."

"Okay."

The two grabbed the stuff and headed into Janet's old room.

Leif unraveled the cardboard, so it was straight, stomping on it a few times to take out some of the creases and folds while John tried to figure out how to connect the bike chain onto the end of the curtain rod.

"This here's a pain in the butt," John said. "How did they do it, way back when—when they didn't have the tools to work with?"

"And they did it? We're having trouble putting it together and we have a picture."

Leif studied it. "Here we are. I may have figured it out?"

"Almost." John attached the chain with a plastic hook that attached with Velcro. "Good."

"Part one. On to part two." Leif raised a brow as he rolled up the cardboard until it was the size of a cylinder the tube was able to fit down into. "Part two. Now we try it out."

"The tubing fits perfectly, the cylinder great, but now, how to work the piston?" John said, wondering. "We have to weight the rod, which is what the chain is for, you see?"

"How do we get it to work? There isn't any reason for the steam to rise. I don't understand. It's strange." Leif scratched his head. "We have to get this figured out, if it's the last thing we do." He took a deep breath. "Suggestions, Mr. Teacher?"

"Well, we have a very long way to go, don't we?" John sighed. "I'm tired. Even though we didn't go down to the park, it's been a long day."

"Ahh, no. We're not done for the day," Leif said. "We'll figure it out by copying this darn book."

"Okay, but if your grandma Frances shows up with cinnamon rolls with caramel frosting, we're quitting. Deal?"

"Deal. I want a couple of those too. You can't eat them all."

"Okay," John said. "This rod goes up and down like a piston, just like this." Up and down John cranked the rod, demonstrating how it brought the tubing upward and back within the cardboard cylinder. "The chain is heavy and will keep it moving."

"It won't though without the boiler, right?" Leif exclaimed. "We're as far as we can go, aren't we?"

"I believe so." John leaned back, crossing his arms. "We'll continue another time."

"Tomorrow." Leif gave himself a nod. "When will Grandma show up with those rolls?"

"I can smell them, can't you?"

They both were setting the materials to the side of the room as the back screen door opened.

"Hellooo! Anybody home? You-hoo!" Frances called. She stepped inside, placed the hot pan of rolls onto the tabletop. "Where is everybody? Do I have to eat them all myself?"

"Nope!" Leif entered and dived into the hot rolls, scooping a large one into the palm of his hand. "It's hot! Hot! Get me a plate!" He jumped up and down. "Hurry up!"

"Stupid kid," John said and reached for the plate to give him. "Here."

Leif slid the roll onto the plate, then went to run his hand under the kitchen faucet. "Oh my God, that was hot!"

"It's the butter." Frances reached for two more plates and forks. "You are the idiot, John. You should've taken out three plates. We all need one. Jessshhh!" She forked out a roll for herself, got a glass of juice before beginning to eat. "Delicious, even if I do say so myself."

Without saying another word, John did the same, only he picked out a beer for himself to drink. All three ate their rolls in silence, but their eyes sparkled with delight.

"The best I've ever tasted," John said, licking his lips. "How about splitting one?" He glanced at Frances. "What do ya say?"

"Nah. They're for my grandson." Frances smiled at Leif, who grinned. "See? I wouldn't want to miss that smile for anything." To John she said, "Don't ever call him an idiot. Ever again! I mean it!"

"Yes, ma'am. I'll never call him an idiot again."

"It's okay," Leif replied, licking the fork. "Soooo gooood, Grandma."

"Thank you. That's what grandmas do for their grandkids." She stared at John. "You apologize or I won't leave any rolls. I mean it!"

"Sorry for calling you an idiot," John said. "I won't do it again."

"Thank you," Leif said. "Grandma, thanks for baking these. Yum-yum!"

"Yes, thank you. I'm very grateful. They are sooo good, just like our grandson says. Absolutely."

They continued to eat the rolls.

"Say?" Frances said. "I've wondered why there aren't fresh flyers up? There should be now that Vicky's case is reopened."

"Good point," John said.

Both adults looked at Leif who dished up another roll.

"Well?" the grandparents said in unison.

"What?" Leif glanced at both, then plugged a large bite into his mouth.

"Talk to Nancy, if I don't, about getting out flyers."

Leif gave a "thumbs-up" instead of speaking since he had a full mouth.

Chapter nine

When Frances and Leif left, and John was finally alone, he went to his easy chair. As his feet went into reclining mode, his eyes closed and he began to daydream. His memory went back to the days when traveling with his dad and sitting in the club car. He'd be able to go wherever he pleased, sometimes in the front beside his dad with an extra seat placed beside him, or he'd roam between the cars. When passing through the cars, sometimes, it was tough. It depended upon the terrain or the outside windspeed as well as how fast the train was moving. He'd have to move quickly, sometimes jump between cars or balance on the rods that connected the cars. There was the patio like platform on either end of the cars to stand upon before opening the next door. It was thrilling. The toilets were scattered in different cars so they needed to be located, which was a game he'd played, and the other was to look for a spy. Of course, he wouldn't have known what a spy looked like in those days, but it was all in fun and kept him occupied on the long journeys. As he drifted into a deeper sleep, his phone rang.

"Maybe I should invest in one of those cell phones?" he grouched as his feet landed on the floor. He picked up the receiver right before it clicked. "Hello!"

"Just hanging up and heard your voice. Nancy here."

"We've been talking around here about the whole thing," John said, stifling a yawn. "Something else has got to be done."

"That's why I'm callin'," Nancy said. "Hold on a minute." She lit a cigarette. "This business is making a mess out of me. I'm smoking again, gave it up twenty some years ago, and now I'm blowing smoke from my ears. What about you?"

"I'm drinkin' more beer. Usually it's one can a day after I'm done for the day. I'm on my second or third already. We have to figure some other means to locate her, one way or another."

"That's right. Dead or alive." Nancy puffed on her cigarette. "This might drive me back to doobies before it's all done."

"How's Judy holding up. Don't see her much but know she's around." He walked to the fridge and took out another beer. "Now, I'm opening another."

"Judy's an alcoholic and has been in treatment. Her former husband is going to come to be with her. She's lucky in that department." She went to her refrigerator and removed a soda. "I almost grabbed a beer. This is ridiculous."

"Has anyone spoken to Diane other than at the funeral?"

"As a matter of fact, no we haven't. Not that I'm aware of, but I'm guessing she's been requestioned by Mark or Ronnie. Why?"

"Frances brought up something about putting out flyers. What are your thoughts on that?" John drank from his beer. "I could speak to her about it."

"It makes me wonder if there are any older flyers stored somewhere. Do you think it's possible?"

"Why not? However, the police could have a sketch artist age her and then there can be a picture of then and now, that type of thing." John drank more of his beer and stared at the plate of left behind rolls. He thought they should be eaten right away or else covered and set aside for tomorrow.

"I like that idea. Let's bring it to Mark's and Ronnie's attention in the morning."

"It's not pouring anymore, just a light rain and the wind has subsided. You can send Leif if you want anyone to run errands, but he's too young to drive so it would have to be on bike or foot."

"We'll get it figured out in the morning."

"Goodbye."

They disconnected and John want back to his chair and tried to fall asleep, but his mind kept turning around and he finally gave up.

Morning came with sunlight poking through the remaining clouds, remnants of the downpour experienced from the day before. His stomach growled because he hadn't eaten anything substantial, but hot cinnamon rolls were super delicious. A roll was wrapped and placed inside of a clean lunch bag. The thermos was filled with extra hot coffee. Next a large sandwich of peanut butter and apple jelly was wrapped and set into the bag. A bag was easy for him to handle, and it was one less worry because the last lunchbox was stolen. Three were bought and paid for from his own pocket and taken from him. No one seemed to want a lonely old bag so this was what he'd used for the past few years. When finished with a soft boiled egg and toast, he dumped the dishes in the sink after a good rinse. He walked through the house, making sure it was locked up tight. His nerves were jittery, and it bothered him as he stepped outside via the back door. With it locked behind him, he was on his way to the park.

Looking over toward the house next door, he hoped to see Leif walking out. It was his hope that Leif would join him on the short walk to the engine, but he didn't see him. At the stoplight, he saw police cars, which caused his nerves to jump. As soon as the light turned, John hurried to the active scene of an ambulance with flashing police car lights.

"Leif!" John pushed through the crowd until he made it to the front. "Leif!" He stopped right when the medics loaded the gurney to the inside. He rushed forward. "Leif! Leif!" A medic prevented him from going any farther. "Is it a young boy?"

"No sir, it's a young woman. A jogger."

"That's a relief," John said, blowing out a long breath. "Thank heavens."

"Sir?" The medic stared at him.

"I thought it may've been my grandson," John said. "Sorry for the rude reply."

John stepped back to wait for the ambulance to drive off. He glanced around him and noticed a long arm in the air and walked toward it. "Leif! Thank God you're here. I was so worried about you," John said, coming up to him, grabbing his shoulders. "Thank you."

"Sure, Grandpa, anytime." Leif hugged his grandpa. "Feel better?"

"Yes." John smiled.

"You don't get hugs anymore, do you? Bet you forgot how to do it?"

"Most likely."

They hugged and walked to the engine.

"Nancy called right after you left," John said, taking hold of his suspenders. "She's onboard for the flyers, but the detectives need in on it."

"That's good."

"Sure is. We spoke of an artist aging one of the photos of a younger version of Vicky."

"Perfect," Leif said as they grew closer to the area.

"I have a favor to ask of you," John said, stopping to look at him.

"I can almost guess."

"No, don't. I'd like a cell phone."

"I knew it! That's what I was going to say!"

"I wanted to beat you to it."

They arrived at the depot and got ready for the spectators to pass or stop by. John always thought it was fun to see the young folks, especially when they had questions.

"I'll get the water," Leif said, grabbing the bucket. "Be back in a jiffy."

"Got it! I'll meet and greet."

Standing back with his hands on his hips, John surveyed the engine. To him, it looked shiny and he questioned whether it needed scrubbing? He glanced in the direction where Leif went, but he'd left so quickly that now he wasn't in sight. Slowly, John walked around the locomotive, keeping a steady eye on all the parts and where there may be smudges left from the day before. He didn't see anything that needed cleaning. At the front of the cowcatcher, there were several larger bugs plus a butterfly that had smashed into it. Fortunately there weren't any birds.

Once he'd set the lawn chairs up, John gathered his thermos and lunch bag and sat down. As he poured his cup full, he spotted Nancy hiking toward him, waving a sheet of paper.

"Guess what?" she called from afar. "We've got one!"

"Let's see." Setting his cup and thermos on the ground, John stood to wait for her approach. "You found one?"

"Ronnie dug this out from when it happened. It's fifty years old. Look at the way it's printed, the lettering is different than what we usually see nowadays." Nancy handed it to him. "Do you see it?"

John took it from her outstretched hand. "It's the font and style. It's not catchy, like."

"I suppose you're right," Nancy said. "However, Diane is being notified as we speak. I hope this doesn't make her any more depressed or upset than she already is. Poor thing."

"When I spoke to her, she was in relatively good spirits. I think it must be the type of thing that you just live with, you know? Either accept it or not, but it's always in the back of your mind. It's kind of like me and Janet. I wish she was here, and then we have Leif." His eyes watered from thought of Janet in a mental institution for depression, that she'd tried to commit suicide at least once. Leif without a father and mother institutionalized for the moment.

"Janet should be getting better," Nancy said. "I know you were thinking of her. I remember you bragging her up at the reunions. You all bragged, nonstop about your kids during the first few decades. Now look at your Leif, he's almost a man. Yikes!"

"What else can you tell me?"

"Oh! That's right! Mark and Ronnie have my number and will text me after Diane meets with the sketch artist. They'll take it from there and will have a hundred flyers printed."

"Will that be enough?" John asked, raising a brow. "I would think a thousand, at least."

"We're not sure how many volunteers we'll have helping us out."

"Oh, sure. Keep me informed."

Nancy gave him a "thumbs-up" as she turned to walk away, then stopped. Turning around, she said, "Get yourself a cell phone!"

"Working on it."

As John sat to drink his coffee, an older gentleman strolled over toward him.

"Good day, sir," John said, nodding to him. "Beautiful day, isn't it?"

"Oh my, yes, better than yesterday," the man said, stopping near John. "I remember riding on an old train with my mother, all the way to Milwaukee to see relatives. So very long ago."

"Loved it?"

"Boy, you betcha! Every second of it. Course I was just a lad of about five or six but remember it well. We were in a coach with bench seats. I'd get on my knees to look out and she'd scold me for not sitting still. We had our own meal with us, of course. It was great fun! Thanks for the memories."

"Anytime." John watched as he walked away toward the waterfall.

"I'm here with the bucket," Leif said, setting it down.

"I bet we don't need it, do we?"

"Nah. I'll climb up there and scrub it down right away."

"I'll get the ladder. You're a good kid."

After the ladder was placed, Leif climbed up and took care of his chore. The morning passed by quickly. When Leif finished, it was time for lunch. They took turns being in front of the engine while the other ate. Leif wanted to be the first to eat since he'd done most of the work for the day.

Sitting close to the depot doorway, John enjoyed the peace and tranquility, sipping his coffee and eating the familiar boring sandwich.

"Hey, you," Judy said, walking toward him. "Things are moving along, aren't they?"

"Finally. I thought I heard you were with your ex?" John drank his coffee. "I don't have an extra cup, or I'd offer you one."

"Nope. Don't worry. My ex has gone back home. He keeps me steady and focused. By the way, Diane brought the photo in right away and the artist has completed the job. It's all in the hands of the printer. Mark supplied the dates. We'll have it here shortly."

"I suppose it doesn't take long to zip out one hundred nowadays with those printers, not like what you and I went through for school. Typing? I had all thumbs."

"You and me both." Judy saw Leif meandering on over to them. "Hey Leif, is it?"

"Yup. You got it right. Named after some Norseman. I compare myself to a Norse God!"

"You should, reddish blond hair, tall, muscular, and kinda cute," Judy said, looking him over. "Dimples too. Smile more, big guy."

"Thanks for compliment. I'll do that, then the girls will be right here!"

"Let's get to the point." John eyed Judy. "You always were a big flirt."

She shrugged. "Loosen up."

"Flyers ready to go?"

"Pretty soon. Someone will bring them over. You got friends to help distribute?"

"I can do it, me and Grandpa."

"Oh, not tonight. I was going to ask if this beautiful woman and Nancy wanted to swing by my house, and we'll talk about old times. Friends, teachers, classes, that sort of thing," John said, looking at Judy. "What do ya say?"

"I think it's a plan. Order in a pizza and we'll pay. Be there at six. Can't be late, we're getting too old to stay out late and can't see well to drive."

"Six it is. Bring your own beverage."

"We're set." Judy gave a quick smile before walking away.

John watched her go and thought of all the good times they'd had in high school, and now they were going to talk about friends long since gone, or how they looked the last time they saw them.

"I'd like to go home to see to the house. Mind staying," John said, getting up. "You're doing great. You can answer questions almost as well as I can, better at times."

"Really?"

"Yes."

"Go ahead. I'll lock everything up. I'll ring when I get home or stop over to see if you need help chasing out the mice."

"I don't have any unless you're counted as one." John picked up what was needed and left for home.

Once he entered the kitchen, all the little chores that needed to be done rushed at him. The house hadn't been vacuumed since Florence did it a few days before—the decorative objects needed dusting. The dishes washed. He began in the bathroom because it called for the most attention. Afterward, the rest of the house was attended to and finally, a change of clothes. What to wear? It was time to put on his new pair of jeans that had been in the closet since Inga passed away. No sooner had he changed than the doorbell dinged and the women entered.

"Come on in, girls, I mean women. Glad you could make it." John stepped aside to allow them entrance. "Have a seat. Let's kick back and pretend we're cool once again."

"Hey man! Super cool!" Nancy entered, wearing a pair of shorts and tank top, carrying two cans of beer, holding them high. "Fridge?"

"Right around the corner. You look great," John said, a little nervous.

"And what do I look like? Cream cheese?" Judy said, entering with two cans of soda. "My doobie's in my pocket, we can share."

"Oh my God, you two!" John grinned from ear to ear. "I'm not sure if I should be embarrassed or not!" He chuckled. "Judy? You look marvelous."

The two women stood in the kitchen and glanced around. "Is it always this clean or did you do this for us?"

"Well Judy, it's only for you two." He knew the grin on his face was going to last through the night and might for his lifetime. "So my lovelies, want a tour of the digs?"

"You did clean for us, didn't you?" Nancy said, opening the first beer. "We want to know. It's important."

"If you really must know," John said. "Yes, I went in circles cleaning when I came home." He looked from one to the other. "However, Frances, the next door lady, does help by coming in and cleaning and scolding me for being messy, drinking too much beer, or generally gets after me for just about everything the way women do. She's Leif's grandma."

"Ahh, like little boys, so much needed," Nancy said, going to the cabinet.

"And expected too," Judy said, following her. "I love these dishes. They must've been doll dishes Janet played with, I suppose?"

"They actually are from my mom, may she rest in peace."

"And then given to her first granddaughter, I suspect," Nancy said. "They're lovely with delicately painted sprays of roses in the center. Very pretty."

"Inga, your wife? Right?" Judy said, picking up the larger picture. "I bet you talk to her every day, don't you?"

"Be careful with it," John said. "The frame is weak."

"Well do you?" Nancy asked, eyeing him suspiciously. "It's a good thing to do. We're not criticizing, really we're not." Nancy stepped back, stopped by the table. "It helps."

"You know what?" John said, getting uncomfortable. "Let's move on."

The picture was carefully replaced. "Is that your wife's ashes?" Judy asked.

John cringed.

"We're sorry, truly, we are," Nancy said. "Sometimes my friend doesn't know how to keep her mouth shut." She glared at Judy.

"It's okay. I needed to hear that, I did. Janet's been after me ever since moving away. Frances raises Leif and Janet barely sees him. It breaks my heart, and at times I take it out on him, the poor kid. What kind of a grandparent am I?" John turned away, sighing. "Let's keep going."

Judy and Nancy looked at each other, raising their brow as they followed him into Janet's room. Inside the doorway, they stopped.

"The other room is my bedroom, and you don't want to see it, but this here is or was Janet's." He shrugged.

"What in the world is that thing-a-mi-jig over there?" Judy motioned to the half-built steam engine.

"Exactly. What is it, pray tell?" Nancy raised a brow.

"Well, it's like this..." John smiled. "Leif wants to experiment to try to learn how in the world the steam rises so this is what we have so far."

"A curtain rod? Seriously?" Nancy said, a hand on her hip while the other held her beer. "Really?"

"And a bicycle chain? Honestly?" Judy said, taking a swallow of soda.

"What about the Dutch oven?" Nancy said, swinging the empty can. "You're cooking the chain in it?"

"You've got an awful lot of explaining to do here, pumpkin," Judy said. "Let's get down to brass tacks and order our pizza."

"Now that's the best idea I've heard yet," John said, showing a bit of a grin.

"No hard feelings?" Nancy said.

"Nope."

"Before we leave this room, I really want to know about the three pieces of 'God knows what'—are used for."

"Piston, boiler, and rod to make it happen. Obviously we're missing a few pieces."

"Got it." Judy said. "I'm starved."

Back in the living room, they ordered pizza.

"Still a rotary phone." Judy looked at Nancy. "We've got our work cut out for us."

Chapter ten

"The pizza's on its way," John said, slamming down the receiver. "I am tired of this old phone. You two here? I feel like—well—all of a sudden I'm out of the blues."

"Good! It's about time," Judy said. "You used to wow me with your moves in junior high. I remember how you used to, "bust a move," don't you, Nancy?"

"You betcha! It was fun. Everyone veered back and you'd do the lindy and got real low!"

"How low can you go?" John said, imitating the song. "Let's refresh our beverages and grab napkins. I'll take care of the paper plates and napkins."

"Right." Judy jumped up. "Mind if I smoke inside or should I go out?"

"I don't care. I just want fun."

John wondered if he should turn Inga's photo over but decided it was a foolish thing to do. He picked up a stack of plates, forks, napkins, and a fresh beer. Before sitting, he closed the bedroom doors.

"Let's tell each other what we've been up to over the years," Nancy said. "You in?" She glanced at each of them. "Judy? You go first."

"Me? Well, okay." Judy lit her doobie, then took a long drag. She let the smoke out, which lingered between them. "So good."

"I never got into that," John said, popping open his beer. He drank from the can then set it aside. "Beer was always enough for me."

"I can see that," Judy said. "Nothing was ever enough for me. Drugs. Alcohol. You name it, I took it and I'm paying for it now. At least this stuff is legal, finally."

"What about marriages?" John said. "You two know most of my business. I've always been a cheap bastard, it made my wife mad. Leif thinks so too. I have asked him to look up phones for me on the internet."

96

"You? After all of these years?" Nancy said, bringing her arm up to her chest. "What is this world coming to?" She brought her hand up and wiped it over her forehead. "Oh, my!"

"You two are hilarious." John chuckled. "Seriously, Judy? Your husband."

"Sadly, my addictions got the best of him. Neither of us are interested in anyone else, but he can't live with me. I am trying to straighten myself out. I've been in treatment. I'm moving along at a snail's pace, but it's better than staying where I'd been."

"Nancy? You never married, why's that?" John said, leaning back in his chair. "I'm not trying to be nosy even if it sounds like it. It's interesting how our lives have taken different twists and turns since graduation."

"Yes, and then there is that frat party where the guys jumped us. It was awful. Thankfully, those days are over."

"You fought those creeps off, though. I gave one a black eye."

"That's right," Nancy said. "Life hasn't been too bad. I got my teaching degree in elementary education and get a nice retirement."

"That's good. Pretty similar to me. Go on."

"I could never love another man. We'd made love in the backseat of the car, my first love. No one after him has ever compared." Nancy breathed in deeply. "I couldn't let love into my life. I never could open my heart. We were so young and innocent."

"Carefree, and such a wonderful time in our lives," John said. "We can't take it back, can we?"

"I sure don't want to," Judy said, snuffing out her doobie. She set it in a small dish to cool, later to wrap and return to her purse.

"I'd love to return and feel him against me once again," Nancy said, a tear sliding down her cheek, "but can't, can we?"

"No, I'm so sorry, Nancy. It's much the same with Inga or missing Janet."

"Janet will move back home, and you have Leif. Don't ever forget that." Looking him the eye, she said, "He's your fam, which is more than what I have."

"I know," John said. "Sorry for making you remember such sad memories."

"They're bittersweet. I knew I was loved." Nancy hugged herself. "If only there had been just one more hug. One more night, as the song goes." She closed her eyes for a moment and the doorbell rang.

"Pizza's here."

John opened the front door to let the delivery man inside, took the pizza boxes to pass over to Nancy who set them on the kitchen table.

"Leave them here in the living room. It's the easiest and most fun," John said. "Chairs are more comfortable too."

"Gotcha," Nancy said.

The two women returned with the boxes and set them precariously on the living room table.

She and Judy each opened a box and took a piece for themselves plus refreshed their beverages. When John finished paying, he followed suit.

After the first few bites, they all agreed the pizza was delicious.

"Remember Beeks? On Hiawatha?" Nancy said, dripping cheese onto her chin.

"Yeah! And Airloha Drive-in?" Judy said, through chewing. "It's hot!"

"You bet! But what about the Juicy Lucy burgers? Sooo good," John said. "Inga and I went there an awful lot with Janet. She loved them." He picked up his next piece. "They are dripping in grease. There goes my cholesterol."

"You only live once, that's my theory," Judy said. "Nummy."

When finished, they took care of the empty boxes, placing them inside the garbage bin in the closet.

"It's probably time for us to leave," Nancy said, rinsing her hands under the sink. "This has been fun."

"I'll say it has," Judy said, grinning. "John, you've given me a new lease on life. It's been terrific!" She reached over to give him a hug. "Let's do it again."

"Me too. Old friends with a lot to talk about," Nancy said, going to the door.

"Until next time," John said, holding open the door.

"Yeah! Tomorrow!"

When they were safely in their car and driving away, John stepped back into the house and shut and locked the door. As he sat down once again, he wondered what it was they were going to talk about because it seemed as if they had talked about nothing but the past. He scratched his whiskers and shut his eyes as his feet went up to recline.

The phone rang, disturbing his sleep. It jolted him upright, causing his hand to accidentally knock over his beer. "Doggonit!" He scrambled to pick up the tipped over can, happy to see only a few drops had spilled out. He hurried to answer the phone. "Hello!" At the same time, he reached for a towel and tried to reach over to wipe the spilled beer but couldn't quite reach it. "Who is it?"

"Daddy? You scared me. You sounded so harsh," Janet said, her voice quavering.

"Oh honey, so sorry. I was on the easy chair and sleeping when the phone rang, and it woke me and in turn I tipped over a water bottle."

"You mean beer can, don't you?"

"Yes, sorry."

"Tell me what you did today to make you want a can of beer? That's what my therapist would ask of me."

John heard, what? Nervousness in her voice? "Two old friends just left. We talked about old times. It was so much fun. They made me forget."

"Old friends? How fun. Who were they? Anyone I know?" Janet asked, more calmly.

"That old girlfriend of mine, Vicky Storbakken, remember? I told you about her. The case was reopened by old classmates. You see?"

"Really? That's fabulous. Tell me more, then I have news for you."

"Nancy and Judy are helping with the search. You might remember them from a long time ago. Both are tall and Judy talks sort of fast, but anyway. Two men, now retired detectives who are looking into the case, Mark and Ronnie, weren't in any of my classes but I recognize. However, the man who escorted Vicky I didn't really know."

"No clue as to her whereabouts?"

"No, unfortunately. Now they're going to send out flyers. I think your son will help with the distribution of them—you know, phone poles and public boards like gas stations. That sort of thing."

"Isn't there a TV program for missing persons?"

"I'm not sure." John looked at Inga's picture, then continued. "What about you? What's on your mind besides your old pop?"

"I'm ready for a visit and asked for it either tomorrow or Saturday, what do you say?"

"Really?"

"Isn't it wonderful?"

"Of course it's wonderful! You took me by surprise, honey. I'll fire up the old '78 Torino. I still have it, you know? We hardly drove it anywhere."

"What day do you want? Tomorrow or Saturday?"

"Tomorrow! Of course!"

"Bring Leif. Just you two for now."

"Wow! Okay. Leif's gotten real interested in the steam engine. We've been trying to build one ourselves. He's spectacular." John could hardly believe his ears. "What time? My God! That's tomorrow!"

"Two o'clock. Check-in and most likely you'll be told to wait outside in the garden area. You can look at all the pretty azaleas while you wait."

"You sound like your mother."

"Do I? Leif's doing fine, helping you out?"

"Yep. He's not as much of a pain anymore."

"Good. See you soon." She disconnected.

Afterward, John stared at the receiver in wonderment. A minute later, in a daze of disbelief, he pushed down on the hook in order to dial a new exchange.

"Hello," Leif said. "You know, Grandpa, if you had a cell phone, we could have your name entered and a picture and then guess what?"

"I don't have time for this. I have news." John hesitated. "It's your mother."

"What about my mother? Did she fall down or something? Go into the rabbit hole?"

"Don't be ridiculous," John said, irritated. "You and me are going for ride to see her. We'll leave at ten o'clock and stop for lunch, then get to the hospital early in case we can see her early on. I'm sure glad it's summer out because I don't want to be driving at night."

"What car are we driving, or are we going by bus or a train or walking?"

"You're being cute again. I'm going to fire up the Torino at nine o'clock. Be over here in case I need help with pumping the gas pedal or something. My head might be under the hood fiddling with the sparkplugs."

"I don't suppose they make parts for cars that old, do they?"

"See you in the morning and no, Frances can't come with us."

"Got it."

They disconnected. With the key in his pocket, John went out to the garage to inspect the car. The battery was dead. Fortunately, he'd invested in a battery charger so he removed the battery and plugged it into the charger for the night. What if the drive to and from was too much? It'd been so long since he'd driven that far in a day.

Half the night, John tossed and turned. His mind went in circles about the day ahead. Morning came and he was so tired he yawned so hard his jaw almost came unhinged. One roll was left from the other day, and he ate it while the coffeepot shot out fresh coffee. By the time Leif knocked on the door, he was dressed.

"Ready?" Leif said, bounding inside. "I'm ready to see my mom. Grandma went over manners like there was no end to it. She also coached me to 'shut my trap' and not put her on edge. I'll be a good boy and tell her she's beautiful and how much I miss her."

"No matter what she looks like, she's still your mother and is beautiful." John finished his coffee. "Ready to start the engine? Fire it up?"

"You betcha! It's the size of a boat, it'll be fun. I wish I was old enough to drive." Leif still stood by the doorway. "Come on, Grandpa! It's already nine. What if it doesn't start?"

"It will."

With keys in his pocket, John locked the house door behind him, and they went to the garage. Inside, Leif climbed in behind the wheel to admire it, sliding his palms up and down the steering wheel before trying out the pedals and opening and closing the glove box.

"I can't wait to drive it alone!"

"Calm down, young man. That day will come." John opened the overhead door. Leif climbed out to walk around to the passenger side.

"Okay?" Leif said.

"Yes."

Leif rolled down the window. John tried to calm his beating heart by taking a few short breaths. He hadn't insured the car and cussed himself out for not calling an agent.

"Here we go," John said, pressing on the gas pedal.

"I can see why we're leaving early," Leif said. "Jed Clampett behind the wheel."

"You've been sitting with Grandma too long watching television."

"*The Beverly Hillbillies*."

Chapter eleven

John intended to take all the back roads to Fergus Falls. The main roads were always congested with cars zipping by, and there was plenty of time to make it to the hospital without being late. He glanced over to Leif who sat with the earbuds in his ears, which in his opinion, made him look like a secret service agent. They kept him quiet, and John didn't have to answer many questions. He decided Leif was most likely as nervous as himself.

The road stretched out in front of him after leaving the city. He was glad the funeral caused him to take out the car for a short spin. At the time, he hadn't called the agent because the church and cemetery were near, but his gut told him to drive and he hadn't regretted it. Giving Diane a ride a home allowed the two of them to talk alone and away from prying eyes. There had been Vicky between them all these years, and Diane's husband had been gone for a number of them. It worked out nicely. The incident with Vicky at the Old Soldiers Home with another person bothered him as well as the other bothersome happenings, such as catching her kissing another man. It helped for Diane to speak to him about what Vicky had accused him of—being mean. That was something he would never have done to her nor anyone. He was glad the air was cleared up between them so that now, if and when Vicky was located, they'd be on even ground and be able to see her again.

Passing along through the small towns of Buffalo and Maple Lake, he continued on the same route, Highway 55. John glanced at his wristwatch and noted the time, it was early at only 10:30. He kept going instead of stopping for gas. He thought Annandale would be a good town to stop in or possibly Paynesville. It made him wonder if the diner where he and Inga and Janet would eat at years ago was still open. John glanced down at the speedometer to check his speed and gas gauge, he was doing fine. There was plenty of gas and certainly he wouldn't starve to death.

Leif pulled out his earbuds. "When will we be there?"

"Don't know. Thought we'd grab a bite in Paynesville."

"Okay." He plugged the earbuds back in and shut his eyes.

"So much for conversation," John grumbled.

"What?" Leif asked, yanking out the left earbud. "Huh?"

"Nothing."

Leif inserted the earbud again.

The open road was what always sent John's heart thumping. The world in front of him. Now that he felt more comfortable driving faster, he stepped on the gas pedal and wished for one of those newfangled buttons to hold the speed steady like in a new car, but he wouldn't trade this one for anything.

The lake was full of swimmers and boaters, he noticed while passing through Annandale—and onward until at last parking outside of the Paynesville diner located near Lake Koronis. He remembered picnicking there with the family.

"Let's get out and grab something to eat," John said, looking at Leif who was holding tight to the door handle. "You look nervous. You're a little piqued."

"Let's take a sandwich with us, Grandpa. I'm nervous and not sure I can eat."

"Well, that makes two of us. Should we get a 'to-go' and have it between us?" John hadn't opened his door either but kept his window rolled down. "Did you like the wind in your hair when we drove?"

"Yes. Why do you ask?" Leif eyed him suspiciously. "Does this mean I can drive?"

"No. I'm trying to make you less nervous." John took another tactic. "How about an order of French fries on the seat between us or onion rings, and we each have our own sandwich."

"How or where do we keep our drinks?"

"Holders under the seat. Get yours out." John reached under his to remove the plastic device and stuck it in the section between the window and door. "See?"

"Cool!" Leif said after he did the same. "Now, let's get something to eat and get on the road."

They each took a turn in the restroom as they waited for their orders of extra-large fries, soda, and two cheeseburgers. Back in the car, after taking a few bites of his burger, John started the engine. He glanced at the gas gauge and figured he'd fill up. A station near the Dairy Queen was the best place and it was on the route, across from the fairgrounds.

"Good fries," Leif said. "Tell me about that place. It's old, like—"

"Go ahead and say it," John said, chuckling, "like me. We'd stop there for a hot roast beef sandwich with mashed potatoes, gravy, and vegetables every time we went to visit my in-laws. Your mother loved the drive. She'd have the window down and let the air cover her face. She'd smile and her hair blew backward. It was as if she had wings and could fly. So sweet looking. Freckles and a smile with wide open blue eyes, like yours."

"Interesting. Never heard that one before. Tell me another story."

"We'd sit and enjoy the scenery. Sometimes she'd read or fall asleep like you did when we first got going. You didn't want to let me know that you were asleep so I didn't say anything."

"Story."

"She talked about your dad nonstop. Even when they were little. They had a birthday party between them. Frances had peppermint chip ice cream for him and your mother liked—"

"I know the answer to that, chocolate."

"Correct. There was always a small cake too. We'd purchase a gift for your dad like a kite or book or bike horn. Something small. No one bought big, expensive gifts in those days."

"This's really cool, Grandpa. Thanks for telling me this stuff." Leif smiled over at him. "When will we be there?"

"We'll soon be in Glenwood. I'll get gas. You go across and get us each a cone. The Dairy Queen is nearby."

"Then how far?"

"We'll be right on time."

They continued to eat and arrived in Glenwood to take care of matters. The trash was thrown out in a can, and Leif returned with two small cones as John paid for the gas. In the car again, they passed Lake Minnewaska, Lake Reno, Elbow Lake, and soon entered the town of Fergus Falls. They followed the road sign directions that brought them straight to the hospital.

"Let's get checked-in," John said, shutting off the engine. "We're almost late."

"Nah, plenty of time," Leif said, turning the volume up on his iPhone.

"No, you don't," John said, tugging the nearest earbud out. "We're going in, right away."

Reluctantly, Leif opened his door. "I suppose we should roll up the windows?"

"Yes. Someone might throw a cigarette inside and burn the seats." John made sure his windows were closed. The side vent and larger window. "Yours all up?"

"Yeah."

They marched into the reception area together and went straight to the front desk.

"We're here to see my daughter. Janet Evans."

"Oh, sure! You're expected. She'll be right out. Go out to the gardens and have a seat. She's excited to see you."

They went out the appointed door and sat nearest the atrium where the flowers were still in bloom—pansies, mums, and black-eyed Susans.

"Lovely out here," John said, standing near a bench seat. "I don't feel like sitting."

"Me neither. Tell me why Mom went back to her maiden name and not my dad's."

"Ask her."

"I will."

They walked a little but stayed near the entrance until Janet strode out ten minutes later.

"Leif! Dad!"

Leif stood to the side, unsure of what to do. He didn't say a word or look in her direction. When Janet went straight over to him, bypassing her dad, Leif collapsed in her arms and began to cry, "Mom."

"Oh honey, I'm so sorry." Janet held him close to her as if he were a younger child. "I'll come home soon, then we'll be a family."

"Promise?"

"Yes. Can I change my name to Evans to be like yours?"

"Nope. I'm going to change mine to yours."

"Really?"

"Yes," Janet said through tears. She turned toward her dad and went over to hug him. "Thank you for coming and bringing me my son."

"He's a good kid and a joy to be around." John kissed Janet's cheek. "Let's have a seat."

"You know, I have an iPhone and not an antique one that belongs in a museum. I can take pictures of all sorts and put them on a fire stick. I know how to set it up so we can look at all of them just like at a picture show, and all for the price of nothing." Leif stood with the phone in his tee-shirt pocket and hands on his hips. "We should take pictures."

"The kid's smart, I'll grant you that," John said, smiling. "Let's do it."

"Leif! That's the best idea I've heard in ages. I'm beginning to think you and me should hang out together pretty soon." Janet reached for his arm and locked hers within his. "What do you say to that?"

"I'm game. Sounds good, Mom." He released his arms and removed the phone from his pocket. "Let's line up. Maybe we can get one of the nurses around here, if she isn't too old," he looked at John, who cleared his throat, "and she can take the picture. It's really easy to do. Even a second grader can."

At the same time, several individuals came out to sit with patients. A woman in a wheel chair and another person who used a walker. Family members attended to the patients, but a man who seemed the same age as John looked after the woman in the wheelchair.

"Let's line up by the flowers, the pansies. Right over here," Janet said, directing them to the row of flowers. "I love the colors, pink and lavender."

The man noticed them getting ready for pictures and walked over to them. "May I take your picture? It's always nice to do this for families."

"That's so nice of you," Janet said. "This is my dad, John, and son, Leif. This man's name is Joe, and he's also a janitor plus he cares for his mother. It's a wonderful arrangement."

"Thank you," John said, nodding for Leif to hand over the phone for pictures.

"Do you know how to take a picture?" Leif held out the phone to him.

"Certainly." He grinned. "I don't live in the dark ages."

"Some people do," Leif said, nodding at John. "He uses an old dial phone, can you believe it?"

"Just take the picture please," John ordered. "I know my shortcomings."

"Stand right there." Joe held the phone and snapped the picture. "Do you want more?"

"Sure. I'd like one of my daughter alone and one with the two of them together. Right over here," John said, indicating the location. "She won't mind, will she?" He meant the woman in the wheelchair.

"No. It won't make any difference to her. She's had so much heartache and trauma she doesn't know which end is up anymore. It's a sad case."

The pictures were taken and Joe returned the phone to Leif. "Thanks," Leif said.

"No problem."

The three, with Janet in the middle, held hands and went over to a table to sit. Lemonade was served and a small piece of apple pie. As they ate, Janet told them what she'd been doing.

"I'm learning to knit and crochet. Next time I see you, the both of you, you'll each get a present from me. It'll be a surprise." She dug into her pie. "Good."

"Hints?" Leif said, eating the pie in two gulps. "I want to be prepared. It won't be something stupid, will it? You know, like from a cartoon or Batman?"

"No." Janet laughed. "I might do something like one of the Muppets characters for Dad."

"How about mittens or a stocking cap?" John said, drinking the lemonade. "That would be perfect." He ate his pie. "Very good."

"You'll just have to wait and see," Janet continued. "I'm also taking painting classes." She finished her pie and began to drink the beverage. "I didn't know I was so thirsty."

"When will we see you next?" John said. "I'd like for you to move back home."

"I want a couple of things to happen," Janet said, pushing her empty plate and cup aside. "I don't want Mother's ashes on top of the cabinet anymore. It's not right. You shouldn't be talking to them all the time."

"See? I told ya it was kinda creepy, didn't I?" Leif accused John. "I was right. What else?"

"No growling when I try to fix up the house."

"Okay. Continue."

"You'll pay since you don't shop and never spend any money, anyway."

"Whatever." John slid his clean plate and glass aside. "Go on."

"Don't forget the phone and all its trimmings." Leif handed his empty dishes to the kitchen help who was collecting them. She removed all the dirty dishes from the table before moving to the next table. "An iPhone for Grandpa and me? If us three have iPhone's we can easily text. Mine has already gotten old."

"Keep spending my money, why don't you two?"

"We can be on a family plan. It's cheaper that way," Janet said with authority.

"I knew that you'd agree," John said, grimacing. "Leif, you've got something else up your sleeve. Now's the day to spit it out."

"I would like a new laptop."

"Good grief." John looked at Janet, reached for her hand. "I'll do anything to have my baby girl back home with me, even if it means I'm overrun with Leif in the house. Anything. He'll help me fix everything up for your arrival. We'll put his bed somewhere, maybe make a room in the basement." He looked at Leif who smiled. "It'll be fine."

"I will Dad. I'll be home soon, and for good."

"That's exactly what I've been waiting to hear." John looked at his pocket watch. "We need to leave before the roads get busy from rush hour traffic."

"All set? Mom? I'll gladly move to the basement and sleep with the spiders to have you back home. Maybe we can get our own place?"

"Eventually."

The three continued inside to the main desk where the two signed out to leave. They kissed each other "goodbye" and exited through the door.

Once inside the car, John turned to Leif who smiled.

"It's going to work out," John said, more to himself, then a little louder, "It's going to work. I can feel it in my gut."

"Me too." Leif put the earbuds in and turned on his music.

John started the car and thought about his daughter and the needed adjustments in the house to bring her back home.

After he'd parked in his garage and Leif went to Frances's house, John went inside of his house. He picked up a can of beer from the refrigerator and went to his easy chair. After a few swallows of beer, he shut his eyes and fell asleep.

One hour later, he woke to Frances and Leif standing before him. Leif shook his arm.

"Wake up, you old coot!" Frances said.

"Grandpa!"

"What?" he growled. He lowered the foot cushion down to sit up. "What?" He looked from one to the other. "You two look ready to jump me."

"See this picture?" Frances said.

"Look closer," Leif instructed, holding the image in front of him. "Tell me who it reminds you of."

"I think it's—"

"Shush, Grandma!"

John took the phone from Leif to hold closer and move around under the lamp light for a better view. He handed it back and looked at Frances. "Do you think it is?"

"It just might be," Frances said. She sat on the couch.

Chapter twelve

"So? Can I text this guy or not?"

"What do ya mean by text?" John said, puzzled. "Oh, well never mind me, I'll give him a call." John stood and started for the phone, then stopped. He realized what kind of an idiot he really was with electronics and should just let the kid text him. "Go ahead. You probably already have the number memorized. I'd have to search my pockets for it." He returned to his chair to sit.

"You should have a cellphone, John. That's the way it is," Frances said. "You're behind the times."

Leif stood with his phone and found the number to send messages to. "It's Mark, right?"

"Yes, and if you have Ronnie, then add him if you can," Frances told him. "It's better that way." She made herself comfortable on the couch after throwing the extra newspapers from the cushions into the recycle bin in the kitchen.

"We don't want Nancy and Judy to know," John said. "It's best when it's all kept secret, especially if it turns out to not be our Vicky." He'd finished his beer and wanted another but thought better of it.

"Have you eaten, John? I bet you haven't, have you?" When John shook his head, no, Frances stood. "I'm going to find us something to eat."

"Please Frances, just rest. All you do is cook for me," John said. "Stay here until we get to the bottom of it."

"No sirreee! I'm scrambling you a few eggs. That liver of yours is going right down the drain, and you're going to wind up in the hospital sooner rather than later. I dare say, if not for me, you wouldn't have anything decent to eat." Frances continued scolding as she dragged out a frying pan. "I know what you want or should I say what you need. A good kick in the seat. If you hadn't been so stubborn then—"

"Stop it, Grandma! The guy has already responded. I only had Mark's number, and he's going to come over right away, so hurry it up," Leif called to her. "You're also hurting my feelings if you're going to say what I think you're going to because I love my mother and want her home more than anything, especially since I, well, never mind."

Frances continued to bang the pan around as she made the eggs and toasted bread to serve Leif and John.

"All set. Get out here and eat," she called. "Hurry up before he shows up."

"Coming." John got up with his empty beer can in hand and went to the kitchen to eat. "I'm truly grateful, Frances. You're very good to me." He smiled at her and began to eat. "It's true. My diet is awful. I don't cook much. I'm a disaster, which is why," he looked Leif square in the eye, "why you're living with your grandma and not with me. I'm a horrible cook and a louse when it comes to taking care of myself."

"Thank you," Frances said, cupping her hands for prayer. "Lord give me strength. Amen."

"I s'pose this means that we go to church on Sunday?"

"All three of us? Good God," Leif said, shaking his head. "I've unleashed two tormentors."

They ate quickly and had just returned to the living room when Mark and Ronnie were allowed entrance.

"Tell us all about it," Mark said the moment he stepped inside.

"That sure looks like her," Ronnie said. "Mind if we sit? We've been reinterviewing former friends and witnesses who may have seen her. It's tiring."

"I bet it is," John said. "Can I get you anything to drink?"

"Water."

"Me too."

"Leif?"

"I'll get two ice water glasses for them." Leif started for the kitchen. "I'm glad you came, so I can tell people I was involved in the investigation."

"He's going to talk my ear off," John said. "My grandson's a great kid. How come he had your number?" The question was directed to Mark.

"I gave it to him in case he should hear something of interest when he's with his friends, or who knows?" Mark shrugged. "One of those spectators may have relevant knowledge."

"As you can see, I have an old rotary dial. He'll bring me into the century."

"It's about time," Frances said, giving John a sideways look.

"Before we start, any news about the headband or sash?"

"No. It's a dead end," Mark said.

Leif carried the two water glasses into the room and handed one to each of the men. "I did all right for myself." He smiled, jutting out his chin. "I know more than the adults, or some of them." He sat.

"The man who offered to snap the photo was very nice, and he'd also pushed the woman out into the garden. There was a familiarity about him, but I can't possibly think of what it may be?" John said. He looked at Leif. "Did you feel that too?"

"I'm not sure what's the meaning to that big word, but he talked as if he'd known the woman forever." He leaned forward, hands clasped. "He spoke like she was really special."

"That's right. He said she'd had a lot of trauma in her day and couldn't take any more. Something of that nature."

"Hmm," Ronnie said, scratching his head. "I know what I'm thinking, but Mark and I will have to have a private conversation and speak with the detective in charge of cold cases to know which avenue to take next."

"That being said, don't say anything to Nancy or Judy and most especially not Diane," Mark said. He drank down his water before he stood up. "If it's not Vicky, then they're none the wiser, but if it is, we'll tell Diane." He walked toward the door.

"This is Fergus Falls, right?" Ronnie stood next to Mark. "John, you still have a good relationship with Diane, don't you?"

"Yes. Yes, I believe I do," John said, getting up to walk over to them. "When and if the time comes, I can drive her to the station or just be with her. It's not an issue."

"Good," Mark said. "Thank you, young man."

"We'll make a couple of prints of the woman to let Diane see first, and we'll need a DNA sample. We'll have to ask permission from both. He should be about Janet's age, right? Let's see if it's a match with Vicky."

"Yes, maybe slightly older. Right around the same ages as our kids," John said. "Good question."

After the two men left, the phone rang.

"Can I answer it?" Leif said, taking a gigantic step toward the ringing device. "Huh?"

"Oh, why not. Make sure that you—"

"Hello! This is Leif. I'm on Grandpa's phone. Who is this?"

"Wow!" Nancy took a breath. "That's great. This is Nancy. You know who I am, and I want to speak to you and not your grandpa, anyway."

"Far out!" Leif said. "I would like to have your phone number, then we can text each other." He turned and looked at his grandparents and winked. "Sure, I'll put you right on to my contact list. Let me open it up." Leif flipped the phone screen photo and it revealed the application needed for him to put in the correct number and her name. "Okay, go ahead."

Nancy gave him the phone number. Afterward she said, "Go ahead and text me a short word or two and then I'll add you to my list. This is how we'll stay in touch."

"Gotcha!"

"Get your grandfather into the century."

"I will. You can bet on it."

Leif hung up the receiver and before going into the living room to join his grandparents, he sent the required message to Nancy.

"What's happening?" Frances said. "We need to know."

"Don't know for sure. She's texting me right away, pretty sure." Leif held his phone in his palm and sat beside his grandma.

"I bet it's about the flyers," John said, yawning. "It's been a very long day. I'm not used to all that driving, and now the car should be looked at since it's been driven. I'll look into a good mechanic to make sure the tires and everything are in good shape."

"Now that you've driven with our grandson all over the state," Frances said, standing, "let's go home."

Leif's phone dinged a message, and he opened it up to read. Out loud, he read, "I'm to meet Judy by the Riverview theater and help with the distribution of flyers."

"What time?" Frances said.

"Ten."

"If you finish up, then come back to the park to help me out, please."

"Okay, Grandpa. You said the magic word."

When the back door closed behind them, John got ready for bed. His thoughts of family gave him a comfortable feeling as he closed his eyes to the night.

Waking to sunshine and the knowledge he may have found his former friend brought him joy as he climbed from the bed and made ready for the day ahead.

After eating his breakfast, John contacted his old car insurance agent and had the car registered with the company, then an appointment was made with a mechanic for later in the afternoon.

With the full thermos in hand, John headed out the door toward the park.

Diane sat farther away from the engine on an old park bench. He could tell she was answering questions and talking to the passersby. John heard her reply several times, "You're welcome," or watched as she gave a nod to individuals. A young woman inquired about her uniform and badges. It inspired John to look into a "railroad day" that would feature the engine and the depot. However, first they had to discover the true identity of the wheelchair woman. John knew it was going to be a rough day since he couldn't spill the beans about the person.

"You're busy," John said. "Leif is helping to pass out flyers."

"Ahh, that's sweet of him. What a nice boy. I'll save him a cookie for a job well done." Diane looked into her basket to count of the remaining cookies. "I only baked two dozen. Not very many." She wrapped up two in an extra napkin and handed them to John. "One for you and one for Leif. My two favorite boys, or should I say, 'men'?"

"Whatever you care to. Sometimes, I feel like a boy, and we already know that the kid is, so it's fine. Call me as you will." He took the cookies and slid them into his pocket. "I'm going to stick them inside the depot so no one else will eat them."

"You go right ahead."

"Would you care for me to bring out your special chair to sit?"

"When you're finished. I'm perfectly satisfied sitting here under the trees. The flowers are gorgeous to look at it. I love it here."

"I'll bring it out with mine, then we'll sit together."

Diane nodded an "okay" to him.

As John walked to the depot to open it and place his thermos and cookies inside, it came to him how useful a cell phone would be. Right now, he could text Leif to make sure the kid was where he was supposed to be. Knowing his whereabouts and friends' phone numbers would be an added plus. Of course Leif would think he was spying on him, but John felt it was in his rights to know a young person's location if not in school. He took care of matters and grabbed the bucket to go after water.

Neither of the women, nor police, were searching the area. It seemed odd to not have so many extra people around. He felt like he walked on pins and needles because he dearly wanted to know if that was Vicky. As he scooped the bucket into the creek for fresh water, his memory went to when they were just kids and walking through the creek to go to the statue of Hiawatha carrying Minnehaha across. It was beautiful and so majestic looking when he was young, and now it was considered historical. It was a treasure to see. With the bucket filled, he trudged back to the engine.

He knew that climbing to the top was now and forever out of the question since Leif had started to do the chore for him. Sponge in hand, he'd circle the engine twice to make sure all the fingerprints and bird poop was removed. When the job met its completion, he emptied the bucket and put it back inside, as well as the sponge. He removed the two chairs and carried them out in front of the engine and motioned for Diane to join him. He wasn't sure if she saw him, so he approached her to let her know.

"Be right there!"

John took the basket from the bench to carry and walked to the chairs with her resting on his arm because the ground was so uneven.

"Thank you." Diane sat and took the basket when it was offered.

No sooner had he sat in his chair and poured himself a cup of coffee from his thermos than an older gentleman stopped to ask a question.

"Hello, sir! Lovely day," John said. "Bet you know more than I do about this engine, eh?"

"I bet we're both quite knowledgeable."

"Do you have a question?"

"As a matter of fact, I do," the man said. "Tell me how the rod is heavier when the piston drops and then pulls itself upward. How does it draw steam into the cylinder? How was the steam cooled?"

"Water was sprayed onto the cylinder to cool it and condense the steam."

"What was the next step?

"The rod was heavier than the piston so it would fall. It pulled the piston upward, drawing steam into the cylinder from a boiler underneath. Water was then sprayed onto the cylinder to cool it and condense the steam."

"That's amazing," the man said, shaking John's hand. "Thank you."

John watched as he walked away.

"I'm getting my car looked over later this afternoon. I can drive you home or pick you up in the mornings after it's been deemed drivable, if you'd like me to?" John said, sipping from his coffee. "It would be my pleasure for such a delicious cookie." He took a bite from his.

"You're so kind." She looked at him. "I rather enjoy the short walk from my house to and from, but for some reason today, I feel out of sorts. I hope you don't eat Leif's."

"Nope. Wouldn't dream of it."

"Tell me about yesterday with Janet before someone else swings by."

"Everything went well, and we talked about her moving back home." He gulped because of wanting to tell her more but knew he couldn't.

"That's wonderful news."

"I'm soon ready to leave. The bench is hard on my back and the chairs aren't much better. Sometimes I think I'm getting too old."

"I don't believe that. You have to hang in there."

"I know." Diane stood up and stretched out her arms and shoulders. "I feel stiff. The weather must be changing."

"I take it you're leaving?"

"Yes. If I want or need a ride, I'll be sure to call you." She placed the basket over her arm. "This is most pleasant sitting here though, isn't it?"

"Yes. Careful and I'll expect a call. Good day."

John watched as she walked and wished he could've told her some good news.

The early afternoon arrived and still Leif hadn't shown up. John was beginning to worry about him. It would soon be time for him to leave for the car appointment. The railroad watch shown two o'clock, and still Leif hadn't arrived. John didn't know if he should leave or not? What if Leif needed his help? John admonished himself for being overly protected. He picked up the chairs and returned them inside the depot, locked the door, and began to walked home as Leif appeared in the distance. When they each saw one another, they waved.

"Leif!" John hollered and hiked toward him. As they came close to each other, Leif looked happier than ever, and John wanted to know what was behind the excitement in his eyes. When they met, Leif stayed near a large old oak tree, which made John move closer to him. "Why are you hiding behind the tree?"

"Grandpa, you're not going to believe this, but guess what?" Leif started wringing his hands. "You won't believe it!"

"Tell me, but calm down." John placed his hand on Leif's shoulder. "Tell me before I pin you to the tree."

"I'm fifteen next week, right?" Leif started bouncing on his toes. "Right?"

"I guess, if you say so. Why?"

"Nancy signed me up to take a driver's training course."

"I don't believe it. I'm going to pretend as if I didn't hear this. It's time for me to drive the car to the mechanic and have it gone through to make sure it's in A1 condition."

"You're not going to say anything?"

"Not right now." John began to walk away. "Come on and tell me about the flyers."

"The images used were of a young Vicky on the top and the older of her sketched below. They couldn't have used the picture we'd taken yesterday."

"I guess so. Where did you go?"

"All the bars and restaurants near Roosevelt and Sanford Middle School."

"No wonder you were gone all day. I really need to get moving. Come with me?" John began walking faster.

"You bet. I aim to learn to drive in that sporty tin can."

"That's what you think."

Chapter thirteen

While waiting for his car to be checked over, the notion hit him that it was up to old Grandpa to find the boy a car to drive. A father always did things like that, so why couldn't he do it? John walked outside to circle around the used cars in the lot beside the mechanic shop but didn't see one suitable for his grandson. Soon his car was ready and he paid before going home.

At home, he opened up a can of beer and went to sit out in the sunshine, by the old picnic table in the backyard. He took a sip and realized it bothered the life out of him not knowing if that person was Vicky. The more he thought about it, he realized how out of touch with living he'd become. Vicky would only laugh at him and say he'd turned into an old grouch. A grouchy old man. Inga had accused him of that too. He couldn't let that happen. As he sat, crunched over and looking downward at the yard, it occurred to him Leif could use a few extra bucks to pay for the driver's training course. He left his beer on the table and went next door to see Frances and Leif.

It surprised him when no one answered the door. He went for his beer to go inside when they called over to him.

"Hey! We went to the store," Leif hollered. "See?" He held the bag of groceries. "Grandma's baking me a cake for my upcoming birthday."

John carried his beer over to them. "I've got a proposition for you." He stayed near the back steps as they continued to climb them and stop on the landing. "How about mowing my yard? I'll pay you for it."

"It's about time you decided to do that. Leif needs to pay for the course, and it shouldn't all be coming from my pocket!" Frances scolded.

"I understand."

"I'm here, you know? You're talking about me. I do know how to talk for myself."

"Well?"

"I'll do it. Show me where the lawnmower is."

"Come by later."

John went back to his yard and into the small hut hidden in the backyard to pull out the old lawnmower. He checked the oil and gasoline after shutting it down and filled them up and made sure the sparkplugs were set. It started with one pull. He left it in the hut in case Leif didn't want to mow straight away.

Inside, John went to his phone book to look up the numbers for cell phone stores in Minneapolis and found out there was one over near the Riverview Theater. He could walk there and not waste gas.

As he pondered whether or not he should buy the phone right now, it occurred to him Inga had saved an old box of calendars. He went in search of them and found them on the top shelf of their closet. He sat with them until the phone rang.

"Will you do me a favor," Nancy said. "I'd like to go to Fort Snelling, but I don't want to go it alone, and I don't care to have Judy join me because she thinks I'm a little wacky over the Marine who's buried out there. She says I should've gotten over him, but I can't."

"You want me to drive you? I haven't been there in years and years."

"I'll buy you lunch. I'll pick you up tomorrow morning at nine, okay? You won't need to drive, and I know the way. It just would be nice to have someone with me."

"I'll do it under one condition."

"What?"

"You go inside that phone store and talk to the person or help me to get a cell phone, but I want the same number. I don't know where to begin, and I don't want the kid to know just how stupid—"

"Or completely worthless you are with modern day electronics."

"Right. Will you?"

"Of course! Love to and we'll grab a bite after we're all done scooting around town."

"Good. Nine o'clock sharp."

They disconnected and John felt the better for it.

Knowing Nancy planned to help him out with the phone made him feel much better, like he wasn't stuck in the wilderness. He wondered how he ended up so behind the times, then shook the thought from his mind. He must concentrate on Vicky. He never really had searched for her and now felt guilty as hell. Something must be done because what if it wasn't her there in the institution?

Instead of making a brief phone call to Mark, he got busy with the box and found the pertinent years to look through. He sat down by the kitchen table to begin his quest.

In January of 1967, they went to a movie. It was, *To Sir with Love*. They'd both fallen in love with Lulu and Sidney Poitier. John grabbed a tablet and pen from a drawer to begin the list of places to search because he'd heard people always returned to their roots in times of crisis. He also reasoned that places of joy and laughter were worth a return to remember happiness. The same year they'd both walked among the pathways, holding hands and sneaking kisses at the falls. Minnehaha Falls was a great place to begin and farther to where the deer pen used to be and onward to the Old Soldiers Home. He placed the lid on the box and set it aside, leaving it on the tabletop, then thought the better of it and carried it to his chair. He hid it on the floor behind his lamp where he was sure no one would look and ask questions that were no one's business. He wasn't sure himself what he was doing but felt it was his time to search for his old friend.

Later that evening, about the time John was going to get ready for bed, Leif came by. He walked right in.

"Grandpa, the boy is ready to see how to start that piece of work out there you call a lawnmower." Leif went into the living room as John brought his legs down for sitting. "Ready?"

"The piece as you call it, is right out in that small hut back there."

They walked over to the area, and John showed him how to start the mower. Leif followed suit.

"Got it?"

"Yep. I'll get on it in the morning."

"If it's wet grass, it won't cut. Wait for the afternoon. By the way, I'm going out in the morning. I might not be here."

"Okay. I'm going in to bother Grandma now," Leif said, starting to walk off. "Really, she does say I'm a bother."

"You're getting interesting and almost likeable, so you're not as much of one, a bother, I mean. Soon your mother will be here and you'll be living with me." John waited a beat to continue. "We must paint the rooms and straighten everything up."

"We will."

The two split and went their own direction—Leif into his house and John in his.

Knowing he had a plan different than sitting in front of the engine, John fell asleep with it on his mind. He'd begun, and planned to continue marking down each important place he and Vicky frequented with the year and possibly correct date.

Morning came with sunshine once again. He felt Inga watching him, which hadn't happened for a very long time. He took it as a sign of her approval. Now he knew he was on the right track to locate Vicky, providing she was still alive.

Five minutes early, he stood out on his front steps to wait for Nancy. She drove up as he was about to call to remind her of their date. Once inside of the car and buckled, he smiled over to her.

"I'm so glad you accepted my invitation," Nancy said, turning her blinker on to drive from the curb. "Phone first?"

"Let's get it over with," John said. "I want one I'll never have to replace and use my old number."

"That might not happen because it'll be a different server, but the guy will get you all figured out. We can return to pick it up too."

Nancy parked in the nearby lot, and they went into the phone store together. He let her do the talking, or as much as possible. The young woman knew what to do and how to take care of matters. They walked out with a new phone and number, which he slipped into his shirt pocket.

"Thank you," John said, fastening his seatbelt.

"You are welcome."

Nancy turned the radio on to a sixties music station before driving from the spot. She followed road signs leading to the interstate that brought her near the international airport. After a few entrances and exits, she entered into the Fort Snelling cemetery.

"After the rush of traffic, it's nice to have the silence," Nancy said, pulling into the front lot. "I really should refresh my memory with a map. Do you want to come in or not?"

"I'll sit here and maybe breathe in the stillness."

Nancy left the car, and he watched as she climbed the stairs to go inside. It was so solemn and peaceful. When she entered, he removed his phone to inspect it, pressing all the buttons. He wasn't sure if he remembered what they were all for, but it sure cost him a bundle. It was almost identical to Leif's. He didn't know what it was that Frances used, but he was sure Leif would help him out when needed, especially to search for things. When Nancy returned, following the given map, they drove straight to the gravesite. John didn't know if he should stay in the car or what to do, but she motioned for him to come by her so he followed.

It was uncomfortable to watch her dry her moist eyes and talk about their first time in the back seat of the car over in the deer pen or the Old Soldiers Home lot and then there were the drive-in movies and how he'd kissed her or the deep kiss before he left for Vietnam. In the end, John's heart bled for both, Nancy for the heartache of never being able to fulfill her dreams with this man, and for Gary, to never have a chance at life with Janet.

"Where to now?" John asked when Nancy turned from the gravestone. "Home? Lunch?"

"Lunch, but let's walk for a minute," Nancy said, reaching for his hand. "It's nice to read the names, it's an honor for them. They'll hear it and know they're remembered."

"I never thought of that. So they hear us in heaven?"

"Of course!"

They strolled for a few minutes before climbing back into the car.

"I really don't know of any place to eat around here," John said. "I never go anywhere, but now Leif is knocking out some of the old cobwebs and shaking up these old bones of mine."

"That's good. It's what that grandkid of yours is for." Nancy started the engine.

They fastened their seatbelts and soon she drove from the cemetery and onto the interstate once again. We'll find a place in the Mall of America. It's right around the corner.

"Never been there."

"I believe it."

As Nancy weaved the car in and out of spaces and onto the exit ramp leading to the parking ramp of the mall, John stared at the signs flashing by him in a blur.

After parking, he said, "Wow! That was something. I never could've driven that. Never." He shook his head. "I don't know how you did it."

"Practice and patients and no talking for me to concentrate."

"I believe it. Where to?"

"Let's hold hands again so you don't get lost." She reached for his left hand. "It's like this—we could easily get separated."

"I can see that."

They passed several unopened stores and crossed into the rides section to watch some of the little kids' expressions as they rode them. Nancy brought John over to the Homeplate stone that marked the spot where it had been in the old Metropolitan Stadium when the Twins played baseball there.

"What a memory. Sixth grade it was an outing to come to a game."

"I remember. Let's go eat!"

Strolling down the walkways, they passed the restaurants but not one struck them as where they wanted to eat until coming up to the Twin City Grill. After perusing the menu, they went inside to sit.

"Next time, we'll go into a different one. We'll work our way around this monstrosity mall," Nancy said, gazing around her. "Even this place is large."

"Next time?" John asked, opening a menu. "So many different kinds of hamburgers and grilled cheese." He shrugged. "I wouldn't know which one to order."

The waitress arrived to take orders.

"I'm going to have a grilled cheese and a chocolate shake."

"I'll have tomato soup, grilled cheese and coffee."

"Bring two waters, please."

"Sounds good."

She left and Nancy looked at John. "You're tired, and something's bothering you. What is it?"

"You know, Frances always hollers at me, whether I deserve it or not. I should've been better with Leif and now that Janet will soon be home, I feel a need to shape up. I've started to realize I need to get him a car. No one else can help him out, really."

"That's not all. Vicky must be on your mind."

The waitress set the water glasses down in front of them and both took a drink.

"I only wish they would've found her by now. I never have really looked for her. I suppose I was still angry over her kissing that guy and so on. I was jealous, no other explanation."

"It's entirely possible to believe you were jealous, but that's a long time ago."

"I wonder how crazy it would be to begin a search, you know? Just me."

"That's really rather sweet. Have you given it any thought of where to begin?"

The waitress carried over the soup and two grilled cheese sandwiches. "Can I get you anything else?"

"My coffee and her shake."

"Right."

They both began to eat. When the waitress returned with the rest of the order, they took a few minutes to continue with the conversation.

"Have you heard any rumors? Anything? What about the bones found along with the animal bones? Were they male? Female?"

"Male, and the composition of them were from the mid-1800s. That makes sense since there were Civil War soldiers buried in the area and Native Americans."

"At least we know that outcome." John continued to eat. He finished his soup. "Very good." He sipped his coffee.

"How do you plan to search? You were going to tell me." Nancy continued to eat her grilled cheese sandwich and drink her chocolate shake.

"Inga collected old calendars and I recently opened the box. They date back to the fifties. I found the year of sixty-five and remembered seeing the movie, *The Sound of Music*, at Riverview. I'm going to go to a movie and pretend to look for her."

"That, alone, is the most romantic idea I've ever heard in my life. It brings tears to my eyes. Can I join you?"

"Join me?" John asked.

"Yes. It'll help me walk through my time with Mike. We can each have our own sites to go to, remembrances, but I bet we visited the same places only at different times."

"Then neither of us would be alone." John warmed to the idea.

"That's right. It'll be our own little club or remembrances." Nancy reached for his available hand to place hers on top of.

"Secret? Me and you? I won't tell anyone." John placed his other hand on top of hers. "I'm in."

"Good. We'll call it our own club."

"The tide of time club," John said after giving it further thought.

"Couldn't have said it better myself."

Chapter fourteen

Upon his return home, John noticed the front grass was mown, but the rows were either crooked or crisscrossed. "Unbelievable." John scratched his head and realized he hadn't worn his old engineer cap, which surprised him. He walked through the house and exited through the back door. "Leif!" He waved his arms at him to catch his attention. "Stop!" When Leif finally saw him, he pushed the mower toward John. Stopping right in front of John, he removed his earbuds and John reached over to shut the mower down. "Turn around and look at the grass."

"What?" Leif looked around him, and his eyes opened wider. "I goofed!"

"Yes. Try to make it look better now, but you'll know for next time," John said, giving him a nod. "I'm going back in." John headed for his easy chair.

At his chair, he removed the phone to set beside him and put his feet up. The hum of the mower put him to sleep. In what seemed like just a few odd minutes, Leif was yanking on his foot.

"Grandpa, I'm done now. Are you paying me or how is this going to work?" Leif stood with his earbuds hanging down over his shoulders. "I want to know."

"I'll pay, of course, and we can begin to look for a car. That will, most likely, come from my pocket since you will not drive my car."

"Understood." Leif stood a moment and looked at him. "Anything else? Such as how will I get money to pay for gas, that sort of thing. I'm not old enough to work."

"I realize that. Go and see if you can drum up lawnmowing jobs. You can use my mower, if needed." John folded his arms behind his head. "Any more questions?"

"How will I get to the jobs?" He balanced from foot to foot, sweat beads still on his brow and he swiped them off. "It's hot out there!"

"Walk. Now let me get in my nap."

Leif glanced at the new cell phone. "What have we here?" He walked over to the table to retrieve the phone, but John got to it before him. "You bought a phone? A phone?" He placed his hands on his hips. "I don't believe it. What is this world coming to?"

John took a deep breath to hold back his temper. "You can go now."

"Ahh nahh. What five and dime did you get it from? The drugstore?" Leif snickered. "I'm shocked."

"For your information, that phone over there will be disconnected shortly or as soon as I call to tell them. I forgot that I must do that."

"Well, I'll be." Leif turned to walk away. "I'll be back."

"I'm sure you will."

John leaned back again and tried to nap.

Into the evening, John had the television on, switching to various stations. He wondered why Mark hadn't contacted him or any other person regarding the investigation. By bedtime, he had exhausted all memorized phone numbers and typed them into the phone contact list. He had trouble sleeping because of the bright moon rays.

In the morning, he was ready for the day. As he left the house, he realized Leif hadn't stopped back in to bug him about the phone business. That would come later, no doubt. Frances didn't holler out the door at him either, which made for a pleasant jaunt to the park. With the thermos and bag with a fresh peanut butter and jelly sandwich in his hands, he crossed the busy street. Once he reached the park area, John resolved to visit the Stevens House during the day since Vicky and him had entered it as young teenagers before going to the Old Soldiers Home to see her dad. It was time to look around the building, even if there was no entrance to the second oldest wood frame house built in Minneapolis. It was known as the beginning of Minneapolis. Colonel John Harrington Stevens of the US Army was a commander at Fort Snelling.

John set about cleaning the engine. Within the depot walls, he set aside his belongings and searched for the bucket. He couldn't locate it. When the two chairs were brought out to their spots and set up, he began the inspection. Slowly he circled the engine, making note of the smudges and fingerprints. After completion, he was ready to set up the ladder when Leif carried the full bucket to the engine and set it down.

"Ready to go!" Leif brushed his hands together. "Got the ladder set up?"

"You're on top of things." John carried the ladder to its normal position. "Go ahead."

As John held the ladder and watched Leif climb, it occurred to him that from the back, he reminded him of his dad. His dad's shoulders were square, and he held himself straight and strong like a soldier. John lowered his arms and reached for the smaller sponge to get to work.

Slowly John worked until at last, the engine shined again. It was a little dirtier than usual since he hadn't been on site the day before because he'd gone out with Nancy. No sooner had he finished and gone for his thermos to sit and relax than a spectator happened by.

"Good morning, sir. How are you?" John said with a smile on his face. "Lovely day."

"That it is." The man rubbed his chin. "Can you tell me if the cowcatcher has really caught cows? I mean, seriously?"

"Oh my, yes," John said, standing up. "Look over here." He brought the man around to the front of the engine. "You see, they couldn't stop or even slow down, but they'd try shooing the cows off the tracks first with the horn."

"The hoot-hoot!"

"Correct. But cattle roamed free. There was no stopping them or the train so the cattle were pushed aside."

"They weren't pushed, mostly shoveled, right?"

"More or less."

"Thanks." The man kept walking.

John removed his watch from his pocket to check the time. Plenty of hours to go, he thought, and walked over to Leif.

"Almost done?"

"Ready to come down." Leif descended and looked right at John. "Perfect timing. Now, I think I should get paid for doing this job, keeping this engine spotless."

"Oh my word." John sighed. "We've discussed this already. Let's get the ladder stored and get out front."

"Got it."

Out front, another group of young teenage girls walked toward them and stopped in front of Leif. John sat back, poured himself a cup of coffee, relaxed as Leif handled the girls. John expressly wanted to observe the scene in front of him.

"Do these kinds of engines still run?" a girl with a ponytail asked.

"Of course they do. In museums or in national parks," Leif answered.

John grinned. So far Leif was doing great, but John hoped to see his face because he wanted to know if Leif was embarrassed or nervous. The telltale sign would be his red cheeks. John did note the back of Leif's ears were pink.

"Have you ever ridden in one of these?" another young girl, who wore a decorative earring in her nose, asked.

"No, I never have but would like to someday," Leif answered. "Thank you for stopping."

The two girls kept walking and Leif stared after them until John loudly cleared his throat.

"How'd I do?" Leif asked, still slightly flushed.

"Great! You'll be a speaker someday. Maybe a teacher."

"Thanks, but I don't think so." Leif pulled out a couple dollars from his pocket. "I'm going for a can of soda."

"Okay." John kept his eye on the passersby and watched the traffic for what seemed forever until Leif's return.

"I wonder where the grandma is today? I could use a cookie," Leif said, sitting beside John. He drank from his can of soda. "Grandma was supposed to make me a lunch but was mad because I hadn't mowed her lawn. Now I don't have anything to eat."

"You take too much advantage of her." John began to eat his sandwich.

"You should talk!"

"I know. She's a great cook." John offered a half from his sandwich and Leif took it. "Let's walk around the Stevens House. Just you and me. No one's around today."

"It's pretty slow." Leif bit into his sandwich. "Tell you what, let's keep a look out for that detective friend of yours. It's been at least two-three days."

"You're right. It's time that we get some answers." John finished his lunch and swallowed what was left in his thermos. "Let's go. I need to walk around."

"Hold on." Leif stuffed the last bite into his mouth and drank down his soda, then belched. "Better!" He wiped his mouth with his arm. "Ready."

"You do need to develop a few more manners." John stood to fold the chair and took his thermos in hand and sandwich bag. "Let's lock it all up. I'll carry my thermos."

The two took care of the chore before starting the short walk to the Stevens House. They followed the pathway that wound through a flower garden and big old grandfather oak trees.

"I bet these trees have been here since the beginning of time," John said. "They're even older than me."

"That's hard to believe because you're old, admit it." Leif looked at him from the side and noticed John frown. "Sorry, that was rude."

They came to the old structure and tried to peer through the windows but weren't very successful.

"We can barely pick out the heating stove and table," Leif complained. "Not fair that it's not open." He held his nose right up to the wavy glass window. "The windows are awful."

"I agree." John began to stroll around the building with Leif following. He kicked in the dirt wherever there was a bump or uneven ground. "I keep thinking that if only something should pop up in my memory by looking around, I might be able to locate her."

"I used to think that about my dad but don't anymore." Leif stared at John and said, "I haven't been to his grave since forever."

"Even with your grandma?" John studied Leif and noticed the way his hair stuck up on his forehead was just like his mother's. "There's something about you, which is just like your dad, but I'm not sure what. You are built like him, if I remember correctly."

"I guess that's a compliment," Leif said, shrugging. "He's buried, you know, at Fort Snelling." Leif turned to walk away.

"We'll take care of that one of these days. The three of us." John began to follow him, stopping on the opposite side where the rocking chair was visible. "Can you imagine sitting on one of those hard chairs all the time?" He yawned. "Well, I'm getting tired."

"I couldn't live like this. No internet. No telephone."

As they drifted toward another location, in the distance Leif spotted a familiar looking car and stopped. He pointed down the horizon where he was sure he saw Mark's car.

"Let's go down there. I think it's Mark's car." Leif began to hurry toward the vehicle. "I'm pretty sure that it's."

John swiftly walked to keep up with him until at last they reached the spot, but there wasn't anyone else nearby.

"Let's just go home," Leif said. "I'm bummed out." He crossed his arms. "Come on, Grandpa!" He dropped his arms and began to walk in the opposite direction.

"Get back here, young man! I see him," John scolded. He removed his engineer cap to wave it back and forth to catch Mark and Ronnie's attention. "Mark! Ronnie!"

When Leif heard the names called, he glanced backward to see where John was facing, then went in that direction. John followed and both converged at the same time where the two men were busy in a conversation.

Mark saw them and immediately signaled to join him and Ronnie.

"Oh! I didn't see you two," Ronnie said when they arrived. "We were just discussing what we've learned about the woman in the institution.

"Which is which?" Leif said, looking at one then the other detective with his arms crossed. "I—meaning me and him," he nodded at John, "want to know what's up. So tell us."

"They'll tell us when they know something," John said, giving Leif a stern look. "We need patience."

"Everyone needs DNA testing nowadays and it all takes time," Ronnie said, then cleared his throat. "That includes you too, young man. Someday you'll want yours done and you'll be waiting like the rest of us." He spread his legs and placed his hands on his hips. "So loosen up."

"Well, okay," Leif said contritely. "Which is it?"

"We did take Diane's, and now have of Vicky's, but the patient's doctor has to request the DNA from the family or caretaker. They didn't take DNA samples because of the date in time. they only saved evidence. We haven't been notified." Mark looked at Leif. "I can see you're anxious to see if the help you've given us, really helped us out, aren't you?"

"Yes." Leif nodded.

"Every avenue brings us a step closer. Don't think that even if it leads to nowhere, it wasn't helpful. It was," Mark said, smiling. "It's very much appreciated."

"Thank you. I'm a star because I noticed it first." Leif grinned.

"Yes, you are," Ronnie agreed. "We're waiting for permission to take a DNA sample."

"Wait and wait," John said, scratching his chin. "There's always a glitch somewhere, isn't there?"

"We've also requested a family history of her, but that hasn't happened either," Ronnie said. "It's all so time consuming."

"In the meantime," Mark said, "we keep looking."

"Does that answer your questions, young man?" Ronnie said.

"I guess. Sorry for being such a pain," Leif said, keeping his head down.

"You are fine." Mark nodded toward the car. "Time for us to head home. Want a lift?"

"Nahh, we're good," John said, "but thanks. By the way, where all haven't you searched?"

"We've been most everywhere. Nancy and Judy have searched in places they thought relevant, but of course, nothing has been found since the headband and sash," Mark said, starting to walk away. "I really must get going."

"We'll see you tomorrow most likely," Ronnie said. He followed suit and left for his car.

John and Leif watched as they walked away.

"I feel like they have something up their sleeve," John said, "but their phones never dinged a message like yours does all the time."

At the same moment, Leif's phone dinged and he looked at it. John made sure to watch how he managed and took care of matters so he could be ready when someone messaged him.

"Grandma wants us home. She's got another idea for us to look into," Leif said. "Here, you can read it." He showed the script to John, who read it.

"She wants to invite Judy and Nancy?" John couldn't believe Frances would offer to do that. "Say no. Tell her, 'no,' that I'll do it," he grouched. "Don't you see? She never knew these folks, but I grew up with them. They were classmates."

After Leif replied to the message, the two walked home and parted at the driveways.

Chapter fifteen

Immediately, John went in search of a beer but didn't find one, realizing he hadn't been into a store in ages. He hadn't thought about groceries since his diet mostly consisted of freezer food. He tended to matters and set out for the store. Along the way, he thought of Diane and stopped to see if she wanted a ride to the market. Outside of her house, he parked and called her on the cell phone.

"Hello, Diane?"

"Yes, is this John?"

"I'm right outside of your house. I'm off to the grocery store. Can I pick you up something, or do you want to ride with me?"

"I could use a carton of milk and loaf of bread, if you don't mind?"

"A small milk?"

"Yes. Two percent. English muffin bread."

"I'll get it and be right back."

They disconnected and out of the cars' side window, he saw waving through the window and nodded to her before turning his blinker on and entering onto the main road.

In the store, he picked up a potato, a bag of apples, and package of ground hamburger. For Diane, he placed into the cart what she wanted and added a package of cupcakes, just for her. The liquor store was around the corner, Minnehaha Liquors, where he parked in the lot and went inside to purchase a twelve pack. Back in the car, he drove to Diane's and parked in front of her house. He carried what she needed to the door.

"Come inside," she said when opening the door.

"No, I need to get home," John said, handing over the groceries.

"Take them to the kitchen, would you?"

John continued to the kitchen with the small full grocery bag and set it on the table. He glanced around the old familiar room, which brought tears to his eyes.

"She's still beautiful," John said, staring at Vicky's graduation picture.

"She is, isn't she?" Diane touched his arm. "It's okay. You haven't really cried, have you?"

"Really? No." He shook his head. "I haven't. I kept thinking she'd return or so many what if's? You know?" He brushed away his tears. "I couldn't really tell Inga how much I missed Vicky, now could I?"

"You met Inga and then you two split, didn't you?" Diane drew him into her shoulder and ran her worn hand up and down his back. "I always thought you two would get back together."

"I suppose that might've been possible had enough time gone by, but then this happened and I met my Inga, and the rest is history." John pulled back and reached for his handkerchief in his breast pocket. He turned to blow his nose and wipe his nose. "A thought just came to mind, actually Nancy and I have been talking."

"Why not sit for a minute?" Diane indicated the chair. "I'll put on coffee."

"As a matter of fact, I thought you'd like a cupcake so I purchased a package of six. Let's have one, and I'll have a glass of ice water," John said. He scooched in behind the table on the nearest chair. "This has been harder on me than I could ever have realized. I'm so sorry for not searching harder for her. Will you forgive me?"

"I knew why you were aloof and now you have dear Leif who has finally been able to get you out of your funk. He is a dear, isn't he?" Diane took care of the water, adding ice into his glass and setting it on the table before him. She opened the carton and offered him the white cupcake with chocolate frosting, and she took the pink one. "Tell me, you sound like you have a plan."

"We were the souls who noticed that woman in the institution and the male caregiver but were instructed not to say anything," he said, then bit into the treat.

"I'm grateful for that. I don't think it's her. She would've been in a nursing home if anywhere. There is always hope, isn't there?" She took a bite of the cupcake and had a swallow of coffee.

"I wonder? This might be too much to ask, but do you have Vicky's diary?" He finished his cupcake before drinking from his glass. "I would like to look through it."

"Whatever for? The police have it, anyway," Diane said, finishing the cupcake. "My, that hit the spot." Her eyes twinkled.

"Do you have grandchildren from Tom?" John asked, noticing pictures on the refrigerator held by magnets.

"No, these pictures are of great nieces and nephews." She smiled and went for them. "They're adorable and I don't see them much."

"This really is tough now that we're investigating Vicky's case again."

"It's been tough for the both of us," Diane said, "and it's okay. We don't grow unless we suffer and heal. You've had the loss of Inga, too. Now you're healing and getting stronger. Let's keep talking, it'll help us both."

"Thank you," John said.

"Count your blessings." Diane smiled. "Take care and I'll see you soon at the park."

They said their goodbyes and John left.

As he carried the food indoors, he thought about Diane without grandchildren. He had his Leif and was grateful, but who did she have besides Tom? She was right, he needed to count his blessings. Leif and Janet. Soon, she'd be home and they'd be a family again.

After starting to fry the hamburger and placing the potato in the microwave, he gave Nancy a call.

"What are you doing, you old fart?" Nancy said. "Been waiting for you."

"Come on over if you don't mind me eating."

"Be there in a jiffy."

They disconnected and John continued fixing the meal. Just finishing, Nancy arrived at his doorstep.

"How'd you know it was me when you answered?"

"It shows up, you idiot."

"Oh." John glanced at his phone. "By golly, it does! Phones nowadays are like magic." John brought her to the kitchen where he quickly ate, then dumped the dirty dishes into the dishwasher. "I know, I should be rinsing." He closed the door to it.

"You spoke to Diane?"

"Actually, beer?"

"Thought you'd never ask." Nancy helped herself and took out a can for John. "Let's go sit outside since it's so nice out."

John followed her out to the picnic table where they sat opposite from each other.

"Tell me now." Nancy sipped from her beer.

"You see, I brought Diane's groceries and we talked for a little while, which reminds me, we both forgot that she didn't pay me." He took a swallow of his beer. "I would've paid for it anyway. I think she lives on next to nothing."

"And still bakes all of those delicious cookies. She's special."

"I always thought Vicky was and then all that happened with her running out on me and now we're searching for her in our own way," John said, frowning. "Well, I asked about a diary. Thought we might be able to discern something from it."

"Judy and I handed over our Barbie Dolls to see if they could get DNA from her on them, you know? Match up with Vicky."

"You did?" John's eyes opened wider. "Never thought of that."

"That's about the size of it," Nancy said. "No word about that business though? You know, with the woman?"

"How do you know about that? It was supposed to be a secret?" John shook his head. "I don't believe it. Nothing is secret around here."

"Frances."

"Of course! Leif and Frances. I thought he could keep a secret though." John sipped his beer. "I have to be more careful."

"She would've been told one way or another since they live together."

"I heard that she wanted to invite you and Judy over to help with the investigation," John said. "She doesn't quit. Was Mike over a lot?"

"All the time. Why?"

"Let's think about where Vicky went and combine that with where you and Mike would've hung out. Where would she have gone? Where did Inga and I go? Maybe drive-ins?" John rubbed his chin. "I've thought of going to the old lots to see which are open for driving around. We wouldn't find anything though, it would be a waste of time." John shrugged. "What's your opinion?"

"I think it's a start," Nancy said. "I think we could walk around Nokomis. People do that all the time, and it would give us some exercise."

"Classmates do that frequently."

"Everyone does," Nancy said, finishing her beer. "Let's start a regiment of searching old sites. "Mike and I went swimming in the lake. Nokomis has the little beach, and that's where we swam out to the raft. Where did you and Vicky go?"

"Same place. You're right. Reliving all of it will be difficult," John said, looking at her with sad eyes, "but very good for us."

"That's right. I know Mike won't return but who knows?" Nancy shrugged, "Vicky just might surprise us."

"You never know."

"It's time for me to boogie on out of here, but let's set a date and time?" Nancy stood. "We could go for a drive around the lake right now?"

"Why not?" John stood, smashed his empty can to a smaller size and did the same with Nancy's can. "You drive or me?"

"Tell you what? What a beautiful night. Let's cruise in that zippy car of yours. I'd love it. Wind in my hair, all the windows open. Old, wonderful memories. It'll settle my heart. For at least tonight, I'll be able to dream of Mike and I out for a spin."

"Then, we'll do it." John carried the cans to a trash can near the garage. "Let me fetch my keys."

While she waited for his return, Nancy walked the perimeter of the car and grinned from ear to ear. As she opened the passenger door, her heart fluttered from the memory of riding in a car similar to this one beside her Mike. "Mike, I'll never get over you. Remember the nights we drove around Nokomis? The water was and still is a beautiful blue, the moon rays were dazzling, and the slight ripple on the lake? So romantic."

John came up behind her and said, "What you say?"

"Nothing, just talking to myself."

"Nahh, admit it, you were talking to Mike. I do that to Inga. It won't be long, and I'll be talking to Vicky." He opened the driver's door and climbed in. "The seatbelts are almost worthless because we still move all over the seat."

"I know. You're right. I talk to him all of the time. He was my man."

"Yes. That's another thing Diane said." John started the engine with one turn of the key. "Bet I won't be driving this winter. I'll have to start being more serious about a car for Leif."

"Pay him to look after the engine. He'd love it. He's too young to find a job." Nancy buckled the seatbelt. "I remember sitting right next to Mike and putting my hand on his knee."

"Vicky did that too," John said, driving from the alley and heading toward the street. "Diane thought we'd get back together with time, I'm sure she expected us to marry."

"From the sounds of it, I bet she hoped for it."

"Let's start with Cedar. It'll bring us to the little beach and then eventually lead us around to the big beach. You're right about where to begin." John opened his vent window and turned it toward him so the wind blew in his face. "Can you reach the back windows to roll down?"

"Pull over. I can't do all that reaching business anymore."

"Right." John drove to the curb and stopped for her to get out and roll the back two windows down before climbing back inside the car. After she buckled up, he merged into the traffic. "Off we go!"

With the wind blowing in his face, John felt as if he was a kid once again with all of his life in front of him. Glancing at Nancy, he could tell by the smile on her face and the way she held herself high, she was ready for the world.

"Ready for what comes?" John said.

"Yes. This all helps. When I leave this earth, I'll be satisfied."

"You'll know it wasn't just a beautiful, wonderful dream."

"Yes."

The drive brought them to the corner of Cedar Avenue and the Parkway, driving past glorious old oak and maple trees giving shade to all the later evening runners and walkers with pets in tow. Older homes built after the war years for the returning soldiers were canopied with oak trees. Turning onto Cedar Avenue, they soon came to a boulevard where the swimmers lined their cars for the day of swimming and enjoying the water. A ramp was farther on where the boaters launched small sail crafts and boats.

"Vicky and I walked and swam along here," John said, parking. "I don't wish to get out."

"No." Nancy shook her head. She pointed to the raft. "Mike and I jumped from that all the time."

"I still have those swim trunks."

"You're kidding me?" Nancy stared at him.

"Inga wasn't much on swimming. I took Janet a few times, then she went on her own."

"So you kept them?"

"I didn't see a need to throw them away. Not sure if I fit into them anymore." John shrugged. "Should we keep going? Tell me, do you still have clothes that you wore when you were with Mike?"

"Yes. One dress."

"See? We're both a little nutsy, but your man passed away."

"We have a different story." Nancy brushed away the tears. "Look at the beautiful moon and the glistening on the water. It's breathtaking."

"Let's keep going," John said. "This is harder than I expected."

"Agreed."

They began to circle the lake once again, coming to the corners where John had to make turns and go around toward the big beach.

"You must've frequented Baskin Robbins for ice cream?"

"We should've stopped there for old times' sake," Nancy said, sighing.

"Next time, we can," John said.

"There is so much change in the neighborhood, it's hard to imagine what it was like growing up. The houses do look the same."

"Only the stores and cultures are different. With us, it was all Scandinavian, and now it's full of immigrants from all over the world." John glanced at her. "Did you do anything with Vicky, like go to a movie?"

"Different circles. When she didn't show for the prom like she should've, there was a buzz, but no one knew anything. It was all rumors."

"I thought so. Well, time for home unless you have anything else in mind?" He took in a deep breath. "I love this cool air against my skin."

"Me too." Nancy did the same and took a deep breath. "If you still have your swim trunks, start to make a pile. Set them aside. We'll do this a time a two more, and we'll see what will come to mind."

"I think my old Twins baseball shirt is in a drawer. I'll put it with the trunks." John kept driving. "I can't see where there would be DNA on it, if that's what you're thinking. They haven't found anything on the dolls."

"Not yet, but you never know about those things. Any little bit is helpful."

"You're right."

John continued toward home, parking in the front of his house. He waited for Nancy to start her car before he drove to the back of his house to park inside of the garage.

After entering the house, he dropped the car keys on the table and went to sit on his chair. It was well passed his usual time for bed, but all the memories stopped him in his tracks. The warmth of Vicky's kisses, especially the last one before he found her with the other man. He'd also driven the same route with Inga, stopping by the side to feel the movement in her belly when Janet moved one of the first times. But right now, Vicky was first and foremost on his mind. She must be found so he could put her to rest. Never had he allowed her memory to haunt him like this before, and it totally unsettled him. Yes, he had been in love with her as a young person, but he was still in love with his wife. There should've been closure for Vicky by now, and he knew he must be a part of the end.

He went back into the kitchen for a new garbage bag to carry into the bedroom. There, he removed his swimsuit from his drawer and placed inside of the bag. Afterward, he searched his drawers for the old shirt and found it. He placed the neatly folded shirt with the trunks. Setting it inside of his closet on top of old shoes, he left them and got ready for bed.

Chapter sixteen

Now seemed like an appropriate time to mention to Mark or Ronnie he had these two clothes items, John decided, while standing in front of the engine. With a moist sponge in hand, he began his daily duty of cleaning the smudge and dirt from the outside of the engine. He knew someday, there would come a time when he'd have to go inside and clean it. That, he figured, might be a good job for Leif since he was young and could get around better than these old bones.

"Hey down there!" Leif called. "Are you in Never-Neverland?" He started to slip but was able to stop the catastrophe of falling off the engine. "Grandpa!"

"What?" John hollered up. "I didn't hear you!"

"Hold the ladder, I'm coming down."

John placed both hands on either side of the ladder to hold it steady.

"What's up? You normally get down on your own?" John stated. "Are you just hungry?"

"I see Diane coming and I want a cookie," Leif said, stating a fact. "See?" He watched her come into view. "There she is."

"Should've guessed," John mumbled under his breath. "Only you would shirk your duties for a cookie."

"Nope! You've told me how Mom would too." Leif bounded to the ground after John stepped aside. It wasn't long before the ladder was folded and brought to the depot to be returned to its storage spot. He came out and swiped his hands on his legs. "I'll return." Leif marched right over to Diane. "It's nice to see you today."

John looked on with his hands on his hips and wondered where Leif got his charm from, then decided it must've been from his mother because Janet could charm a ten dollar bill out of his pocket in a minute, and his wife would scold him for doing it. He lunged the sponge back into the bucket, wrung it out, and continued cleaning the engine. When finished, he joined the two in front of the engine as a group of five cheerleaders stopped to ask questions. He noticed Leif was all red once again.

"Why is this old thing still here?" one of the girls wanted to know, smiling at Leif.

No wonder Leif was red, John thought. He cleared his throat and was ready to speak when Leif stood.

"It's like this," Leif said, coughing. "It's for us to look at and realize how lucky we are to have a car."

John stifled a laugh and glanced at Diane who in turn handed him a cookie and then winked.

"Do you ladies like cookies?" Diane held out her box. "What school are you from?"

"Roosevelt. Why are you in a uniform?"

"Because that's what we wore back when we passed out food to the World War II soldiers."

"Is that why you're giving away cookies?" another girl asked, reaching for one. "Chocolate chip. Just like my grandma's."

"Your grandma may have stood right beside me and passed out sandwiches to the soldiers as they went off to war. The train left right from here and that engine, my dear, may have been one that took the first war soldiers off to France and never returned."

"Yeah! So don't start thinking this engine isn't important!" Leif declared. "It's spotless because of me and my grandpa, and we plan to keep it that way."

"What's the significance of it, anyway," another girl said.

"It turned heat into energy. Now we have cars because of it."

"The engines of a car?" another said.

"Yes, I just said that," Leif replied, arms folded.

"Okay. We get it." They began to walk away.

"Thanks!" one of the girls called over her shoulder.

The three returned to their chairs to relax, and each ate a cookie.

"You did great, young man," Diane said. "I'll bake extra cookies for you next time I come." She looked across to him. "Perfect answer."

"Well, thank you." Leif smiled. "Got any left?"

"Just two. One for each and then I'll leave. I have a matter to attend to."

"Thanks!"

She passed the box down before standing.

"We'll take care of the chair, of course. If you need anything just let me know," John said, looking up to her.

"I will."

Both watched as she walked away.

"You haven't seen either of the detectives or women, have you?" John asked.

"Nope."

They sat for the better part of the day, each taking turns walking about for a short while.

"I should've brought my fishing rod."

"Maybe tomorrow. Let's go home."

They returned the chairs, picked up their stuff, and left for the walk home. When they stopped for the light to change on 42nd and 38th street, John remembered walking almost the same route with Janet piggy-back.

"Your grandma walked your mom to school. We're walking in their footsteps." John proceeded to cross when the light changed to green. Leif hung back, so John said, "Hurry-up!"

"I am! What bothers me is that she's never said anything about going to school, not really. I'll have to ask her. Are we calling soon?" Leif was beside him. "I want to speak with her and tell her what we've learned."

"Okay. I'll let you text her. She'll most likely call you since she won't know my phone number."

"Sometimes, you're absolutely hopeless." Leif's mouth dropped open and he shook his head.

"That's what you're for, to keep me in line."

They continued until they reached their respective backyards and stopped.

"I have hamburger and potatoes. Come on over and I'll fry you up something to eat."

"I've given Grandma your number since you didn't."

"Thanks. Maybe she'll call?"

"I'll text Grandma and let her know I'm going to eat at your house." Leif dug out his phone to text her. When finished, he stuffed it back into his pocket. "Let's get into your house but take your time cooking."

"You're absolutely correct."

They continued into the house and dropped their lunch items onto the counter. Each grabbed something to drink before going to sit down in the living room. John plopped into his chair while Leif spread his legs out across the couch.

"It's nice and comfy in here," Leif said, drinking from a fresh water bottle. "What's in store for tonight? Old movies?"

"I have the perfect one for the two of us to watch, and I think you can locate it on some place like this Netflix. Do I have it? I think I do. You might have made me get that device to stream on."

"You don't have it." Leif looked at him. "It's called Roku. It hosts different platforms, and that's where Netflix and these other places are. That's where you find them."

"Do you have it at your grandma's?"

"Yes. Want me to get it?"

"I suppose your grandma paid for it?" John drank a few sips of beer.

The backdoor opened and Frances entered. "I bet you two are waiting for dinner?" She carried a large chicken salad inside of a covered bowl. "I have a chicken salad with fresh buns."

"That's very kind of you." John looked at Leif and both rolled their eyes.

In the kitchen, Frances removed two plates from the shelves and set them on the counter. When they entered, she said, "It's filling. Loaded with meat and veggies."

"Thanks."

The two guys sat down and were waited on by Frances. Finally, she served herself by buttering a roll and eating at the sink.

"What is it you two were discussing? Me again, I suppose?"

"Grandpa wants me to watch some old movie," Leif said, chewing. "This is good."

"Well? What movie?" Frances looked at John.

"*Von Ryan's Express*, about a steam engine. It's got enough excitement in it to keep him attentive, and it's got that train ride. It'll be good for him to see how it helped to win the war."

"You're absolutely correct. But you have to go buy your own *Roku*, you can't take mine. I might never get it returned."

"You're joyful. At least I know how you think. I always return everything, and you know it."

"Excuse me," Leif said, taking another bite.

"Don't talk with your mouth full, young man," John said. "Manners, remember them."

"Right." He swallowed. "We're going to pick up one of them, and I'll spend the night here in case Mom should call."

Frances looked at John. "Did you call and leave your new number?"

"No. I forgot." John felt like he was in the principal's office. "She has Leif's number."

"I'm sure she does. It's a good thing I remembered to do that for you because now she does have your number." She took her last bite of the roll.

"May I eat now without being harangued by either of you for my lack of remembering?"

"Go ahead," Frances said, offering more salad. "You do have enough, don't you?"

"Yes. Thank you, Grandma." Leif dished himself more food from the bowl. "Very good."

"No, thank you," John said, refusing to be intimidated.

Frances placed the cover on the bowl. "I'm going home. You can stay with your grandpa, Leif, I won't mind."

"Thank you, Grandma." Leif kissed her cheek.

When they'd finished and John placed the dishes in the washer, they went into the living room.

"How can I get one of those things?" John asked. "Do you know how to install it?"

"Of course! I put in Grandma's."

"Let's go get one."

Leif's cell phone rang and he read Janet's name. "It's Mom."

"Great."

"Mom! I'm putting you on speaker phone since I'm with Grandpa."

"Okay. How are my guys today?"

"We're fine, Mom, but when will we see you again?"

"How about fetching me tomorrow for your birthday, honey? I'll stay overnight and we'll see how that goes."

"I'm looking forward to it, honey," John said.

"Leif, have you been able to get Grandpa into the current year?"

"Trying hard, Mom. He'll pay for my driver's ed course and is going to buy me a car." Leif smiled.

"That's super. I've been taking pictures and drawing but want to know how it turned out with the search for Vicky?"

"So far," Leif said, "nothing has happened. We don't know anything."

"That's a shame. What time will you pick me up tomorrow?"

Leif looked up to his grandpa. "Eleven o'clock. We'll stop to eat at that old place in Paynesville on our way home."

"Will that work, Dad?"

"Of course, honey! Whatever is the best for you and Leif."

"Boy, have you changed and for the better," Janet said. "You don't even lecture or get grouchy anymore."

"It's all because of this kid."

They disconnected and Leif looked at the time. "We'd better go buy it before the stores close."

"You're right." John went to grab his keys while Leif finished drinking his water. "Let's go!"

The nearest mall was on Lake Street, which was where they went. It didn't take long for Leif to find what was needed and John to hand over his credit card to pay for it. It took about the same length of time to return home. Leif opened the garage door for his grandfather to drive inside and then closed it down.

"Let's get this installed," John said.

"Right away!" Once inside, Leif set about installing the device. "It won't take long."

In a few minutes and after pressing a few right buttons, the streaming apparatus was installed.

"This is confusing."

"Not really. I'll show you," Leif said, going to sit on the couch. "It's like this." In a few minutes he reviewed the workable buttons and how to turn it on and switch to and from the television and on to Roku. "It's easy."

"Complicated. Let's put it down for now. We have a big day tomorrow." John handed the control wand back to Leif. "I'm going to bed. We have to be on the road early. Did you tell Frances?"

"Yes, I think. I'll send it again."

"The bed is right in there, but remove all the experimental items left from our lessons about steam engines."

"What will I do when Mom is here?"

"Sleep with me."

"Sure." Leif took a breath, trying to picture himself in bed with his grandpa. He got up and got busy straightening the room so it would be ready in the morning. "I need clean clothes."

"However you want to do it. The back door can stay open."

John took his bedclothes and went to shower. When he was finished, Leif was sacked out on the living room couch with a small bag on the floor by his feet presumably full of clean clothes.

The morning found them up early, and they fought over the toaster but not coffee or orange juice.

They drove straight through to Fergus Falls, stopping for gas and another donut and coffee from the gas station. After they signed in to let the staff know they'd arrived, Janet was allowed to join them.

"Honey!" John gave her a hug.

"Mom!" Leif hugged her too.

"Happy birthday, sweetheart," Janet kissed his cheek. "It's so good to see you two. I'm excited. Let's get going."

Leif retrieved his mom's small suitcase to carry it to the car, walking beside her. "I'm looking forward to this. Will we be able to have time alone?"

"We'll plan on it." She leaned in to kiss him on the cheek. "It'll be almost like old times."

"I hope so."

"Dad? You haven't said anything," Janet said at the car. John opened the door for her and she crawled into the front seat. "I think I want to sit near Leif." She crawled back out and Leif stepped aside, allowing her entrance to the back seat. "Better. Right beside my son."

"Mom! Really?" He hesitated to climb inside until she patted the area beside herself. "Okay."

"I'll be the chauffer. I won't mind sitting alone."

John took his role seriously and drove them straight over to Highway 55 toward Paynesville, stopping to eat.

"We'll order as quickly as possible. These folks have a tendency to be slow because it's all home cooked."

"I remember." Janet squeezed Leif's hand. "You'll enjoy it."

"We stopped the last time."

The three ate and returned to the car. Janet stayed behind with Leif. He smiled and held her hand.

Leif jumped out to raise the overhead garage door to let John drive in and park. They stepped into the yard, and John pulled Janet close to him.

"It's good to have you home."

"I'm thrilled to be here."

Leif led the way into the house, carrying her bag.

"I'm so happy to be here," Janet said again, swiftly walking up the stairs. "You're staying, Leif, aren't you? I want you with me. I don't want to be without you ever again."

"Mom, I'm spending the night on the couch. You can have the bed. The sheets are clean."

They continued into the house. Leif carried her suitcase into the bedroom.

"Thank you."

"We have the rest of the afternoon ahead of ourselves," John said, standing in the living room. "I have a favor to ask of you, Janet, and it's fine if Leif stays. In fact, I don't mind at all."

"What is it?"

"I need help going through my clothes. I'm trying to remember dates with Vicky and what I wore to see if I have any leftover clothes. I found my swim trunks and old baseball shirt. Will you help?"

"I would love to later. Now, Leif and I have a date. We're going to the movies."

"What?" John said.

"What movie?" Leif asked.

"Sit down you two," Janet said. "I've made a video of old pictures from years ago that I kept with me from your childhood, back when you were in diapers."

"Holy cow!" Leif sank into the couch. "I can't believe it. You have pictures of me as a kid? A baby too? Mom, this is spectacular!" Leif took a breath, his eyes filled with tears, and he wiped them dry. "Grandma, Grandpa, and my mom, all on the video." He shook his head. "You sure have surprised me."

"There are several pictures of when I dated your dad on the video."

"I want to see it right now!" Leif said. "*Now*!" Leif grabbed the video and inserted it, then started it." Holy shit! Look at me as a baby! *My Dad! My Daddy*!" Leif held his breath as he watched the image of his parents' kissing. "Who took the picture?"

"One of my friends."

"Now he's in uniform!" Leif sat with tears streaming down his cheeks as Janet pulled him into her arms.

"You're my boy and now I'm home," Janet whispered in his ear. "Time for your grandma and the cake."

"I can't wait to have you to myself."

"I know, sweetie."

"I want to watch this all night long, over and over."

"You'll be able to."

Chapter seventeen

After blowing out the candles, Leif declared he wanted the most frosting and the biggest scoop of ice cream. "First, I want to open presents."

"You're the birthday boy," Janet said. "Let's go into the living room. I have to finish fetching my gifts from my suitcase." Janet went to pick up the wrapped gifts and returned with them, then passed each out. "One for everyone."

"Sure, Mom. My birthday and I get the same presents as everyone else." Leif winked at her. "Not fair!"

"Don't worry," Janet grinned, "we're going to be together tonight."

"Okay." Leif ripped his package open and held the picture. "Wow! It's really cool! A picture of me in diapers with something hanging out of my mouth." He stared at his mom. "I don't get it."

"Slow down, sonny boy," John said. "Your mother painted that from an old photograph. She's put all of her love into it. You best apologize."

"What have I been trying to teach you?" Frances said, glaring at him. "Manners. And respect, which you're lacking in both departments."

"Mom?" Leif turned to her with mournful eyes. "I'm sorry."

"It's my fault. You expected something better, more from me," Janet said with tearstained eyes. "I'm so sorry."

"Oh, Mom. Don't think I don't love it. I'm a spoiled brat. I've been told that. Is there any wonder why Grandpa calls me 'the kid' or 'the boy' once in a while?" He gave his mother a hug.

"Much better," said Frances. "He's beginning to grow up."

"At last," John said. "He's a fine young man."

"I'm still here, you know," Janet said, pursing her lips. "I've plans for tomorrow morning."

"Time for the cake and ice cream," Leif said, ready to go to the kitchen.

"Nope! We're opening our gifts," John said, ripping away the wrapping paper. He removed his picture to hold up for display. "It's beautiful. Me and my fishing pole."

"You like it?" Janet said.

"Of course. Why wouldn't I?"

"I couldn't find a photo with you and fish." Janet grinned. "Frances?"

"I love it! It's a picture of you and my son. I never realized how much alike Leif and Gary are in looks. Thank you." She held it close to her chest. "It's beautiful."

"I'd like a picture of my dad. Just him."

"You'll get one." Janet clasped his hand and began to sing the birthday song and the grandparents joined in. Afterward, it was time for ice cream and cake.

When the cake was eaten, Frances went home with her gift. Janet and Leif turned to watch the video again after popping a bag of popcorn. John went to bed, knowing Janet and Leif could use as much time alone as possible. While Janet was still at home, he really wanted her assistance with sorting through his old clothes and with any luck, she'd help with the sorting of her mother's clothing.

In the morning, John peeked into the living room where Leif might be snoozing but found the couch empty. Softly, John walked to his daughter's room and quietly cracked open the door to peek inside. He found Leif cuddled up beside his mother, softly snoring. John silently shut the door and went to the kitchen to begin the coffee brewing.

He set out the cereal boxes. Since Leif invaded his house over the summer months, a variety of cereals were displayed, not just Cheerios. By the time the bacon started to fry, he heard rustling around in the bedroom. In a few minutes he heard the bathroom shower run and expected Janet to walk over and swipe a slice of the bacon. Continuing with the breakfast fixings, John set out bowls and spoons, knives and forks. He slid the napkin holder over for easier usage.

As the bacon finished frying, he poured himself a hot cup of coffee and stood in front of the window. He thought of the many times he'd stood in the same spot and remembered all the early mornings when first married and the birth of Janet. How much he'd loved his wife and daughter. Then the subject of miscarriages came to mind, and how after three, they quit trying. Neither of them could go through another one. It was horrible to have lost a child, but to lose three was the worst feeling in the world. They were so thankful to have Janet. If only she'd move back home and get settled, see to Leif like a proper mother. He prayed that now, it would finally happen. The bathroom door squeaked open, and there she was.

"Morning, Daddy." Janet's smile lit up her face as she walked over to him. "I'm glad to be home."

"I'm so thankful you're here, honey." He hugged her and didn't want to let her go. "Please live here for a time before you and Leif move out."

"You won't mind?" Janet stepped back to study his eyes. "I want to. I need a job, that's for sure."

"Any thoughts about what you want to do?" John refilled his cup and offered her one, but she declined.

"I'll have a glass of water." Janet helped herself. "I've had a thought about being a dental assistant. I might be able to get loans and go to the tech school."

"I'll back you up in any way possible." He removed the bacon from the pan and set it on a plate. "Help yourself."

Janet reached for a bowl and poured herself Cheerios while she chuckled. "Fruit Loops for Leif, right?" She grinned. "I've really missed him. I've messed everything up, haven't I?"

"I don't think so." John went to her and pulled her into his chest. "It's okay, really. He loves you and has looked forward to you and a proper family."

"Thanks," Janet said, wiping her eyes. "We'd best keep going because I have to be back by five, which means we don't have an awful lot of time to spare."

"Do you mind helping with the clothes? I'd like to also go through your mother's."

"We'll take care of it," Janet said, pouring her cereal. "Let's take care of your clothing first and Mom's when I return. She'll take the longest time, since well, think of all of her shoes."

"Understood. Can we get busy while Leif's still sleeping?"

"Sure. We're going to spend a good part of the day being together, and at times, away from you or Frances so we can better get to know each other."

"That's fine."

They continued eating and afterward, Janet followed him into the bedroom.

"Nothing has changed," Janet said. "It's like it's all been broken in this house." She collapsed onto the bed. "This is going to be tough." After a deep breath, she glanced around the room. "The curtains are ready to fall down. They need to at least be washed. The carpet too."

"Honey, life stopped without you around. It's been awful between you being gone and your mother's death. That cancer is awful stuff."

"I know, Daddy. It's time for me to toughen up, stop thinking of just my needs and wants. It's also time for me to show Gary what sort of a wife I could've been, and Leif deserves his mother whole. Not broken." Tears flooded her eyes. "I'm ready, Daddy."

John sat beside her, placing his arm around her shoulder. "We'll get through this together, the three of us."

Sounds of squeaking floorboards and running water drifted to them.

"Leif! You showering?" John called.

Leif squeezed his head out through a slightly opened door. "Yeah."

"Let's you and me go through my clothes." John stood and pulled out the bag he'd already thrown the two pieces of clothes into. "Where should we begin?"

"Your dresser drawers or basement?"

"Basement. It's horrible down there."

They got up and went to the stairs, John carrying the bag. Janet went first with him right behind. At the bottom, Janet turned on the light and the room was illuminated.

"Let's begin right back in here," Janet said, leading the way to the storage room. "It's still full of old decorations and Mom's coats and boots. Mine too. I can't fit into most of these coats and neither would I want to."

"I'm a hoarder. I admit it." John followed her into the space. "Let's begin with those large plastic boxes. They're stuffed." He lifted three down to the floor. "I'm almost afraid to find out what's in it."

"Me too. There might be a dead mouse." Janet reached over to pull the cover off the first. "What is that smell?" She marveled at how full the container was. "Oh my God! What on earth?" She pulled out some of her baby clothes. "Look at these! They're beautiful. My little dresses. I want all of them." Pulling them out, one by one, she held them high to inspect them. "They're still in great shape. No moth holes."

"Nope. Your mother wouldn't have allowed it to happen. She set out mothballs, that's what we're smelling." He removed the bottom few items and looked at them. "These are your little diapers from infancy. Everything is in here. I bet there are bottles somewhere down here too."

"I'll close this up and shove it aside to be scrutinized at a later time," Janet said. "When I'm here for good and Leif is with me."

"Maybe you're right," John said. He slid it to another corner. "What about the next?" He lifted the lid. "Look at that." He pulled out his letter jacket. "I always wondered where this ended up." He lifted it up to view. "I wonder if it'll fit?"

"I bet it will." She gave him a wink. "Good luck."

John pushed his left arm into the sleeve, then his right. He shifted it a little to better fit and pulled the front together. "What do you think?" He turned around. "Look good?"

"Spectacular, but what will you do with it?" Janet said, helping to remove it from his arms by pulling down on them. "Pretty tight."

"Shush now." He thought a minute, then folded it tight, and dropped it into the bag. "Let's continue. I wonder what else will be found?"

The stairs squeaked and Leif called out, "Mom! Grandpa! Where are you?"

"Down in the dungeon," Janet hollered back. "We're going through Grandpa's old clothes." She reached into the box to remove a set of hockey pads. "These are odd to have in here and probably adds to the odor. Pew!" Janet plugged her nose, picking up each one between her fingers and dropping them to the floor. "I hope you're not going to turn these horrible stinking things over to the police?"

"Nope. We'll either throw them or give them to an antique store."

Janet waved Leif inward. He stood in the doorway."

"I didn't know this room existed. It's full of all sorts of antiques. The school theater department could use some of these crazy things." Leif reached into the box and removed a set of old skates. "I can't believe you skated in these old things."

"Set them in that pile over there with the pads. I fear we'll be going to the junk store soon," John said, shrugging. "Let's keep going. There must be my old running shoes from football." His thoughts went to the last day of football of his senior year when Vicky had walked over to him. She'd reached down to prevent him from turning away and touched his shoes. "They go in the bag."

Leif glanced down and saw a brightly, albeit faded, set of gold and maroon pom-poms and brought them to the light. "Look at these! Wow!"

"Whose were they?" Janet inquired, studying John. "Mother's?"

"No. They were Vicky's. She'd given them to me." John took them to place into the bag. "I think I have enough items to turn over."

"Why did you save these, Dad? Tell me why?" Janet crossed her arms. "They should've been thrown immediately."

"Yeah, Grandpa." Leif did as Janet had and moved closer to her.

"The tide of time has uncovered many things, such as relationships." John looked from one to the other before tying a knot in the bag. "I'm going to take this upstairs. I'm sure the rest of what's down here is either from your mother or was Leif's when he was little."

"Man, I gotta see this," Leif said.

John left them behind as he climbed up the stairs and right outside to deposit the bag inside the trunk of the car. When he'd closed the trunk lid, he considered walking over to see Frances but thought the better of it, certain she'd lecture him about not doing something right. He wandered around the yard before going back inside.

After refreshing his coffee cup, John took it outside to sit in the sun to reflect on the items to bring to the authorities. He knew a phone call was in order since neither Mark nor Ronnie had appeared the last few days at the park. Fortunately, he and Nancy were able to spend together talking and laughing over there younger years. Yes, he did miss Vicky, but would he have married her knowing what he knew? That he couldn't answer truthfully. It was something he'd never know. Why had he kept the pom-poms? John rubbed his chin to ponder the question and the only answer that satisfied was that he had loved her and never wanted to forget about her. John took a final sip of his coffee and threw out the rest as Janet and Leif arrived.

"Grandpa, Mom is going to take a photo of me," Leif said, grinning. "I can't wait. She wants me to stand in front of the falls for the backdrop."

"I'd like to draw a picture of my son while I wait for my release papers to come through."

"That's a wonderful idea. Someday, you might draw from a picture with us as a family?"

"Hey, that would be super but we must have Grandma in it."

"Do you mind if we go it alone?" Janet said.

"Not at all," John said. "Do I need to shut lights off downstairs?"

"Probably better check," Leif said.

"We'll leave before two o'clock."

As John watched them walk away, he knew there was one small box for him to see to but wanted it kept a secret. His thoughts wound between Leif and Gary. It was as if the two were the same—father and son. "She'll return and stay," he said to himself.

Inside, John immediately went downstairs to finish what had been started. Knowing there most certainly were more of his old clothes hidden away, he began to sort through one more box that sat under the coats.

He lifted it out to open, setting it on the narrow counter. Inside was his winter paraphernalia from school days—neck scarves whenever hockey practices were held outside. Old winter gloves he placed on the counter and then he came across the gloves he'd thought lost forever. The pair of white gloves Vicky had worn during their confirmation ceremony. She'd given them to him to get rid of because they were uncomfortable and too warm. Her excuse to her mother was that they were lost. John boxed everything back into the box, keeping the gloves separate, and marched up the stairs to the car. The box he set into the trunk and opened the bag, settling the gloves inside it before tying it up once again. Knowing later he'd turn it all over, he went back inside.

John drove his car to the filling station to have it ready to drive Janet back to Fergus Falls. On his return home, he went by the Riverview Theater and the featured show was none other than the old movie, *Murder on the Orient Express*, another great train movie to take Leif to watch. He made a mental note of it as he drove to the garage to park outside.

When he and Leif dropped Janet off at the hospital, she informed him he was to clean up the basement and make it livable for Leif. Once home, he went for a beer to sit and contemplate this in his chair.

His phone buzzed a call.

Chapter eighteen

"This phone is such a nifty thing," John muttered aloud. "Hello, Leif! What can I do for you?" He took a sip from his beer. "I'm relaxing."

"Good! Then I can come over with a bunch of my stuff."

"I bet you're already out the door. I hear someone on the back steps." John sighed and thought he'd never get any more peace until he died. "Come in. You know what to do." He disconnected and set the phone aside.

Leif opened the door and walked inside, dropping his large garbage bag of clothes onto the floor. He entered the living room. "I knew I'd find you here. I'm going to move in right away."

"That's okay, John said. "Sit. We need to discuss rules around here."

"Uh-oh." Leif sat upon the couch. "Here comes the bomb."

"Nope. Nothin' like that." John sat up straighter. "It's easy. Curfew is ten on weekends and nine on school nights. No drugs or alcohol or girlfriends. You're too young for that business. Can you live with it?"

"Sure. I know my limits, Grandpa. You'll throw me to the dungeon or back to Grandma if I mess up." Leif stood. "Now can I get busy in the basement to set up my room like I want?"

"Sure. No naked women posters."

"Okay." He grinned and walked away.

Leaning back, John knew he had to become the household chef but didn't know what to do about it. What to serve? It'd been a number of hours since eating, and he was tired from the day and drive and wished he hadn't had to leave his daughter behind once again. His consolation was that today was the last time, she'd soon be home for good.

His thoughts went to odd or different projects she may be interested in, like a neighborhood event or interviewing women who served in the troops as they went to war. It was a possibility, something for him to consider before talking to her about it. The noise downstairs alerted him, and John knew Leif needed time alone.

He gave Nancy a jingle.

"Hey, Nancy."

"Hey to you! We're meeting up with Mark and Ronnie at The Howe. Come join us."

"You mean Judy?"

"Yes."

"Good. I have some of my stuff for the authorities to go through, maybe find some evidence of wrong doing. Who knows."

"Bring it along. See you there."

John finished his beer before going to the kitchen. After plopping the can into the garbage, he went over to the basement stairs to call down to Leif.

"I'm going out. Meeting friends." John descended two steps with the sole purpose of listening to Leif's response, but the music was too loud. He climbed farther downward. "Leif! Did you hear me?" He walked right up to Leif and tapped him on the shoulder. "Shut that thing off so I can talk to you!" John hollered.

"What?" Leif shouted, then shut down the speakers. "Man, I didn't know this old radio of yours had so much zing to it. Cool."

"I'm going to lose my mind." John shook his head and began to chuckle. "I'm sounding like my parents. Sorry, but I'm going to meet friends for supper. You'll have to feed yourself or go to Grandma's."

"Okay, Grandpa. I'm on my own for supper. Got it! Bye." Leif turned the speaker controls on to loud and went back to his business.

John covered his ears as he climbed the stairs. With his keys in his pocket, he shut the door behind him as he walked out.

Located on the corner of 36th Street and Minnehaha, The Howe had been a local haunt for over one hundred years. Marge and Ole's was the former name of the business in the time of his parents. He knew the place like the back of his hand. It was the establishment where he'd sit and drink soda and eat popcorn or play pool while his parents had conversations with friends. The corner was busy and he figured it always would be. It was the area of Minneapolis where the first Scandinavian immigrants migrated because of the many lakes.

It took John approximately five minutes of drive time and longer to locate a parking space. At last, he parked down the block, shut the engine off, and stepped out from the inside, locked the door by pressing on the button, then shut the door. He wondered about taking in the clothes but decided to wait for someone to take it later.

Once inside the large room, John realized it appeared almost the same as when he was a kid, even though it'd been many years since he'd been inside. Of course the booths lined the outer circle of the bar, but the bar was new, or was it? He couldn't tell. The inside was brighter than remembered but no one smoked anymore, which explained the brighter atmosphere. Glancing around, he saw Nancy wave so he walked over to them and chose to sit beside her rather than Mark.

"It's been years since I've been in here," John said, sitting. Nancy and Judy slid closer to the wall. "It's quite nice."

The waitress came by and four ordered a beer, Judy a soda before they took menus.

"When were you here last?" Ronnie said, chewing on a toothpick. "I think everyone's parents came in here at one time or another. Mine did."

"Me too," Mark said. "It was called something else, wasn't it?"

"Marge and Ole's." John leaned back for the waitress to set the tray down with the beverages.

"That's right."

"Ready to order?" the waitress asked, holding a pad and pencil.

"Not yet." They all agreed when Mark answered, "Come back in ten."

"Got it."

"What's the news so far?" John said with the menu in front of him. "Any news?"

"Hold on," Mark said. "You're getting anxious like the rest of us."

"Of course! I want to find her." John decided upon a burger and fries, rather than try to eat anything different. His stomach didn't feel right after the long drive during the day. "I have a bag of clothes I'm sure she's either worn or touched. It might help."

"Anything will," Judy said, drinking her soda. "

"I've got good news too," John said. "Janet will be moving back soon."

"Great!" Mark said, noticing the waitress returning. "Here she comes." He stacked up the menus as each told their orders. "Here."

"Thanks!" She walked away.

"Tell me what you have so far about Vicky," John said. "I've never really searched for her, but now I want to be all-in. I think, like most of us, I thought she'd return." John sat back and enjoyed the time with his old friends. "Diane reminds me of her whenever she brings us cookies." He grinned. "Leif loves them."

"I bet he does," Judy said, sipping from her soda. "Have the flyers generated any new leads?"

"It's hard to say. A few phone calls," Ronnie said, resting his elbows on the table and chin within his hands. He pushed his glasses farther on his nose. "No one had anything different to say, mostly that she was remembered."

"Which is what we were afraid would happen," Mark said. "Diane wants to find her daughter."

"That's what she's told me," John said. "I brought her a few groceries the other day, and she was so happy for it. Even though her son isn't too far away, she's still very lonesome."

"She's hanging on until Vicky is found, I bet," Nancy said. "We'll have to keep digging."

"I agree," John said, nudging Nancy under the table with his knee. "We'll keep going."

"For sure," Nancy said, trying to ignore him.

The waitress carried over the food and placed it in front of each of them.

"Correct?" When all nodded, she said, "Anything else? Beer? Water?"

"Water," John said.

"I'll bring a glass for all."

She left for the water and returned as they began to eat their burgers and fries.

"Tell you what," John said, between bites, "I have a pair of her old gloves."

"You're kidding me!" Nancy said. Her mouth dropped open and she had to wipe her face. "That's absolutely incredible!"

"How in God's name did you ever come by them?" Judy said, leaning forward to look at him. "Did you yank them off her when you—"

"Shush now, we were kids," John said, enjoying the ribbing. "It's a secret, anyway."

"I know. I could swear I saw you wear girls' gloves to church once," Mark said, elbowing Ronnie. "You did too, didn't you?"

"Yes. It was the Sunday after confirmation, right?" Ronnie said between bites of his burger. "Or was it Easter?"

"John? Did you wear them twice?" Mark said with a twinkle in his eye.

"This is great. My friends think I'm a lunatic," John said, pushing his plate aside. "I'm stuffed. Do you want to hear what else is in the bag?"

"You're not going to explain yourself?" Nancy said, grinning as she stared at him.

"You guys are something else," John said, drinking down the water from his glass. "I have my old letter jacket, which she wore many times. No one else would've put it on except maybe my parents."

"You've got a few great pieces I know the team will appreciate." Mark finished his last French fry. "What else?" He pushed his plate aside.

"An old Twins shirt, she may have worn. Don't say anything, you four hoodlums, you know it was all innocent in those days." John shook his head. "Has anything at all developed from the woman in the wheelchair. I know she is a dead end, but how about the man caregiver?"

"We're not looking into him because there isn't any reason since the woman wasn't Vicky," Mark said. "What else do you have?"

"A bunch of other miscellaneous items she may have worn. She did give me back our going steady ring I forgot to bring along." John reached for his wallet at the same time everyone else did. "I now have Leif moving into the house and I can tell you one thing, I'll never be the same. The noise from the basement."

"Get used to it," Nancy said, laughing.

"Do you want to take the clothes now, or what should I do with them?" John wondered. "They're in my trunk. That's another thing you people will laugh at, my swim trunks are in it also."

"Your swim trunks! When would she have put them on?" Judy said, "Or is it take them off?"

"See? I knew it. I thought maybe because she stood beside me," John replied, sheepishly. "Come on now! Don't tell me you four dum-dums were pristine."

"Ahh no, this is about you," Mark said, "you've opened yourself wide open!"

"No end to it," Ronnie said. "We all knew what you were up to before you two split."

"Let's change the subject," Nancy said. "He might turn his attention to other matters such as the size."

"I'll go home and look for the ring, you four morons, and bring the goods to the station in the morning," John said, handing the waitress his money. "Keep the change."

The other four friends did the same, then they walked out to their respective cars. Nancy was the nearest to him, and he said, "Want to walk around Howe School since we're here? We can go and come back, talk about anything that comes to mind. Something might strike a chord."

"Let's, but wait until they've all left." Nancy walked to the sidewalk and John followed.

"Would you want to see what I have?" John asked, standing beside her. "I wasn't making an advancement, I wanted you to know it's important for us to keep searching. It's pulling further away from the past and reconciling my future."

"I know exactly what you're saying," Nancy said, glancing around to look for a recognizable car. "They've left." She began to walk toward the school, which was three blocks down from where they stood. John was by her side. "This is a great idea."

Casually they walked the three blocks until arriving at the corner of their old grade school.

"Front first?" John said.

"Sure, why not?" Nancy said. "I remember entering this school so many years ago. I don't remember much, but know I had nice teachers."

"Me too. Most elementary teachers are nice. I think they have to be," John said, "or the kids would cry to their mothers, and then they wouldn't go to school."

"They have to have patience galore."

They continued to walk to the front of the school and then down the side of the back playground area.

"I really don't remember anything from the playground, do you?" Nancy asked.

"Nope. Maybe we should've gone to Sanford Middle, our old junior high, or Roosevelt?"

"We'll do one at a time, walk the perimeter and try to think of places she may have gone to," Nancy said. "Mike never went to our grade school, instead, he went to Hiawatha.

"Do you still think of him an awful lot?" When Nancy nodded, he said, "I can see that in you. It's almost like me and Inga."

"I don't think it's Inga that you miss the most," Nancy said as they turned the corner to cross the rear of the playground.

"What is it then? Janet? I have Leif invading my house and playing loud noises. I'll never have a decent nights' sleep until after he grows up."

"Don't be so grouchy."

They continued walking back to their cars.

"You never answered my question, Nancy. What do you mean, not Inga?"

She stopped and turned to face him before climbing inside of her car. "You've missed Vicky all of these years. You loved Inga, I'm not saying that you didn't. Certainly, you love Janet and Leif, but Vicky's always been on your mind."

"How can you say that? It's not right," John said, opening her car door for her.

"You believe what you want," Nancy said as she climbed inside but held the door open to talk. "We'll talk another time, but think about what I said."

"Right." John got into his car and started the engine, letting her breeze past before driving from the curb. "What is she talking about?"

Instead of going straight home, he went to the Minnehaha Falls parking lot and parked. He paid the amount required before walking to the falls. Standing alone, he paid little or no attention to the onlookers. Memories of walking along the pathways as a kid came to mind, but her voice was so loud in his head he turned to see if she wasn't standing behind him. "Inga?" John moved closer to the cascade of waterfall and felt the sprinkle of the sparkling water gushing to the floor bed of the rushing water below. Away from spectators, the voice spoke in his ear. "Vicky?"

With the rising moon, John drove home.

Chapter nineteen

As soon as John entered the house, he knew something was different because there wasn't any noise and the kitchen was a big mess. A moist towel was in a heap on top of the counter and when John glanced down to the floor, he noticed a pile of paper towels. "The kid spilled something and didn't want to be around to hear my lecture!" John wasn't quite sure how to handle the situation. It'd been a long day for both of them, so he picked up the paper towels that revealed a pile of cooked, mushy spaghetti noodles. After scooping them up with a few more handfuls of toweling, John took the wet mop to clean the flooring.

A text message popped onto his phone screen and John took the time to read it: See the basement.

Pleasantly surprised at the basement room because it was filled with a single made bed, and the area was neat and clean. The kid was learning and he was still young, and he loved having him around.

John texted Leif. "There must be a sign outside on the door which reads, Leif's room. Grandpa." He sent the message.

The old "going steady" ring came to mind that should be found, and John got busy in his bedroom. Never in his wildest dreams could he imagine holding on to it for all these years. It had been well over fifty years since they'd split up, and he'd been married to his wife for fifty years. Where on earth was it? Or simply, had he thrown it away? John looked for the old brown pine box given to him as a youngster by his mom to hold all his secrets such as a special stone or Indian head from when the family camped by the shores of Lake of the Woods. He located the box behind a larger one full of collectable dolls that had once been Janet's. The doll box was carried into her bedroom and placed upon the bed, but the pine box he carried to the living room to dig through.

Sitting on his chair, he first checked for messages, but there wasn't a return from Leif to read. Frowning, he opened the box and peered inside. Slowly he removed each item, placing them aside. There were plenty of those Indian heads and old fish hooks, a couple of stones and rabbit's foot for good luck, jacks to play with marbles. All brought a refreshing smile to his lips and a twinkle in his eyes, but in the bottom corner was something that glittered. It was his half of the heart necklace that went with the one he'd given to Vicky. He was to wear his half but had set it aside during football practice, never to be picked up again. John went for a plastic bag to drop the necklace into. Afterward, he dropped it into his chest pocket and began to place everything else back inside of the box. As he stood, John glanced toward the doorway and there stood Leif.

"How long have you been standing there? I never heard you come in." John still held the box in his hand. "I suppose you'd like to see what's here?"

"Of course!" Leif reached for the box. "What else have you found?"

"A box of dolls that belonged to your mother. They're on her bed." John followed Leif into the living room. "It's my half of the necklace. I suppose I just didn't know what to do with it and left it in this box."

"Could be." Leif sat on the couch. "I can't believe you're not hollering at me." Leif opened the box and looked into it. "Pretty cool stuff."

"I thought so, many long years ago." John made himself comfortable on the chair. "It is getting late, you know? We should be going to bed."

"We aren't punching a time clock," Leif said, removing the items and placing them on the table. "What are you going to do with all of this garbage?"

"Aren't you going to ask about the rabbit's foot?"

"Nope. Did you kill it?" Leif narrowed his eyes when he looked at John. "You didn't, did you?"

"Of course not! I bought it for good luck."

"Arrowheads and a few stones." He rolled them around between his fingers. "That's all there is." He picked them up and dropped them inside. When the cover was closed, he pushed the box aside. "You're right. Time for bed and Grandma fed me. She said you should apologize for not taking me with you. So apologize."

"Good grief!" John scratched his chin. "I'm showering and you can come with me to the police station in the morning before we go to the park, but I'm not parking over there. I'll park at home and walk over, drop you off there if you want."

"Okay, it's a deal. I'm part of this investigation too, you know?" Leif stood. "Remember that." He waited a moment then continued. "Grandma told me to say that."

"She did, did she? Why am I not surprised?" John headed for the bathroom. "I'm first since I'm the ancient one."

"Got it." Leif left for the basement. "No loud music! There, I said it for you." He continued downward.

As John fell asleep, he wondered if he'd live through having another teenager in the house as well as his daughter. He saw his wife smiling down on him through his dreams, then he knew he'd manage.

Morning came with the shower running and music blaring. Yawning, John grunted his way into the kitchen to make the pot of coffee. Quickly he dressed and returned to the coffee maker brewing the pot, and as he reached for his cup, the pot finished its last drop. He poured his cup full and drank his first swallow before making himself toast. When Leif walked from the bathroom, he hollered, "Do you want an egg?"

"Sure. I like the yolk cracked and cooked. I don't like that slimy stuff." Leif started down the staircase, then stopped. "Two!" he shouted.

"Two! Coming right up!"

He dished up the eggs as Leif entered the kitchen. "It's getting late. Let's eat right up."

"Got it." Leif dug into his meal and finished as John did. "I'm ready."

"Let's rinse the plates because eggs stick. You do that, and I'll make the sandwiches unless you want to?"

"Go ahead, I'm through with food for now." Leif began to clean the dishes.

John made the sandwiches. While wrapping them up, he realized the necklace wasn't inside of his pocket.

"I'll be right out." John handed the sandwich bags to Leif. "Go open the door."

Leif did as told and John appeared in the garage soon after with the necklace in his breast pocket. After John started the engine and backed the car from the garage, Leif closed the overhead door and climbed into the car. Seatbelts were buckled and John drove to the police station. He parked nearby. "Don't forget to push the button down to lock the door and make sure the back door window is up. It's something that always needs seeing to when you ride in an old car."

"Got it, Grandpa." Leif followed the instructions.

John removed the bag of goods from the trunk and handed it to Leif. "You carry it, you're stronger than me."

"Younger too," Leif said, grinning.

Ronnie saw them enter from a makeshift desk by a window where he sat with Mark and came out to greet them.

"You've got your grandson with you this time, so we don't rib you about the—"

"Never you mind now. Be nice," John said. "I also have a necklace that matches one Vicky wore." He dug the small bag from his pocket and turned it over. "Take all of this and let us know if anything comes of it."

"Sure will, but we received a tip last night," Ronnie said. "Why don't you two follow me around the corner to where Mark is." He motioned for them to follow. "It's this way. Not far." He led them in. "Mark. Tell them."

"Someone left a tip and we're going to follow up on it. There was a little boy born in a certain hospital nine months after the crime."

"I don't see how this birth can be connected, but every lead must be followed," John said.

"Every tip is being looked into," Ronnie said.

"I have a good feeling about this," Mark said.

"All gathered DNA will help us to identify this man, if the data lines up correctly," Ronnie said, sitting on the edge of the desk. "We have Vicky's but let's see how it all comes together."

"What about the clothes?"

"We'll take them from here," Ronnie said, placing the bag on top of his chair. "We'll be in touch."

"Okay. It's time for us to go to the park, anyway." John advanced toward the door and looked over his shoulder at Leif. "Coming?"

"Wait. Hold on," Leif said. "What does it take to become a detective?"

"Brains and good listening ears," Mark said.

"Yeah, and no loud music so you go deaf too early!" John said, walking out the door.

Leif hurried to catch up to John.

The street was too busy for John to pull over to let Leif jump from the car so he drove into the lot.

"I know, you don't have to tell me," Leif said, closing the car door. "I'll have it all shined up by the time you get here."

John drove home and soon parked in the confines of his garage. Since Leif hadn't taken the lunch bags from the car seat, John lifted them out to carry to the park. He'd also forgotten about the thermos of coffee. While a fresh pot was brewing, John took matters in his own hands to make sure the house was straightened because his gut told him there would be visitors soon coming to the door. He gave thought to his four friends he'd been with last night, the four people most likely to stop in unannounced. The pot finished it's loud gush of coffee, so he filled his thermos and took what was needed before leaving.

When John made it to the park, it impressed him to see Leif standing with his arm outstretched and shaking hands with a spectator. As he got closer to the scene, he realized who Leif spoke to. It was the industrial tech teacher who'd attended with the students a few days before. John hurried toward them.

"Good morning," John said. "It's good to see you again, but what brings you here?"

"You mean besides talking with this bright, young man?" Mr. Olson said. "We're always trying to figure out lesson plans, you see? That's what industrial tech teachers do to draw students into the field, and the steam engine seems to resonate with the higher grades."

"What do you propose?" John asked. "Let's go around the engine so we can talk without interruptions. Leif here, he can take over for me. I think he's smarter and certainly better looking."

"That's for sure," Leif said, smiling. He looked over toward an approaching couple.

"This way." John began to walk around the engine while the teacher followed beside him. "I need to set down our lunches and my thermos. Ever been inside of the depot?"

"Nope. Never have."

"Let's go inside." John unlocked the door and they entered the inside of the building. "Pretty small as far as depots go."

"Oh yeah, but just as grand," he said. "Call me Bill. By the way, I also grew up in the area. School and the whole nine yards but went to South instead of Roosevelt."

"Same neighborhoods, almost, and skated in the same parks," John said. "It's good to meet a fellow from the old neighborhood. What can I do for you?"

"Isn't there lighting in here?" Olson walked the interior. "It's so dark."

"That, I'm not sure about. It's been closed up for a number of years now. I know they had lighting, there must've been. Why? You got something in mind?"

"It's sort of turning around in this head of mine. I'd like to showcase the moveable parts of the steam and how it's compacted in order to turn it into energy."

"We've already got a contest going between the schools. What are you sayin'?"

"It might be interesting to open the depot up for an event type thing for the public to come," Bill said. "Are you open to something like this?"

"I would love to see that sort of thing happen, but it's not up to me. The park board must approve anything of that nature. They only approved of me because I'm an old fart, and my dad was an engineer for the Milwaukee Road. I'm not supposed to be allowed inside of this building, either. I sneak inside. Leif and I are the only two I know who do this and keep chairs for sitting." He glanced over to the chairs.

"I'll go to see the person in charge of the park board and propose this idea." Mr. Olson finished walking the perimeter. "I'll let you know what comes of it. I'll contact Tiffany too. Got a number where I can reach you?"

"Sure." John removed his phone from his pocket and opened it up. "Right, here's the number. I never remember it." When Bill finished adding John's name and number into his phone contact list, John closed the app and placed it into his pocket.

Outside, Bill carried a chair and John the other over to where Leif stood. As Olson left, he said, "We'll be in touch."

"I'll be waiting."

Both watched him walk away until out of sight. John removed his railroad watch to check on the time, and Leif glanced at his phone.

"I have eleven thirteen," Leif said. "See if you can beat that."

"Eleven thirteen and forty-five seconds. There! Now it's eleven fourteen!" John gave him a sideways look. "Do phones tell seconds?"

"Sort of," Leif said, a little frustrated. "I thought the phone would be the best."

"You mean most accurate?"

"Of course."

"Let me tell you something. If not for the railroad, there wouldn't be regulated time. The arrival and departure of the locomotive brought changes, not only for the ability to move from place to place faster than a horse and buggy, but it brought schedules. Trains ran on seconds for arrival and departure, not approximate time schedules. The whole world changed because of them, and this baby right here, helped to make the change."

"I believe you." Leif's stomach began to grumble. "I'm hungry."

"Don't forget my thermos," John said to him as he walked away.

As John waited the few minutes for Leif to return, a spectator approached. John stood to shake his hands.

"Yes sir, how can I help you?"

"How did the steam become energy?"

"The pressure of the valves harnessed the heat, causing the combustion to produce the energy."

"How does the gasoline engine get its energy?"

"There is water in the radiator. It works like the heat from coal or wood burners, it heats and makes the pistons work."

"Plus the rest of the engine works like a sparkplug."

"Correct. Without the knowledge, we wouldn't have our car or modern technology."

"Thank you." The man nodded to John and walked away.

Leif set the sandwich bags on the ground but offered the thermos to John. "Couldn't have said it better myself." Leif opened his meal and began to eat. "I don't have anything to drink."

"Did you get the engine cleaned? It looks good," John said, reaching into his pocket. He pulled out a dollar to hand over to Leif. "Did you?"

"You didn't come right away so I did get the top cleaned. I don't suppose you noticed the water bucket? It's by the rear wheel."

"Oh. I'll snap to it after we're through. Anyone come around earlier besides the teacher?"

"Nope." Leif gulped down his sandwich. "I'll be right back." He left John alone.

While John poured a cup of coffee, his phone dinged a message. He finished pouring before reading the message from Nancy.

"*Another clue. Mark and Ronnie are going to extract DNA from a woman in a nearby nursing home.*"

"*What about the birth of that baby*"

"*Someone will check into the county birth records for the indicated time frame.*"

"*Thanks for letting me know. We're finally getting somewhere in our search.*"

"*Yes, we're pulling it together.*"

John set the phone into his pocket, instinctually knowing Vicky would be soon found.

"Get yourself something to drink." He popped out a handful of change from his pocket to turn over to Leif. "That should get you a can."

"Right. Ever heard of a bankcard?" Leif said, folding the cash into his fist. "It works nicely, then your pockets won't get holy. You know what I mean?"

"You and your new fandangle stuff. Leave me to drink my coffee for a few minutes in peace, will ya?" He sat back, sipping on the coffee as Leif sauntered away. John wished to be young again while wistfully gazing out onto the flowers and beautiful wilderness of trees and scampering squirrels, gophers, and chipmunks. When Inga and Janet came to mind, his memory wove to when they rode the bus and trains to all different places and resolved to take Leif for a trip, like to Milwaukee or Chicago like his dad had or him. Leif came back with his beverage and sat beside him.

"Where do you think Vicky is?"

"No clue. None at all. My hope is she had a proper burial if she died and not that her bones were thrown in the ditch and never found."

"Except by animals." Leif popped open his can of soda and drank from it. "It's like a horror movie."

"Let's hope this guy is dead because I might kill him myself," John said. He looked over Leif's shoulder and saw Diane struggling to walk toward them. "Good grief. Go help her!"

The two set down their beverages and hurried toward her.

"What happened to you?" John asked, taking her basket and handing it over to Leif. "Diane, did you fall down?"

"Why are you on crutches?" Leif said. "Did you break something?"

They helped her by tucking her arms around their own while John held the single crutch over his shoulder until at last able to set her down in his chair.

"My goodness, little lady!" John declared, standing over her. He placed the crutch beside her on the ground, and Leif waited for her to be settled before handing the basket to her.

"Take a cookie, young man," Diane said, looking up to him. "That was very kind of you to help. Both of you, very helpful." She opened the basket to offer the delicious chocolate chip cookies. "Fresh from the oven."

"Thanks," John said, "but, you didn't have to."

"Well Grandma, it was mighty nice of you, if I do say so myself!"

"You're a sweetheart," Diane told him.

"Ahh, here comes a few young ladies," Leif said, standing up. "What can I do for you?"

"You're kinda young," the eldest replied, "but can this little grandma tell us why she's all dressed up in a skirt that resembles my old Girl Scout uniform?"

"Have a cookie, girls," Diane said, offering the basket. "I passed food out to the soldiers when they went to war, and so had my mother when my dad fought in the Great War."

"World War I, right?" another young woman said. "They're chocolate chips."

The three reached for one and cooed from the taste.

"Absolutely delish!"

"Thanks."

"Yummy!"

The three young ladies strolled farther down the pathway.

"Very sweet girls," Diane said, her eyes glistening. "I remember being that age and standing out here, which reminds me, John?"

"Do you want a ride somewhere?" John said. He'd moved to the third chair when the girls were asking the question. He slid his chair over to see Diane easier. "My appointment book is pretty open." He grinned.

"There is a meeting at the History Center in St. Paul about the women who passed out the sandwiches and beverages, support, and love to the troops. There also is talk of having some sort of celebration in their honor. I would like to be part of it, but I can't possibly take the bus, and a taxi is too expensive!"

"I'll drive you. Leif is on top of everything. I'm considering giving him a salary anyway—"

"Really?" Leif's eyes opened wider. "I don't believe it!"

"Quiet now! Let your grandpa speak!" Diane said, winking at John.

"Oh, sure!" Leif pretended to zip his lip.

"When is this meeting?" John asked. He cupped his ear since the traffic became louder.

"Tomorrow morning at ten. We'll have to leave early because of parking and so on."

As the two were discussing the plan for the following day, a spectator approached and John gave Leif a nod to take care of the person.

"I'll pick you up at 8:30, Diane. If we're early, that's okay. It'll give us time to find a good seat and use the restroom if needed before it begins."

"Thank you. I can't walk very fast since the accident." She lifted the crutch, then set it back down. "I snagged my slipper on the corner of the bed frame and hurt my foot. I might've sprained it."

"Did you call the doctor?" John leaned closer to her.

"Yes. I can stand on my foot but it hurts so much, and he said to stay off it."

"Being here isn't staying off it."

"I'm fine."

Leif continued to speak to the spectator. "Oh, sure he's ready now. Grandpa?"

"What can I do for you, sir?"

"Do you mind if I go inside of the depot? I'm being allowed to have my best students build a new ticket counter and set in new seats. Measurements are needed. I'm the wood working teacher from Roosevelt."

"Come on, Anderson, let's get you started." John turned away. "Follow me." Upon reaching the main door, he opened it wide for the two to view inside. "Shall we?"

"Let's," Mr. Anderson said.

"I'm John." John led the way inside. "I believe the counter was set in this corner. There also was space over here," John stood at the spot, "where the telegraph was."

"Oh! Sure there would've been. Even if there was a phone, few people had one. Second thought, I'm sure there was one. Where would it have been?" Anderson scratched his head, his strawberry blond hair was brighter from the light through the small window where he stood.

"Right over here!" John tapped his foot near where a capped outlet was. "All the electronic business had to have happened right here."

"I believe you're right," Anderson said, hands on his hips. "Now I know what needs to be gotten done." He looked to John. "I'll be bringing the students around the first of next week. Will you be here?"

"My grandson and I are almost always here. You'll be able to get in, if that's the question, and he'll be told to stay out of your way." John headed for the doorway. "Where will you get the seats from?"

"We'll set up old wooden chairs."

"Sounds right."

When they exited, Anderson shook his hand and said, "I'll give you a call to let you know the date and time."

"Sounds great. I'm happy to hear of it happening. The depot seemed lonesome, in a way. It doesn't make sense, really." John looked at him.

"I know what you're saying." Anderson walked away.

When John returned to his former place, he tasted what was in his cup and threw it out. "Yuck. Too cold." He looked toward the woods and the road ahead. "It'll be wonderful when it's finished."

"Really? It'll be so much fun to see the depot back to where it once was though without the tracks? Do you think they'll re-lay them?" Diane said, puzzled. "It seems that should happen."

"It would be fun, wouldn't it?" John said. He glanced around and didn't see Leif. "Where on earth did he go to?"

"Leif? He's a fine boy, growing up tall and thin just like his dad," Diane said. "I remember seeing Janet whenever she'd come around to the store when I worked."

"Well, I suppose we could call it a day, but I'll take you home."

"No. You don't need to. I can go the short distance on the bus. Only in and out once, so it's not bad," Diane said.

"Not on your life," John said, "but wherever is he?"

"He'll be back. Get your car and he'll be here waiting." Diane nodded. "Just wait and see, and he'll have good news to tell."

"When Leif returns, have him walk you to the parking lot but first lock everything up."

"I'll relay the message."

"Okay! Be right back."

Swiftly John walked toward home, only having to wait for the stop light to turn green. As soon as he arrived, he retrieved his car keys. After opening the overhead door and closing it once back outside, he drove toward the park. In the lot, he parked in a slot in the front row. When he shut the car engine off and stepped from the car, he looked over to the engine and noticed both Leif and Diane approaching. He waved and Leif acknowledged with the same sign.

Leif crawled into the backseat while Diane was safely seated in the front. When everyone was ready, John backed out of the spot to drive to Diane's house.

"Do you have news to tell?" John said, looking in the rearview mirror. "Leif, you look like you're ready to burst. What has someone told you?"

"That the detectives and your lady friends are stopping by tonight for a few minutes."

"That's all? No other news? Nothing about Vicky?"

"All I know is you won't need to cook me a meal tonight because they're bringing over pizzas."

John looked over to Diane. "Do you know what this is about?"

"I'm not sure. I know someone may have come forward who may have known my daughter. But I don't want to talk about it. I get my hopes up high only to have them dashed."

"I'm sorry," John said. "We've almost got you home. Leif?"

"Huh?" He leaned over the front seat. "Want me to walk her to the door?"

"Of course!"

John signaled to turn into the parking lane and stopped in front of the house. "I'll pick you up at 8:30 sharp."

"I'll be ready." Diane opened the car door. "Thank you, John, you're very thoughtful."

"Take my arm now, Grandma," Leif said, grinning. "I'll hold on to the crutch."

John watched as they walked/limped to the doorstep and Leif helped her inside of the house before returning to the car.

"Typical grandma's house, full of all sorts of old things," Leif said, climbing into the front beside John. "Home?"

"Were you able to lock up the chairs and the depot?"

"Certainly."

"Then it's home, and you're going to tell me what you learned."

John turned onto another street to avoid the stop lights and entered his back driveway, stopping to wait for Leif to open the overhead door. Soon he drove inside and parked. Together they walked to the house.

As they began the ritual of taking a beverage from the refrigerator, John's phone dinged a message. After reading it, he said, "They're coming by with two large pepperoni pizzas and a six pack of beer."

"I knew it. I overhead what they were talking about. That's why it took so long for me to return to the engine. Truth will set you free, that's what I've been told." Leif drank from his soda. "I bet you don't know who first said that, do you?"

"Well Mr. Know-it-all, who?" John grinned.

"Einstein."

"You can do better than that," John said, chuckling. "It was Jesus."

"I quoted the Bible?"

"Yes, you did."

"Oh, wow!"

As they sat in the living room, three cars parked out front. Mark and Ronnie each carried a cooler from their respective cars. When Judy and Nancy exited their car, they each lifted a pizza from the backseat, bumping the doors closed.

Leif opened the front door, allowing them to enter. "I knew you guys were coming. I overheard you."

"We knew you were there," Nancy replied, walking straight to the kitchen table to set the box down on top. "Let's eat!"

Judy placed the pizza she held next to Nancy's, and both opened the boxes. Ronnie and Mark opened the coolers.

"Help yourselves!" Mark called. "Come on, Leif!"

Leif helped himself to a slice of pizza while John removed plates from the cabinet, forks and napkins.

"Here, folks!" John stepped aside to allow his friends to dish up first and then he followed. "Will someone please tell me what's going on?"

"Well," Mark said, chewing a bite of pizza. He carried a can of beer into the living room. "We have a wonderful lead. It's not to be spread on Facebook or any other media source, Leif." He looked at Leif. "Understand?"

"Of course!"

"I guess that I've been told what kind of an old geezer I truly am," John said. "On that note, let's give a toast to Vicky. We'll soon know what's happened to her."

"Nope. The toast is to you, old friend, for being such a miser and holding on to almost everything. To John!"

"To John!" they said. "Cheers!"

"That's enough! We still don't know anything or are any closer to finding her," John said. "Diane should be congratulated. Tell me about this woman at a nursing home, or isn't there one?"

"How did you find out?" Mark looked over to Leif. "You have ears everywhere, don't you?"

"I sure do, and there's something else," Leif said, facing John, "Grandpa go ahead and tell them."

"I want to hear more about this woman, first."

"We have someone searching birth records, which you already know. We'll know in a day or two about it." Ronnie bit into his slice of pizza. "The woman is a nurse who remembers a patient who reminded her of Vicky's picture. The police were granted access to files, and there are officers sifting through them as we speak."

"My gut tells me we're very close," Mark said, smiling. "Now that we've shared information, what is this business about a teacher and the depot?"

"A woodworking teacher is coming with his best students. They'll rebuild the interior where the ticket counter, telegraph, etcetera used to be. And, chairs."

"It'll be as before?" Nancy asked. She finished her pizza.

"Sure sounds like it."

Chapter twenty

John parked the car right in front of Diane's house and shut off the engine. She began opening the main door as he walked to the steps.

"Leave the crutch, and lean on me," John told her. "No need to have you be troubled with finding a place to sit because of it. We'll manage." He reached out his arm and she folded her arm around his. "Ready?"

"Let's go." Diane leaned into him and they slowly walked. "It doesn't hurt as much as yesterday or the day before. I can step on it a little bit, but the doctor said not to overdo it."

"I'll keep that in mind." John led her to the passenger car door. He helped her inside before closing the door and going to his side. "I wasn't sure about traffic, and I'm not real familiar with St. Paul. We never did hang out in the city. I suppose it was because of all the gangsters in the 20s, 30s, and 40s." He signaled before driving into the traffic. "My folks always told us not to go to St. Paul. It's a holdover, most likely because they were of the age where it did happen. The gangsters from Chicago found refuge in St. Paul. The police chief let them escape justice. His pockets were lined pretty thick from bank robberies. They'd rob a bank in Minneapolis and nothing happened to them when returning to St. Paul. Brothels were acceptable also and not in Minneapolis. It was a whole different life back in those days."

"And now we have little kids getting in trouble because of treatment center closures for the young. Life doesn't mean anything. Church attendance is way down too. Nasty business nowadays."

"I'm in agreement and just as guilty," John said, merging onto Interstate 94 and converging with the busy traffic. "I'm not used to driving, so hold on to your seat!"

John chugged along the best he could before exiting to the Minnesota History Center. Once arriving, he parked in the given parking lot and found a space closest to the main door. After shutting off the engine and locking the car, he escorted Diane to the door where they entered. There was a short window of time for them to explore the exhibits of the Native Americans and the Scandinavians who settled in Swede Hollow before being able to assimilate into the American lifestyle. The hollow was destroyed for many reasons and located near the riverbank and Hamm's Brewery, a stalemate of the Twin Cities for jobs.

"Look here, it's all about the Donut Dollies! That's me and my mother!"

"That's why we're here. Let's go find a seat up close. I too want to learn more about it. It shouldn't take too long before visitors are able to learn all about the Donut Dollies."

"That's exciting!"

Following the signs, they continued toward the main room where chairs were ready for sitting. Since they were among the early attendees, they circled the room and took advantage of reading the displays without interference. The displays spoke of women's involvement in the war effort without being an enlisted soldier. As other individuals arrived, they decided to pick a seat in the front row so no one was able to block their view.

Sitting, Diane glanced around her. "I'm glad we sat up front."

"Me too. We'd never see anything or hear if we sat farther back."

"I wish my mother could be here. I should've worn my uniform."

"No more should've, Diane. You wear it every day you sit with Leif and me." John leaned in closer to her. "Last night, Mark and Ronnie, Nancy and Judy stopped in and brought pizza."

The sound technician went to the podium to make sure the mic worked properly by tapping it and saying, "Testing," a few times. He also placed a water bottle under the podium for the speaker to drink.

"I know there's something happening, but I haven't been contacted of late. Don't tell me anything. Let's keep it that way. My feelings go up and down like a yo-yo, and I want to enjoy the day." She looked at him then smoothed down her dress. "Deal?"

"I only wanted to let you know that we're in touch."

"I'm sorry." She saw a well-known figure advance to the podium. "It's going to start."

"Don't be," he whispered.

The room became silent as the speaker stepped up to the microphone.

"Good morning! And thank you to everyone who put this presentation together and to the History Center for hosting this event." She looked out onto the audience and repeated, "Thank you. Thank you to all who are here to hear about the Donut Dollies and how special they were to our troops and still are."

The audience clapped in response.

My name is Mrs. Barton, and no, I'm not related to *The* Clara Barton."

Another round of applause.

"But I wish I was so I could say it's all in the family."

The applause and laughter filled the room once again.

"Let's get started. If there are questions, please wait until the end, otherwise I just might lose my place in the notes. I'm not getting any younger, you know?" She smiled up to the audience. "As you can see, and I noticed that a few of you are wearing much the same clothing, this is the uniform style the young women, girls, if I may, wore as they distributed the needed food and clothing to our brave young men. How many of you women have heard of the Donut Dollies." She stared out in the room. "I see that most have, which is good. Was anyone a Donut Dolly?" She looked out again and saw Diane raised her hand. "Tell us about it, if you would please? Someone bring the lady in the front row the microphone."

When the person stopped to hold the device in front of Diane, she said, "I stood next to my mother. I was very young but helped none the less. To this day, I wear a skirt, white blouse, my mother's old sash, and her beret. I give out cookies at the Minnehaha Falls near the old train depot. The Minnehaha Depot." There was a round of applause. "Thank you."

"How interesting. You're a Donut Dolly! One of the younger of us at the time. Do you use donated money or where do the cookies come from? A nearby bakery?"

"No." Diane shook her head. "I bake at least two dozen either in the morning or the evening before if I know for certain I'm going. I carry a small basket and away I go, staying until they're gone." Diane smiled. "I love it. So many youngsters stop to talk and sometimes, they call me grandma or tell me I remind them of their own."

"That's fabulous and I thank you, we all do, for doing that," Mrs. Barton said, indicating the crowd. "Would you mind standing for everyone to see you?"

"Sure." Diane stood up and turned around to see the attendees before taking her seat again.

"Thank you," Mrs. Barton said. "Let's give her a round of applause." When the noise subsided, she continued. "I wouldn't advise everyone to bake cookies, if I did, everyone would end up eating burnt goods."

There was laughter.

"Time for us to get serious. I'm looking or should I say my partners and I would like to bring the Donut Dollies to the attention of the public. There are few that remember us and maybe, just maybe, there will be a few former soldiers who will join us and tell us their stories, such as taking the train to the ships or airfields where they were carried overseas. They'll talk about how the bagged meal from the lot of ladies was the only meal they had until landing overseas. It kinda makes you wonder what went into their stomachs once they left their homebase?" She took a deep breath and flipped over her notes. "As you know, Clara Barton was known as the 'Angel of the Battlefield.' She was known to risk her life to bring supplies to the soldiers on the battlefields of the Civil War. Besides supplies, she also brought food and clothing, nursed the sick and wounded. She started the Red Cross."

She stopped for a moment, shifting from left to right before taking a drink from the given water bottle. "Let's shift gears for a moment. I believe you'll find this interesting. How many of you know why the soldiers wear, 'dog tags'?" As she looked out into the audience, another drink from the water bottle was taken. "I see you ladies are up to date on history. Let's see if your information is the same as mine. I investigated the Defense Department and copied right from the site. Here goes: Unofficially, identification tags came about during the Civil War because soldiers were afraid no one would be able to identify them if they died. They were terrified of being buried in unmarked graves, so they found various ways to prevent that. Some marked their clothing with stencils or pinned on paper tags. Others used old coins or bits of round lead or copper. According to the Marine Corps, some men carved their names into chunks of wood strung around their necks. Those who could afford it bought engraved metal tags from nongovernment sellers and sutlers—vendors who followed the armies during the war. Historical resources show that in 1862, a New Yorker named John Kennedy offered to make thousands of engraved disks for soldiers, but the War Department declined.

"By the end of the Civil War, more than forty percent of the Union Army's dead were unidentified. To bring that into perspective, consider this: Of the more than 17,000 troops buried in Vicksburg National Cemetery, the largest Union cemetery in the U.S., nearly 13,000 of those graves are marked as unknown.

"The outcome of the war showed that concerns about identification were valid, and the practice of making identification disks caught on." She looked up to the audience. "According to the Army Historical Foundation, the term "dog tag" was first coined by newspaper magnate William Randolph Hearst. In 1936, Hearst wanted to undermine support for President Franklin D. Roosevelt's New Deal. He had heard the newly formed Social Security Administration was considering giving out nameplates for personal identification. According to the SSA, Hearst referred to them as "dog tags," similar to those used in the military.

Other rumored origins of the nickname include World War II draftees calling them "dog tags" because they claimed they were treated like dogs. Another rumor said it was because the tags looked similar to the metal tag on a dog's collar." Mrs. Barton smiled and said, "The nickname is very apropos, isn't it? But we're here to talk about Donut Dollies. Florence Nightingale added to the presence of the Red Cross, helping in the hospital rooms, sitting with soldiers waiting to die, writing to their mothers. All were volunteers, much as the Donut Dollies. All brought nutritious meals as needed and cared for the needy and poor of spirit during wartimes.

"The Donuts supplied all of the above. Sick soldiers were welcomed by a good meal and someone to listen to their stories before going home. What I'd like to see is for committees arranged from as many depots as possible to choose a day to represent us before the summer is gone." She smiled. "Us meaning the Donuts!" When the clapping ended, she asked for questions. When none came, she said, "Let's put together a list of individuals from that time and have a caller. The lady in the front will be helpful." To Diane, she said, "You won't mind taking charge of the Minnehaha, will you?"

Diane nodded.

"Good!" Mrs. Barton said. "Anyone who lives near Minnehaha Depot, come see this woman. Don't forget, it's separate from the Milwaukee Depot." She walked from the stage.

When Diane had a list of ten names typed into her phone for future reference, she and John left the premises, walking straight to the car. As the engine purred, John put it in reverse and backed out from his spot and then turned toward the road home. It took fewer minutes to return home than it had to arrive. After assisting Diane to her house, he left for home. Afterward, he went inside to make sure all was in order since Leif was left to his own devices to make it to the park. John made sure Leif's room looked presentable and his bed was made. Then John pressed the buttons to contact Janet.

"Janet."

"Daddy! What a surprise! I'm waiting for tomorrow!"

"I can pick you up at eleven?"

"I'm ready, Dad. Something's up. Tell me. Why did you call?"

"It's not Vicky, but there will be students rebuilding the inside of the depot and today, Diane and I attended a speech about the Donut Dollies! Those women who served meals to the soldiers as they left for points beyond. It was exciting. She'll be putting together women who either were one or remember helping, whatever, and they'll be with us one day at the park. I haven't told Leif yet. He's already at the park."

"I'll call and tell him about tomorrow," Janet said. "I told him to keep his room clean. Is he?"

"Absolutely." They disconnected. With the door closed behind him, John hiked over to Frances's house and entered. "Anyone home?" When no one answered, he began to leave but stopped when footsteps echoed on the basement stairs.

"What's going on?" Frances said, stepping on the final step. "Now, I'm here. What is it?"

"I spoke to Janet, and we're picking her up for home tomorrow at eleven. I thought you would like to know. I can't wait."

"That's really good. Great for our grandson, and I'm happy to see you two are getting along. Should we plan for a welcome home meal?"

"I was thinking along those lines, but I'm not any good at cooking. She would like to see you too." John hoped Frances would offer to cook and bake a welcome cake.

"Why don't you have Leif pick out an ice cream cake for her return and pick up table flowers. She would like that." Frances went right to the freezer. "I can make sloppy joes real easily and potato salad. You can supply another salad."

"Where are we eating?" John hoped it was here and not at home.

"We'll eat at your place since she's your daughter and Leif and is already living with you," Frances replied. "Now I must get busy and finish cleaning."

"Okay. Supper tomorrow night at my house. You'll supply the buns and sloppy joes and potato salad. I'll get the ice cream cake and another salad. Anything else?"

"Nope!"

"See you tomorrow."

John left for the park, trying to figure out what kind of a salad would fit with the meal? He decided cole slaw. Period. If she didn't like his choice, that was too bad. He continued with his walk. At the stop light, luck was on his side, he walked across the street. At the park, he hiked right over to the engine where he noticed Nancy talking to Leif.

"Hey! What's up? Find out anything?" John asked, approaching them.

"Grandpa! 'bout time you showed up." Leif cocked a brow. "It's getting late, you know. You might be in trouble."

"That's what I put up with all the time," John said, turning his attention to Nancy. "We don't have answers yet, do we?"

"Not yet. We're all sitting on pins and needles. I have to do something to occupy my mind right now instead of thinking about Vicky."

"Where's Judy?"

"She's at the Mall of America shopping. That's how she's managing. I can't do that, shop, I mean." Nancy shook her head. "How about a movie?"

"Movie?"

"This guy here can take over since he might be more aware of how to speak to kids and wow the older spectators than you are. Besides, we can talk about places or movies from the past while in the theater. The Riverview has "Mr. Ed," on the screen all afternoon for five bucks."

"Leif," John questioned, "what do ya think? Do you mind?"

"Nah, go ahead." He smiled. "Did you talk to Mom?"

"Yes. I called and we're picking her up at eleven. By the way, when you leave, would you mind stopping at the grocery and picking up a container of cole slaw and an ice cream cake that your mother would like for a celebration? Grandma is making the rest of the meal."

"I can do it. Hand over the money." He held out his hand. When John gave him a twenty dollar bill, Leif frowned. "We really need to update this guy. A bank card is the way to go."

"We must take it slowly with him," Nancy said, grinning. "Some people are slow learners."

"I'll see you at home. Make sure you don't make a mess."

The two adults walked away.

"I don't have my car."

"I do." Nancy led him to where she'd parked, down near the Old Soldiers Home. After climbing in, John told her all about the morning's talk and how interesting it was to learn about the Donuts. As she parked, John said, "I can't count the number of times I saw a movie with either Inga or Vicky."

"I know the feeling. Boyfriends, girlfriends, and so on. This landmark has sure stood the test of time."

They went to the booth and both paid for a ticket. After arriving inside of the theater, they walked the rows to look for the perfect seat to watch the comedy, *Mr. Ed the Talking Horse.*

"It's been years since I've seen this crazy movie," Nancy said. "I never saw it with Mike. I do wish I had more memories."

"You and me both," John said, sitting down. Nancy was beside him. "Right off over there," he pointed, "Vicky and I usually tried to sit. We'd neck the whole time."

"Mike and I were over there, in the dark shadows," Nancy said, motioning to it. "We should sit at one of the places."

"Together?"

"Sure. Why not?"

"Your place or mine?" John said, standing. "Yours? Inga and I sat closer to the front."

Together they sat as they reminisced about watching Road Runner and Bugs Bunny cartoons began to play onscreen.

"Right. I don't feel a sense of Vicky, either," Nancy said. "This will give me a chance to imagine or at least think of Mike and me together once again."

The movie began and they got comfortable.

Chapter twenty-one

Leif stood in the middle of the kitchen at an early hour, scratching his head. He yawned until he thought his jaw was disconnecting. He glanced over to his grandpa's bedroom door and heard more noise. He couldn't figure out where all the noise was coming from. It had woken him up. To him it sounded like a bass drummer right in the middle of the house, only the musician didn't know how to drum! It had to be snoring. Then he heard someone cussing.

It was Grandma cussing. Grandma never cussed! Never! Where on earth was she?

The sound came from his mother's bedroom, but she wasn't here. Leif went to Grandpa's room to open the door but wished he hadn't. Grandpa gave him a sleepy-eyed blank look, sitting on the edge of the bed with his knobby knees and long straggly hair poking from the knee caps. Leif almost laughed at the sight but decided he'd better not.

"Grandpa? Where's all the noise coming from?" Leif asked, entering. "It's so loud. It sounds like Grandma, but she doesn't cuss. This person in cussing."

"Did you look in the living room?" John said, yawning. "I'm tired, but I suppose we'd best get going, eh?"

"Living room?" Leif held the doorknob, "Really?' He hurried to the living room, peeked inside, and found his grandma tugging the furniture away from the walls. "Grandma!"

Frances fell backward and landed on the floor with the hammer still in her grip. "What are you trying to do? Scare the life out me? You—you—you—help me up instead of standing there and staring at me like I'm some kind of freak!"

"Are you hurt?" Leif reached out his hand to help her stand. "Maybe we should call an ambulance?"

His grandma dropped the hammer beside herself, then placed her right hand on top of his extended hand, but he couldn't raise her higher. "Grandpa!" Leif turned to see his grandpa stood in the doorway with his pants on but not wearing a shirt. "I need help!"

"Frances, what on earth were you doing so early in the morning that you couldn't at least wait for help from one of us?" John looked down at her. "Do you hurt anywhere?" He reached over, and she placed her left hand inside of his, her right still within Leif's palm. "One, two, three!" The two raised her up to standing. She collapsed on the nearest chair. "Rest for a minute."

"I intend to but you, young man, tell me why you scared the life out of me." She looked at John. "Well don't just stand there! Get me a cup of coffee, or are you such a donut that you haven't made any yet?"

"I'll take care of the coffee." John said to Leif, "You figure out what the devil she was doing pounding holes in my walls so early!"

"Got it. The grand wars. The G war." Leif chuckled. "Mom will love this."

"I bet," Frances said, staring up to him. "I'm trying to decorate. There's nothing wrong with a few decorations on the wall and the nails are tiny. No one will see the holes once they're removed from the wall." She motioned to the back of the furniture. "Look at all of it. I wanted to surprise you two before you left. You'll have something to get her real excited about." Frances reached into her pocket to remove a tissue to blow her nose and wipe her eyes. "I've got my ideas too."

"Aren't you happy for me? For Grandpa? We get her back home again. This time, it'll work out too. She'll be home for good and we'll be able to have our own place and I'll have my mom and we'll be able to be together and she'll have a job and she'll watch me graduate. Aren't you happy about that, Grandma?"

"Of course, I am. Good grief, what do you take me for, some kind of monster?"

In the background, the coffee pot perked. John removed two cups from the cabinet. "Want sugar?" He peeked from the corner of the living room. "Cream?"

"You know what I want. A little milk," Frances hollered.

"Of course." John went back to the kitchen and quickly returned with the two full cups. He glanced at Leif. "Go get ready. We have to leave in a few minutes."

"Got it." He made the "okay" sign before leaving the room.

"Let's see what you had in mind to hang on my walls," John said, looking behind the furniture.

"A welcome home sign in big bold letters that will spread across the back wall," Frances said.

"Wouldn't it be better to hang it on the open kitchen wall? It could've gone above the china cabinet. Then you wouldn't be in the predicament you're in at the present time." John crossed his arms and peered down at her. "Now, before Leif and I leave to pick up my daughter and his mother, I would really like to know what else you have in mind so when we return, I won't be completely surprised or in the dark. Hmm—" He massaged his chin. "Understand?"

"Don't expect me to wash Leif's clothes or yours before you return," Frances huffed, standing toe to toe with John. "I'm only going to clean."

"You'll clean? Like vacuum?"

"Of course!"

"And what else?"

"I'm going to dust and wash the kitchen floor since it's a big mess from spills never wiped up and then there's that dishwasher in need of a good cleaning. The bathtub is a disaster from two men and all their dirt from cleaning the engine day in and day out and the bedrooms are a disgrace with the odors. You must fart all night long."

"Is that all or do you have more to say?" John kept his eyes on her.

"I can't have my grandson's mother return to her house and have it ready to be condemned!"

"That's enough! We're leaving as soon as I dress, and we'll eat on the road. Leif has purchased an ice cream cake for his mother and cole slaw. You better not forget your end of the bargain for the meal!"

"I won't."

John stepped back and she went around him. "What seems to be your problem, Frances? You're grouchier than normal."

"Nervous. I want it to work out. I don't want her to leave again."

"No one does so don't be so ornery! Got it! That'll make her want to leave." John stormed into the bedroom to dress. "Damn woman."

As soon as they both were dressed, Leif and John went straight to the car to leave for Fergus Falls to pick up Janet for the final time.

As they drove from the garage, and after Leif had taken care of the doors and climbed into the car, they gave each other a huge smile.

"Ready?" John said.

"Yep," Leif said. "She scared me. Honestly, she did. Why would she do that?"

"She wants everything to be perfect," John said, driving from the vicinity and onto the main throughfare. "Your dad wasn't like that. I think it must be a 'woman's thing,' as they say. She's nervous, very nervous. She doesn't want you to go far away, either. You have a grandma who dotes on you." John glanced at Leif. "Am I right?"

"I guess," Leif admitted, keeping his focus straight ahead. "Where will we stop to eat? I'm starved?"

"What would you like? I'm willing to go to the nearest drive-through."

"Seriously?"

"Yes, anything to keep going and get a fresh cup of coffee to drink in the car."

John drove into the nearest fast food joint to order egg sandwiches, coffee, and juice. It didn't take them long before they were on the road.

"Are we still stopping for lunch?" Leif began to eat his meal.

"We will with your mother unless we eat in the cafeteria with her first. It depends upon when she's formally released." John tried to eat but food particles kept dropping on his shirt. "I'm making a big mess!"

"Nahh! You look fine. Mom won't mind what you look like." Leif didn't speak for quite a while, then said, "It'll be fine, won't it?"

"Of course! Positive," John said, choosing not to think about Leif's last comment. "Do you want me to tell you about your dad?"

"Yep." Leif leaned back in his seat, opened the front windows before reaching back to roll that one down. It didn't take long for the breeze to bring back old memories. "Let the stories begin."

"You're causing me to relive old times," John said, finishing his sandwich and taking the last drink from his coffee cup. He tucked it into the bag Leif set between them. "It's like this—many years ago, your dad and mother celebrated their birthdays together. Did you know that?"

"You may have told me but go on. Tell me again."

"Your grandma invited the boys over and your mother to bob for apples or sink a clothespin into a jar from on top of a chair." He glanced at Leif. "More?"

"You betcha, Grandpa."

"Your dad always won because he had the eye of a sharp shooter. However, his friends began to make fun of him always inviting a girl, so your parents had ice cream and cake on a separate night. Another added reason for the individual parties was that your mom's birthday was two days later and she always had girls attend and they'd play dolls or talk about boys. Your dad, of course, didn't want anything to do with that business, so your two grandma's came up with the idea of the private party. It worked quite well. We'd purchase your mom's favorite and they'd purchase your dad's favorite ice cream and cake. Two days, two parties apart from each other. They enjoyed it. I'm not sure what they talked about, but it was probably school related, at least initially."

"Man! It's my favorite cake." Leif stared out of the window for a few more miles. "I see it won't be long until we get there. She'll be ready, won't she?"

"Of course! She's all packed and waiting, if not by the front door, it'll be her room." John turned the corner to follow the signs for the hospital. "It won't be long."

"One more story about the two of them together. Short one."

"Your mother hates mice. The two of them were watching a movie and there was a mouse in the house. I don't remember what Grandma and I were doing at the time, but we heard a scream and came running. We found your mom standing on top of the sofa while your dad held a mouse, squirming, by its tail. It was funny."

"He was brave."

"Yes, he was." John drove into the lot to locate a place to park. "Here we are."

"Thanks, Grandpa. Now I know why my dad went to war. He was brave and courageous." Leif unbuckled and reached behind to roll the windows up.

"All that from a dead mouse?"

"Yes. Either a dummy or someone brave would hold a live mouse between their fingers for the woman sitting beside them. That's when they fell for each other."

"Good grief! There might be something to you, after all."

They hiked up to the front doors where Janet stood waiting.

"I thought you would've just stopped in front of the doors so I could've climbed in," she said with two suitcases beside her. "I'm ready. All checked out."

"Let's go, then," John said. He reached over for the smaller of the suitcase.

"I've got it." Leif took the larger. "I'm ready to see what Grandma has in mind."

"What are you talking about?" Janet said, walking between the two. "What's going on?"

"It's kinda funny, really."

John opened the car doors, and they piled the suitcases in the trunk before climbing into the car.

"I'm sitting in the front," Janet said. "You can roll all the windows down."

"We'll let the wind take us home," John said, getting inside and starting the engine. "Country roads, take us home."

"Mom? You wouldn't believe what happened this morning."

"Go ahead, tell me."

Leif gave her a rundown about the morning's event. "It was sort of funny," he said. "Grandpa told me about the mouse Dad caught when you two were watching a movie. Tell me more stories about you and Dad. Normally, I don't know anything because you never wanted to talk about him."

"It'll be hard to speak of him, but I'll keep going. You see? We were meant for each other, your dad and I."

"Tell the story about the snowball fight or the time you two went skating." John said, glancing over at Janet. "Do you mind if we keep going, or should we stop to eat?"

"We should keep going. I want to see what Frances has been up to today," Janet said, turning sideways to talk to Leif. "It's like this—your dad was full of the-you-know-what, and we went skating in the nearby outdoor park rink. It was so incredibly cold, and we played crack the whip with a bunch of friends."

"I know what that is. A bunch of kids hold hands and then you all skate around but the lead of either side jerk the arm of the person beside him, which is like a big crack, and then they have to hold on so they don't split. Right!" Leif said. "It's why it's called, 'crack-the-whip!'"

"You know what your father did?" She smiled. "He grabbed me and threw me into the snowbank. My rear went down so fast, and then he covered me with snow! I had a horrible time trying to stand. He had to help me up."

"He flirted constantly with you, Mom. He was a big flirt and that's that."

"We're approaching the city now, it won't be long before we're home."

When John drove into his driveway so Leif could open the overhead door, he suddenly got a weird sensation.

"I feel weird like."

"Me too," Janet said. "I hope Frances didn't invite some of our old friends."

"I wouldn't put anything past her," John said. He drove into the garage and parked, shutting the engine off. "Let's hope not."

They removed the suitcases and closed up the garage before walking to the house.

"I think something's going on," Leif said. "There were cars out front. Did you see that?"

"That's why I feel so nervous," Janet said. "Leif, Dad, hold my hand. Don't let me go."

"Don't worry. We won't, Mom." Leif took her hand into his right and John took her left into his as they walked up the path to the door.

Frances greeted them by opening it. "Surprise and welcome home!"

John and Leif took Janet's suitcases to her bedroom and joined Frances and Janet in the kitchen.

"Don't be afraid to go and sit, honey." John said. He took her hand once again and so did Leif as they escorted her into the living room.

"I love the decorations! Frances, they're beautiful!" Janet dropped their hands and took in the beautiful welcoming sign. "The flowers on the table remind me of when Gary and I were kids and you'd set the birthday table." She leaned over to smell them. "I smell something cooking and I'm starved."

"Me too," Leif said. "Grandpa barely fed me."

"The house is nice and clean, Frances. Thanks, but why do I feel as if something is afoot?"

"Ready!" she called.

From the basement stairs, three couples climbed up and entered the kitchen.

"Surprise!"

"You! You guys! The old group we hung out with? Who stood with Gary and me while we pledged each other our hearts?" Janet's eyes opened wider and tears streamed down. "I love you guys!"

They had a group hug.

"Frances? You outdid yourself," John said, smiling at her. "I wish Gary was here."

"He is," Frances said, reaching for Leif's hand. "See? This is your mom and dad. This is how great he was, friends from when he was a child and they still love him just as much if not more. That's love and that's a life worth living."

"Wise words," John said, placing his arm over Leif's shoulder.

Chapter twenty-two

One week later.

John drove Leif to the park and pulled into the space closest to the waterfalls. The sound of water gushing over the edge filled his ears with joy. It reminded him of his bride walking down the aisle, so beautiful. Inga was like the mist in his heart, lingering until they met again. As he and Leif hiked over to the engine, he noticed the lineup of students following Mr. Tiffany's approach from the opposite direction.

"I see that we're arriving with them," John said, speeding up to reach the depot before them. "I'd hoped to be a little earlier."

"Yes, to wash the beast. The big guy," Leif said. "I forgot what it is that you want to call it." He shrugged. "It doesn't really matter though, does it?"

"Not anymore."

"I'll fetch the water and you can clear out our stuff," Leif said, starting to move away from John.

"If only I had the energy," John said, "to keep up with him." He grinned, keeping his eye on Leif. When he reached the depot, Leif had it unlocked and was already heading toward the creek bed to scoop up a pail full of water. Right away, John removed the chairs, ladder, and anything else of his left inside. He set the ladder up in anticipation of Leif washing the top.

"Back!" Leif set the full bucket down right at the foot of the ladder. "I see we're in for a full day at the park. We're going to be invaded by students."

"That's real good news," John said with his hands wrapped around the ladder legs. "Let's get you up here and clean the beast."

"I like The Beast, don't you?" He began climbing upward. "Time to get busy."

"Your mother said she will come by later," John said. "I think she and your grandma are up to something, and that usually means lecturing me about something."

"Today will be special. No fear." Leif reached across the top of the engine and began to clean the surface. "I don't see any bird shit!"

"That's good. Thanks for the pep talk," John said, picking up the large sponge. "Time for me to get to work."

As John busied himself by circling the engine and wiping down smudges and gang related signs, Leif took care of the top. When completed, Leif emptied the bucket and carried it and the ladder to the car.

Mr. Tiffany raised large tents for displaying the steam engine models with demonstrations to come. Each student with their own model began to set up their tools and equipment after the tents were assembled. Each had a numbered tent, and a classmate to stand beside and work with on their model.

With envy and joy, Leif observed and joined in to see how the steam engine harnessed the energy. "I hope to take classes to learn all that I need like you guys."

"We're seniors," one of the students replied. "What grade are you going into and what school?"

"I'll be a junior at Roosevelt," Leif replied, hands on hips. "Can I help?"

"Sure, join us," the other student said. "We can use a lot of help. The teacher makes us think for ourselves, not just follow in the book."

"I've studied from Grandpa's old books, but it's not the same. I couldn't get it all right, you know?" Leif watched as they began to set the piston into the cylinder. "Grandpa and I used cardboard and a baseball bat for the piston."

"That's ingenuous," another student said.

Strolling around the tents, peeking inside and making suggestions at times, John found it was rather enjoyable. At last he entered the tent where Leif assisted a student.

"Having fun?" John asked the group. "You kids are terrific. So knowledgeable. Don't forget the water, it's crucial."

"We won't. Thanks." They nodded to John.

"I'm going to see to the Donut Dollies."

"I'll be out in a jiffy. I want a couple of cookies."

"Cookies? Count us in!"

With Leif by his side, John walked to the depot. "Have you been inside yet?"

"Nope. Too much to do," Leif responded. He suddenly walked faster than John, passing him out, and went right inside of the depot. "Amazing." His eyes opened wide. "Grandpa! It's so cool!"

"Oh my goodness, it looks just like it did back in the day," John said, admiring it.

"Over here," Mr. Anderson, the teacher motioned, "come here, you two."

They hurried over to where Mr. Anderson stood and witnessed him tapping on the telegraph machine.

"To think, this is how communication developed across the country. Look what the railroad did for the world, really," Mr. Anderson said, showing them the bars and where the tickets were purchased. "The first person to send a telegram stood right here. This was back before women were really allowed to work outside of the home."

"Far out!" Leif said. "Who sent the first telegraph?"

"None other than our own First Lady, Dolley Madison. Mr. Madison had passed away, and always with a twinkle in her eye, she sent the message to a relative. It read, *What had God wrought?* Unbelievable, isn't it?"

"Amazing," John said. "That woman was a wonder." He looked across the floor. "I see it's all swept and cleaned, ready for the chairs."

"They'll be here at any moment."

"That's a relief because I'm pretty sure that the women, the Donuts, will arrive soon."

"Good! It's all on time. Everything is in its place." Mr. Anderson took a breath. "The woodworking class has really enjoyed themselves."

"Those kids with the engines have also." John's phone dinged a message and at the same time, so did Leif's.

"We gotta go, Grandpa. Nice seeing ya," Leif said, marching out the door.

"I guess that means me." John followed behind.

Outside, they hurried toward the side of the engine where thirteen ladies lined up all dressed in uniforms similar to what Diane usually wore with a basket over their arm. Brown skirts, white blouses, sashes with little pins or buttons showing they'd served coffee, sandwiches, and pastry items. On their head was a brown beret or beanie similar to what the Girl Scouts of America wore or the Brownies.

"Take a picture," John told Leif. "Take many of them. Go back into the depot and do the same. Fill up your camera. This is a day to remember for the ages."

"Right." Leif began snapping images, lining up each lady to take a picture. One right after another and then he stopped. "Grandma? You too?"

"Snap it!" Frances said. "Don't forget your mother. She's beside me."

"Man, am I stupid." He shook his head. "I never even saw you guys." He snapped pictures of each. When finished, he said, "Miss Donuts, you know where to find me if you want a picture. I'm Leif, the grandson."

The women murmured, "Thank you."

"Would you like a cookie young man?" one of the ladies asked.

"You betcha!" When Leif snitched several cookies, he popped one in his mouth and a couple into his pants pocket then went to the depot to begin taking pictures.

While friendly spectators stopped for questions with the women, John strolled the area. Up ahead and close to the Stevens House, he noticed Nancy and Judy walking toward him. John waved to catch their attention.

"What's up?" Judy asked. "So much going on."

They stopped farther from the busy area to be able to talk privately.

"The Donut Dollies. The Depot is being refurbished inside. It's so beautiful and amazing. You'll have to walk through it and stop to talk to a Donut and ask for a cookie before Leif eats them all."

"Sounds like an all American boy. We have news for you," Nancy said. "You won't believe it."

"Tell me. It must be about Vicky because Diane isn't here, and she hasn't contacted me either, nor shown up the last few days."

"Tell you what, John," Nancy said, tears springing to her eyes, "it's over. Unbeknownst to us, they went through nursing home records on a hunch, here in Minneapolis. A former nurse saw the flyer and reached out."

"And?"

"They think she's found, they're pretty certain of it. It's got to be Vicky. That's where Diane is. She's sitting at the grave of her daughter." Judy bit her lip. "Not sure how to tell you this but—the name given at the time of her admittance was Vicky Evans. They can tell you all about it later because I don't know the specifics."

John's eyes teared up. "I can't believe it. She took my name?" He faltered, and they helped him to the nearby bench seat. "Where is it?"

"Lakewood."

"It's where Inga will be when I pass, then we'll be buried together." He wiped his eyes dry. "The friend bonds from school are never broken, are they?"

"No, we'll always look after each other."

"May she rest in peace," John said, bowing his head and wiping his nose.

"Amen."

The End

About the author

Barbara Schlichting was born and raised in Minneapolis, MN. After marriage, the family moved farther north to Bemidji. She has an elementary teaching degree plus a master's degree in special education from Bemidji State University. Writing has always been her passion, her master's thesis was titled, "Learning Language Through Written Expression."

THE GIN GAME

Buck turned on the radio to the jazz station. It was hard to locate one that played strictly jazz in Walnut Grove, MN in 2022. The song played was "Boogie Woogie Bugle Boy (From Company C)" by the Andrews Sisters. It brought back memories of his time as a fighter pilot during WWII and stationed near London, England.

He'd loved the serenades by the Glenn Miller band. The blue skies and freedom it brought to fly on heavenly wings. His best friend from grade school, Ed, enlisted with him and was usually his gunny. They'd been blood brothers since childhood.

Buck's love for flying and building model airplanes came from his grandpa Olaf. By golly, he planned to bring joy to one of the four youngsters in the art of model airplane building. It was time to get up and go to the old schoolhouse in Heritage Square where Laura Ingalls Wilder attended as a child. He was employed, volunteered, to teach a model airplane building class to the enrolled boys.

The glaring morning sunlight burned his eyes. It was as if he got sun blindness. Buck had been this way ever since his plane went down in the ocean way back during the war. The Great War, the Greatest Generation. *As if—we were all just a bunch of scared shitless youngsters still pulling on our mommies' apron strings.*

Just because he'd lost his footing and fallen a few times, he'd been forced to live with his son and daughter-in-law. The ground seemed unsteady at times, but that had to be expected, he reasoned, since his birthdate was nearing a hundred years ago.

Buck grudgingly walked down the stairs, past the living room filled with all kinds of new electronic fandangle thing-a-ma-jigs, including a seventy-two-inch wall-hanging television. Such crazy stuff nowadays. He couldn't make sense of all the new toys in the house he lived. *Why on earth do they need a TV that huge?* Just plain old-fashioned lunacy. Spending money recklessly. Someday, he figured, they'd be sorry about wasting money on nothing. He'd look down from the great beyond and laugh when another depression like the one in the twenties hit again. By God, what about the one in the eighties, and they still kept buying nonsense! He wasn't sure if he should believe in God and all that good stuff or not, but his late wife of seventy years had. She'd gone to church every Sunday and even coaxed him into going a few times over the holidays such as Easter Sunday. Why, he'd even bought her a bonnet. She'd fallen in love with one that reminded her of what Judy Garland had worn in the old classic, *Easter Parade*, also starring the dancing nut, Fred Astaire. Those were the days. He could wake up, have his morning coffee, go outside, and stretch and smell the sweet smell of the cornfields and the barn without having to look around to see if anyone was watching. Now he lived in a small house right in the middle of a city block in the small town of Walnut Grove where Laura Ingalls Wilder had lived in that dugout, and Pa had played his fiddle.

As he passed through the living room, Buck growled. The damn son of his, who should be out working the fields, sat by the computer.

"Why ain't you workin'?" Buck said, passing through. "Go find a job that makes sense like farming."

"Same to you, Grandpa," Donnie said. He scratched his bald head. "In case you'd like to know, I do my work from home. Ever since that crazy pandemic, lots of workers are staying home and doing their jobs. It frees them up to take care of family matters as long as their work is completed at the end of the day. It's good for people with—"

"I'm on my way." Buck continued to the kitchen.

"Time for coffee? Sleep well?" Sandy held up her cup, put on a pasted grin. "I'm glad you're here, Buck. Donnie worries about you."

"I'll keep that in mind, but I'm just old. Not dead," Buck said. "I'm taking my coffee and going back up. I've got reading to do." He poured his mug full and swiped a large cinnamon roll. "By the way, my name isn't grandpa."

"He called you that? Shame on him," Sandy said, shaking her head. "I'm sorry. Do you want me to show you how to use the microwave? Then the roll will be nice and warm. It'll taste really good. They're homemade, just like you like them," she said, smiling again.

"Thank you kindly. I appreciate your graciousness. I don't necessarily need looking after, Sandy, but it's right kindly of you."

Buck proceeded to leave and return to his upstairs cave. Sipping from his mug, he slowly circled the room, inspecting his creations. Two shelves of model airplanes lined all four walls. All from the war with one exception, the Wright Brothers' *Glider*. The Wright flyer came next. He picked up the *Glider,* and his heart skipped a beat or two before the flyer was returned to its spot on the shelf. Moving over, he settled down on his chair beside the bed to listen to the music on the radio.

His old transistor radio announced the news as it had when purchased back in the sixties. He slurped the hot coffee and chewed down on the roll. His eyes opened wider as he listened to the broadcaster speak:

"The Wright Brothers' *Glider* plane will be on display in Walnut Grove, MN in the county park. The Laura Ingalls Wilder festival is happening at the same time. Two impersonators who look like Wilbur and Orville Wright will speak as well as Laura Ingalls Wilder. And...there's a rumor floating around the station that someone just may fly in for the festival on a Lancair Columbia 300 small single engine aircraft. Remember, though—it's just a rumor!" He cleared his throat. "More news at the top of the hour."

"What? *The New Spirit of St. Louis?* Right in my lap? But—but—*Kitty Hawk*! In my own backyard!" Buck turned the volume up higher, then louder in case he hadn't heard the news correctly. It didn't take long before Donnie pounded on the floor from the ceiling with a broom handle. "Damn kid. Can't even have my radio on loud enough so a person can hear it."

Since the family insisted upon him living upstairs in a room that reminded him of a cave, Buck made sure he wouldn't go along with any kind of phone family plan. He insisted on an old-fashioned dial telephone with his own separate number. Buck cranked the radio as loud as it could go. He glanced at the clock and saw it was the top of the hour. He sat on the foot of his bed to listen.

"The Wright Brothers' *Glider* will be on display around the state of Minnesota. It will have a certain route to follow and will be in Walnut Grove. It's part of a nationwide road trip sponsored by the Air and Space Museum. The Minnesota tour kickoff will begin in Little Falls to pay homage to Lindbergh's transatlantic flight in the *Spirit of St. Louis*. From there the Brothers' *Glider* will travel by semi-truck around the state and will stop at several historical sites such as Fort Snelling, in St. Paul, and it will continue on to Walnut Grove."

Buck was about to reach for the phone when it rang. Only two people had his number: Ed. He'd known him from childhood, school, military enlistment, and fighting the krauts through WWII. Dave was the second. Since he'd flown helicopters in Vietnam, Buck figured him as a comrade in arms. He picked up the ringing phone.

"Ya hear it?"

"You betcha," Ed said. "And both, coming here."

"I can't believe my ears. It's our lucky day," Buck said.

"We've talked about this for years. Since we were kids."

"Don't get your shorts in a bind. We've got planning to do."

"Yeah, and we'd better get Dave onboard," Ed said.

"We will, but first we need to purchase some lumber and do it fast," Buck said. "Your sawmill still running?"

"Yep."

"Meet me at the caves after my class in roughly two hours," Buck said.

"Gotcha."

Buck put aside the old newspaper pile full of old war headlines but left the Glenn Miller front page on top. Man, he loved listening to that man's music. Who was he kidding? He was a product of the big band era. Before going off to war, he'd set the radio on the jazz stations out of Chicago at night and swoon. Now he wished for a chance to play the old sax again like he'd played in high school. He remembered the fingering to a T for the tune, "Moonlight Serenade." The beautiful memory of dancing with his wife while he inhaled the fragrance of her sweet perfume choked him up. He sighed, knowing he was stuck with this damnable kid downstairs who played on a computer all day. Sandy was so sweet. She was sweet in a way that made him sick to his stomach because she reminded him of his late wife.

Buck grabbed the box of five Wright Brothers' *Glider* models and headed out of his bedroom door, locking it behind him. He marched down the steps. Stopping at the bottom, he remembered that a large package from UPS was expected. It was another model airplane, the *Spirit of St. Louis*. This model, he was sure, would prove harder to put together than all other larger fighter planes assembled down in the basement or across the shelves in his upstairs cave. He walked quietly over to Donnie and stood behind him to watch.

"You really do know how to hunt and peck efficiently," Buck said. "I'll have to give you credit even if it is a girlie-type job, sitting by a keyboard all day long." He snorted.

"I'm not sure if that's a compliment or not? However, you should remember that I pay the bills," Donnie said, glancing over to him. "I see you're going out, and I know you've brought a plate and coffee mug upstairs. Did you remember to haul them downstairs and place them in the kitchen sink like a grownup?"

Buck growled. "I'm going out to teach the youngsters how to build airplanes, and I'm expecting a package. I'll be home later."

"Does this mean you've ordered another unwanted toy airplane? Another of about two hundred and ten, but who's counting?"

"I'll take care of the dirty dishes upon my return."

"Please do," Sandy called from the kitchen. She peeked her head out from around the corner. "I'm running short of clean mugs and dishes."

"Such a shame. Take it out of my retirement to purchase more since it's already directly deposited into your joint account." Buck held the box holding all five glider boxes tight. "See you later." He walked out the front door, gritting his teeth.

The 1978 pickup truck, Old Blue, still got him where he wanted to go. The old Ford never let him down. He'd given it the name and liked it. Buck missed his wife and wished he hadn't been such a rotten cuss to her over the years. He couldn't decide if she died just to piss him off or she really did have cancer.

He swore to God he'd be a better person if only she wouldn't die, but He took her anyway. Now Buck didn't know if he really hated God or not. He rubbed the back of his neck as he plunged the key into the ignition and turned it. Old Blue started right up, just like a brand new babe. As the truck rolled down the streets of Walnut Grove, he drove past the farm that had once belonged to him and his wife, where his son, Donnie, was raised. Buck's eyes filled, and he wished that son of his had had some interest in farming. Instead, his centennial farm was sold to strangers.

Buck didn't think it possible to ever forgive his son for selling his grandfather's farm. Now he'd never be able to legally walk the fields, check on the corn crops, milk the cows, or taste sweet peas or beans from the garden. Picking the windblown apples from the ground was a pain, but the applesauce, apple butter, apple jelly, and apple pie was so sweet and good his mouth watered thinking of it and how much he missed it all. Seeing Donnie sit in front of that contraption all day only reminded him of his age. My God—ninety-eight. He knew there wasn't a whole lot of time left and the reason for the move into the house really did make sense, but he felt like he lived in a jail cell. Couldn't Donnie have driven the tractor across the fields and smell the fresh air and fallen in love with it? Just like he'd done with his father and his father before him? Why didn't that memory pull on Donnie's heartstring and make him want to farm? Didn't his palate yearn for another jar of homemade jelly or fresh fruit and vegetables? Buck's wife's strawberries had won awards at the county fair. Why weren't there grandchildren so he could've been like Grandpa Olaf and taken them on a spin around the pasture and fields?

Buck parked in the lot nearest the schoolhouse and got out. He expected the door open upon his arrival, but instead, he had to wait. The four boys soon were by his side, and the woman with the key arrived and opened the door.

Once inside, the boys took their seats.

"Call me Buck. You are? Tell me your names, and I'll write them down on a name tag for you to put on your collars. Oops. No collars, the front of your shirts."

"Tony." Buck gave him his name tag.

"Jethro."

"Jed for a nickname?" Buck asked. When he nodded, Buck handed him his name tag.

"Tim."

"Nick."

"Done," Buck said, passing the final name tags out. "Today we'll talk a little about what's expected before we get going on the project."

"Are you a real teacher?" Jed asked.

"Nope." Buck held up the box to reveal five boxes inside. "What we'll do is open your box and on the side—hold on. Do we have markers?"

"Over on the counter." Tim pointed. "Want me to get them?"

"Yes." Buck kept talking. "We'll place your name on the box sides."

"Should I pass them out?" Jed asked, still standing.

"How old are you twerps?"

"We're seven and eight," Nick said.

"Don't we need trays to put our stuff on like at school?"

"Great idea, Nick. Go ahead," Buck said. "We'll place each piece on the trays from inside the box."

Once Nick had passed them out and the students printed their names on the boxes, Buck instructed them to look at the directions. As he read aloud, they carefully followed the instructions.

"That's all for today," Buck said. "Next lesson, we'll apply the decals to the wings. I assume the glue is supplied. I'll check on that. Where can we place these trays so no one gets their greedy, dirty little fingers on them?"

"Up on the top shelf," Jed said, pointing to it.

Buck went to stand below the shelf and said, "Okay boys, bring them over here, and I'll place them up there. Don't try pulling any down yourself next time because it'll just dump over and you'll lose pieces. We don't want that to happen."

Buck placed the four trays high on the shelf and said, "See you guys later."

He watched them leave, picked up the mess he'd made of his model, and dumped everything into his box. He'd placed the cover on as two women strolled in, one shorter than the other and about the same age. Both women had more gray hair than colored.

"You done?" the taller woman called.

"I'm not standing around without kids here for my health," Buck said. He started for the door.

"Don't leave on our account," the shorter woman said. "I'm Maggie. We're here to teach little girls how to tie flies for fly fishing."

"Well, Maggie, that's all fine and dandy."

"I'm Patty, in case you're wondering. We'll be here each time you are, so don't mess things up," she said with a wink.

"Got it, but the same for you, sister," Buck said. "And by the way, those trays up there belong to my class. Don't touch them." Buck headed out the door to the truck.

"Nice guy," Patty said.

"The biggest buzzard in the county," Maggie said.

They stood and watched Buck hike to his truck and drive away as three girls entered.

***

Patty and Maggie turned their attention to the girls.

"Good morning, girls! We're going to have fun. Call me Patty."

"I'm Maggie, the smart one."

"Yeah, right," Patty said. "Maggie, find three trays for the girls, would you?"

"Sure." Maggie glanced around the room. "I don't see any except for the four up there Mr. Grouch told us to leave alone." She walked toward the back of the room. "We've got cardboard boxes out in the closet area."

"Bring three." Patty found the sticky paper used for name tags. "Names, please?"

"Sarah."

"Jane."

"Debbie."

When the name tags were passed around, Patty opened her kit and explained about the string used, the colors for the fish types, and the hooks for the catch. The scissors and other instruments used for tying. When finished, the girls had their names written on their respective box.

"Where should we put them?"

"Right over here," Maggie said. "Right on the end of the boys."

"How about the shelf in the clothes closet?" Patty said. "I think it's better."

The girls carried their boxes to the location.

"Grab your belongings, girls," Maggie said.

"I'm waiting for my mom," Jane said. "I'm to wait here on the steps."

"That's fine."

The other girls left.

Jane turned around and went back inside. "I forgot something," she called.

"We'll wait outside," Patty said.

Jane hurried to drag a chair over to the shelf where the boy's trays were and reached for her brother's. It tumbled down to the floor. Quickly she placed everything inside the box and was going to bring it home but stopped when the door reopened. She left it on the floor.

"Jane," Maggie called from the doorway.

"Coming." She raced back outside. "I wanted to bring my brother's model home so I could see it."

"It belongs here," Maggie said.

Patty and Maggie waited for Jane's mom with her.

When Jane left, Patty and Maggie jumped into their camper.

"This was a great idea to rent a camper, Patty. Now we can cook inside or out and each have our own bed."

"I love it," Patty said.

"I'm glad we have it."

"Yes, me too. I glanced around as we stood waiting. It doesn't look like it'll be too hard to police when the Wright Brothers' display is here," Patty said.

"It doesn't seem like it," Maggie said, "but that remains to be seen."

"True, but remember, we have to keep it secret that we're going to be used as security extras. The Wright Brothers' *Glider* is the utmost important plane of all time. As outsiders, we won't be suspected."

"I can see why Mark and Ronnie mentioned it to us. As detectives for Minneapolis, they'd know that extra policing such as the citizen's patrol would be necessary," Maggie said.

"That's right! A perfect undercover job for us, and it'll pay for all of our camping expenses such as the site rental for a week," Patty said.

"And extra fishing time!"

They drove to the creek. It was time to get the poles in the water.

**

Buck drove back home to retrieve his transistor radio and in turn he carried his dirty dishes downstairs to the kitchen. He went back outside and jumped into his truck, driving toward Plum Creek. Laura Ingalls Wilder used to tickle the fish in the creek, and it was located right on the shoreline next to the caves. Buck stopped and parked. After shutting the engine off, he headed for the cave and noticed the same two women who taught fly fishing at the school. Patty was already reeling one in. Buck wanted to see the fish but decided against it because he didn't want to get caught up in all the useless small talk that women seemed to enjoy. It wasn't that he was against it, but not now. However, he planned to investigate who these women were and why they were here. Women didn't normally fly fish.

He hightailed it into the cave.

Dave always brought his radio and played that rock and roll shit from the sixties—that Beatle bullshit. Ed liked country and western, and Buck loved jazz. He made it inside the cave first and placed the radio just outside the entrance to pick up reception and turned up the volume once he'd found the right station. Ahh, it was Old Satchmo—Louis Armstrong on the air.

Inside the cave he opened a folding chair and card table that rested against one of the sides. He'd studied the drawings more times than he cared to remember of the Wright Brothers' first flight in Kitty Hawk, North Carolina, on the Outer Banks. Buck smiled. He would build his own and compare it with the original.

While Buck studied the drawing that he and Ed had drawn several years ago, Ed entered the cave.

"I can hear that damn radio all the way home, and I'm hard of hearing," Ed shouted. "What the hell's the matter with you?"

"Point taken. Shut it down, will ya?"

Ed turned around and shut off the radio, bringing it to Buck and set it down.

"You do realize there's two women out there fly fishing, don't ya?"

"Those two teach how to tie fly knots at the school right after I'm through my class. They'd better not mess up the boys' trays. Period."

"They'll be careful, just wait and see," Ed said.

"I sure hope you're right." Buck rubbed his neck. "Have a seat. Let's figure out how much spruce and ash we'll need."

"Let's get busy, you ornery old bastard," Ed said. "One of us will have to go and buy the French sateen. I wonder if it's possible to purchase it?"

"Already did about two years ago. Been waitin' for this day since I was born. Grandpa Olaf used to talk about it," Buck said, smiling. "It's going to be our finest hour."

"We'll have to get that old fart Dave onboard real soon. He gets to be a royal pain in the ass if he's not included from the start."

"Does he have a woman right now?"

"Nope, none that I'm aware of," Ed said, drumming his fingers on the table. "That means we have to start planning."

"What the hell?" Buck stood, pointed his nose upward and sniffed. "Don't tell me—" Swiftly he walked to the entry and peered out. After he'd seen enough, he went back to Ed and said, "Ahh shit. They're frying up fish."

"Don't spook 'em, or they might not leave," Ed said, scratching his whiskers. "Remember what happened last time when two women walked by?"

"Those two young 'uns? Earlier in the summer?"

"They weren't young, at least not that young. They reported you to the police and filled out a report against you for swearing like a sailor for no good reason. So leave those two grannies alone. They're harmless."

"This spot has been ours for years. They'll catch our fish," Buck said.

"You have to learn to play nice, as they say nowadays, because they won't be here for long. They're vacationers."

"Okay. I'll try to make nice, but they'd better not catch that old rainbow, Sammy, that's been lying in wait for many years."

"Let's get out of here. I've got the dimensions written down and figured out the amount of wood needed already. We should pick up the wire too, all at the same time," Ed said. "I'll check out things at home and make sure my wife isn't around when I begin to cut and plane the pieces. We don't need anyone to know what we're doing." Ed took a moment and sucked in a deep breath. "Can't you just smell those fish frying? I haven't tasted fresh fish cooked over an open fire like that in years. Norma hates fixing fish like that." He removed his cap that had a fish on its bill, then plopped it down on his head. "Land sakes alive."

"Get your head outta your ass and think of *Kitty Hawk*. Your sawmill should take care of our project, shouldn't it?"

"Yes, you bastard," Ed said, shaking his head. "Tell you what, I'll go home and make the order and put a 'rush' on it. We should have planks by midweek. That gives us plenty of time to measure and cut."

"I'm going over to Dave's. I don't like the idea of anyone hanging around, especially those two women."

"Don't bother them." Ed left the cave, shaking his head, stopping near the women. "I don't know of many women who fish."

Hearing Ed's voice caused Buck to hustle. He folded the chairs, the card table, grabbed the Wright Brothers' *Glider* drawings and rushed out from the cave. He went right over to them.

"So, you really do fly fish," Buck said. "No bobber, Ed."

"I'm Patty, and this is Maggie. We find it enjoyable to fish the state," Patty said. "We're teaching how to tie knots at the school. We met your friend at the schoolhouse."

"Yes, he said," Ed said. "His name is Buck."

"I'm here, you don't have to talk about me behind my back," Buck barked. "Why here?" He flipped his cap on and off. His bill showed a facsimile of the Wright Brothers' first flyer.

"I bet you're also here for the Laura Ingalls Wilder pageant," Ed said.

"Nah. We're over all that historical stuff," Maggie said. "We're here to laugh and have fun, catch fish."

"Actually, that isn't completely true. We're going to make a few bucks from teaching to help pay for our hobby," Patty said. The fish was fried, and she lifted it onto a plate, split it in half, sliding a half onto another plate, then handed it over to Maggie.

"Get paid? I'm volunteering."

"We asked for a stipend since we're from out of town and got it," Patty said. "Fishing is a fun hobby. Fresh fish. Fresh air. See the countryside."

"Hobby?" Buck said. "Women? Fishing?"

"Why not?" Patty said. "It's not the fifties anymore, Grandpa. Women don't wear bras anymore either."

"Or dresses, Grandpa," Maggie said.

"Call me Buck. That's what you call me. Period."

"Got it," Patty said. "Ed. How about you? Does your wife take to fishing?"

"Nah, she hates fishing but will fry it over the stove." Ed was eyeing the fish on Maggie's plate.

"Tasty fish," Maggie said, taking a bite.

"This rainbow is really good," Patty said, taking another bite. "Almost as good as what we caught in Colorado last summer. Maggie, let's do that again."

"You betcha."

"At least it's not Sammy, the old rainbow we've been trying for for a few years," Ed said.

"How long are you two little grannies planning to spend your time here fishing?" Buck said.

"You should talk. You call us by our names, Patty and Maggie. Got that?" Patty said. "Now do you mean hours? Days? Weeks?"

"Don't be funny," Buck said. "I grew up around here, and there's not much to hold anyone's interest."

"Which is exactly why—oh never mind," Maggie said.

"Well you see, we're here at Plum Creek to see if we can catch some of the good fish that Laura did. The creek is full of fish of all kinds," Patty said. "And to see the *Glider*. The flying machine of all time."

"We're excited about seeing it firsthand," Ed said. "You two have fun fishing, but don't catch any of ours. We have our secret spots. Only our best friends know about our secret location."

"I hate women hanging around," Buck said. "Laura fished upstream. Go fish over yonder." He nodded his head in the general direction.

"As your grandchildren say—get over it. We're not going away," Patty said.

"I don't have any," Buck said.

Did you love *The Tide of Time*? Then you should read *The Gin Game*[1] by Barbara Schlichting!

[2]

THE GIN GAME is loosely based on the historical events of the Wright Brothers first flight on the Glider. Laura Ingalls Wilder historical sites in Walnut Grove, MN are used as a backdrop for this fictional tale. A festival occurs during the nationwide Smithsonian touring semi of the historical plane. During the festival the Wright Brothers impersonators and characters from the Laura Ingalls Wilder television show. Three former servicemen pull their imagination together and will try to hijack the Glider. There are two women snoops who are quite meddlesome. The men devise tricks to keep them from learning what's happening in the barn.

Read more at www.barbaraschlichting.com.

1. https://books2read.com/u/4AdxZq

2. https://books2read.com/u/4AdxZq

About the Author

Barbara Lindquist Schlichting grew up in Minneapolis, MN and graduated from Roosevelt High School in 1970. After marriage and two children, we moved to Bemidji. I attended Bemidji State University and earned a four-year degree in teaching elementary education and a masters degree in special education.I am also a playwright.

Read more at https://www.barbaraschlichting.com.